THREE MONKS FROM FLORENCE

THREE MONKS FROM FLORENCE

Hendrik Hoitinga

Printed in the United States of America
ISBN 978-1-967279-12-8 (hc)
ISBN 978-1-967279-11-1 (sc)
ISBN 978-1-967279-13-5 (e)

03.31.2025

This book is printed on acid-free paper.

Blue Ink Media Solutions
1111B S Governors Ave
STE 7582 Dover,
DE 19904
www.blueinkmediasolutions.com

Table of Contents

BOOK 1
THREE KEYS.
THREE CLUES

PROLOGUE;
Cannes, Southern France 1963.

The white open topped Mercedes 230sl Pagoda drove at high speed along the coast road from Nice, heading for Cannes.

Despite the weather being overcast and several dark clouds looked threatening to deposit rain any time soon, the female driver wore large round dark sunshades. The scarf she had tied over her hair and fastened under her chin, was billowing, and struggled to contain her long red hair.

It was a little before one o'clock in the afternoon and though driving at speed, she had control of the vehicle, regularly checking in the rear-view mirror.

Her face was set in full concentration, her red lips almost a grimace.

With ease she passed two cars in succession, checked her rear-view mirror again and began to relax a little.

Cannes was not far away now.

Roberto Solari finished his lunch in the harbour front cafe, nodded goodbye to the owner and left the premises. He walked along the waterfront and looked out to sea.

He took in the fresh air, looked at the dark clouds above and figured he had better get a move on if he didn't want to get wet.

It was the first week of May and posters were up on fences and in shop windows, the film festival was coming. Commencing on the 9th.

Roberto reflected as he followed a path away from the seafront leading to an apartment building. He had moved from Monaco, where in Monte Carlo he had previously lived and worked, after a few sizeable commissions had afforded him to do so.

This had been in the year 1948, after the film festival had relaunched the previous year, Roberto having a sense that there could be good business to be had.

His apartment was on the top, the fifth floor, and comprised of a large room which he had transformed into his studio, then a further four rooms, made up from a small dining room that opened into the kitchen, then two good sized bedrooms, one of which had an ensuite, and a further bathroom. Already over fifteen years ago, he mused, since he moved here, getting ready to cross the road.

The sound of a car approaching added by several beeps on the horn, stopped him in his tracks.

The white Mercedes braked, skidded a little, then stopped, the woman behind the wheel calling out,

'Roberto!'

She switched off the engine and got out. She was very slim, Roberto noted, wore a tight-fitting pencil skirt which hampered a bit as she got out of the car. Her shoes, white, had sharply pointed toes and heels that were surely three inches or more. The blouse was white, partly tucked into the skirt, partly out.

He didn't recognise her, but she obviously knew him. Crossing the road, after letting another car pass, he walked towards the woman, who was now leaning back against the car awaiting his arrival. As he drew near, she took off those big sunglasses and her green eyes focusing on him, said, 'Natalie Umbrego'

Then he remembered her, the red hair tucked under the scarf prompted his recollection.

'Ah, yes, what, two weeks ago, the party on the yacht?' He asked, stopping several feet away and recalling a redhead in a black evening dress, though he had only briefly seen her. Noticing that on those heels she was taller than he.

'Si, yes, I need you to do something for me, I will pay well..' she began, then anxiously looking past him down the road.

He sensed her tenseness, in the body language, in the voice, speaking French with an Italian accent, which was somewhat rushed. Then, looking in the car he noticed it tucked behind the passenger seat.

'I know, somebody tell me,' she said, ' tell me where you live, tell you lunch at same time,' then reached in and drew out the parcel, wrapped in a large beach towel, ' tell me you paint, make copies, but, no, I don't want that, I need you to clean and fix, is very dirty and ripped in places, you can do this?'

She handed him the wrapped painting, then looking past him again, she said,' I have to go, can't explain, I'll be back, in a week or so!'

Then manoeuvred herself with that tight skirt back into the car, turned on the ignition and sped away.

Roberto stepped onto the pavement, clutching the painting, watching her disappear. Then, as he walked up the path that led to the foyer of his apartment building, he heard another car, heard the loud engine, turned, and watched as a dark brown coloured car, what looked to him to be a Jaguar, speed past.

He frowned, then shook his head and turned to enter the building, thinking about what she had said. Lunch at the same time? Was he that habitual?

Stepping into the old elevator, the blanket wrapped painting under his arm, he figured that he must be, thinking that he ought to perhaps vary his routine. Pressing the button for the fifth floor, he then wondered what might be revealed when he took the blanket off.

THE PRESENT; Paris

Thursday 23rd April 2020

Hospitals were struggling to cope. The death toll was rising in vast numbers every day around the world. The Covid 19 virus spreading throughout nations, affecting rich and poor, making no distinction of race or colour or creed.

Though it was the elderly that were at most risk, as were those with lung related illnesses. Travel was now severely restricted, cities were in lock down, people were urged to work from home where they could, wear masks everywhere and wash hands, keep distance and drink fluids.

Sophie Pontiac was home. The Paris Fine Arts Auction House, where she was the manager, was closed. The Director, Emmanuel Sauvonne, had caught the virus, thankfully just bed ridden and not in hospital.

Sophie just got off the phone with his wife when there was a ring on the doorbell.

Donning her mask she went to the hallway, and tentatively opened the door leading into the foyer area.

'Special delivery ma'am' the courier, a female, also wearing a mask, said, 'no need for a signature, have a good day' and with that she left, leaving the parcel standing against the wall.

Sophie sized up the package, wrapped in cardboard, taped securely, it was around sixty centimetres in height and close to forty-five centimetres wide. It was less than four centimetres in depth.

'Merci' Sophie called out, then leant to pick up the parcel.

It was not heavy.

After having taken the cardboard wrapping apart, leaving just, what Sophie assumed to be a painting, inside a plastic sleeve lined with tissue paper, she then disposed of the cardboard, washed her hands thoroughly, and proceeded to uncover what it was that had been send to her.

There had been no return address, no inkling, yet, as to who it was from.

Slicing the cello-tape loose, Sophie slid the painting out from the sleeve. A sealed envelope fell out along with it. Ignoring the letter for a moment, she studied the piece. It was an oil painted on wood, it was old, she was sure of that, very old.

It wasn't a masterpiece, in some places it was almost naive, a little crudely painted.

It was a monk, in a typical monk's attire, the clothing, the staff he had in his hands, the cross and some sort of key that hung around his neck, these were all rather nicely detailed. The hands and face of the monk were less refined. This puzzled Sophie, as she carefully studied the piece, it was as if the monk himself, wasn't important. After scrutinizing it for some time, she was sure of several things.

First, it was old, judging by the style, the composition, the wood upon which it had been painted, which was likely poplar, she figured it to be mid-16th century and Italian.

Secondly, it was on a panel, and she was sure, looking at the edges, that it had been a triptych, it was one of three panels. Moreover, she was certain, that she held the centre piece, at the top and bottom of the painting, ever so faintly, in the centre, she noticed lines, where the other two side panels, would have closed upon it.

And lastly, she felt sure, that the important aspect of this painting, was not the monk himself, but the attire he wore, the staff he held and the items that hung around his neck.

Time to read the letter.

It was from Roberto Solari.

'Dearest Sophie' the letter, type written in French, began,' it was very nice to see you last year when you and your English friend Victoria came to visit.

It was afterwards that I made up my mind that it was to you that this painting should go. Let me tell you Sophie, this is not a forgery,

I cleaned and mended several gashes it had, this was some time ago, I believe it to have been painted in the mid to late fifteen hundreds, most likely, having a long time ago done some research on it, it was done in Italy, probably Rome, but there is no signature, or date. Let me tell you the story of how I come to have it..'

THE PAST; Period 1

The year 1578 – Florence Italy

In what was once a formal dining room, Father Dominic had set himself up, using the long, polished, oak dining table, as a desk. Here he had sat and scribed the detailed letters, here he had scribed the instructions for the three monks he had chosen. Here he had scribed the letter for the woman.

He had chosen her with care. She was young, merely two decades, but she came from a good family, a loyal family.

Whilst the plague that had wiped out half the city's population was already some two hundred years behind them, a current illness was sweeping through the land.

It was this virus, this disease, that had been the cause of the difficulty Father Dominic now faced. He had to think fast, to think clearly and to make sure, that everything was in place, that everything was accounted for, everything was protected. And the first thing, was to make sure the baby was safe.

A little girl.

The young woman he had chosen, he felt, could be fully relied upon, also knowing she had a feisty nature, even though she had just entered a convent, wasn't afraid to speak up and would not be easily intimidated. He had organised for her to come and see him, nearly two weeks ago.

She had been wary at first, had stood in front of the table that he was now using as a desk, having not taken up the offer to be seated. She stood straight and her eyes were totally focused on him. In that moment he knew he had chosen well.

He began to explain, then handed her the letter.

She took it, looked at him, and decided to sit down.

When he had looked at her, and she had looked up after reading the letter, questioning with his eyes, she had merely nodded.

His next object was twofold, find a painter, good, but not

established, not well known, and secondly, a master craftsman, that knew about locks.

Then his last task, was to select three men. Three monks, that could be totally trusted, could read and write, and be physically fit enough to travel a long distance.

It was early evening, Father Dominic sat at his makeshift desk. One table lamp already lit and glowing on the polished surface. Nearly time to move, nearly time to leave. Everything was in place, the last part of his plan had been the painted triptych, this was now ready and he himself would take it with him.

He praised the Lord that it had all been accomplished in time, for he knew, that trouble would come knocking. Finishing up, tidying up and taking himself of to the room in which he had slept for the past seven weeks now, he was ready.

They came the following morning.

If they thought they might surprise him at this time of day, the sun having only just made an appearance, they were mistaken. He had been up for hours already.

Someone, a man Father Dominic recognised as a local tradesman, usually seen sharpening knives and tools in the town, unlocked the front door and let them in, a woman and a man.

'Well, figured you would be here Father, where is she?' the woman asked, noticing him, standing ever so still, in the large foyer as she entered the house.

'Who?' he asked.

The woman, glaring at him, said, 'You know very well who.'

'Very well, follow me' he said, then turned and headed for a door that led from the main foyer of the large house. Opening it, he said, 'One moment, I need to get a lantern.' There was one on a small shelf just inside the door and Father Dominic fetched it out, it was already lit, then looking at the woman, 'Careful down these steps' then turned and led the way, thinking that, although he shouldn't feel this way, he secretly had no wish for her to be careful on these steps.

The tradesman, who had opened the front door, receiving a nod from the woman, turned, and left, closing the front door behind him.

There were some twenty stone steps, at the bottom, making sure to hold the lantern up to see the floor clearly, he turned left, then, taking a moment, he lit another lantern, placing it on the floor.

They were in a small crypt. Three coffins, two normal sized, one small.

'She died' Father Dominic said. His voice calm and without emotion.

Making sure they could see the child's coffin, in particular the name on the copper plate he had engraved. Anna Kastanje 1575-1578.

The woman and the younger man beside her, stood for a moment, then the woman said, her voice, hard and with a tone of menace, 'How can we be sure they are actually in there, especially the girl...' turning, she noticed that he had gone. 'Father?'

She looked up the long steps, was sure he hadn't gone up there, where was he?

The lantern he had held, was on the bottom step, in the dim light the man and woman looked at each other.

Using the lantern, the woman walked around the small crypt, but there was no sign of him, no sign of any other doorway.

'Come on' she said to the man, 'we'll check through the house, 'then, having already moved back up the stone staircase, the man, picking up the other lantern following, she continued,' and have someone check those coffins, all of them!'

Alexandria Wenschelburg was furious. Sitting in the very chair, behind the very same dining table in the former dining room of the big house, where Father Dominic had sat earlier in the day, and for most days these past weeks, prior to their arrival, she glared at the young man who had accompanied her when they had entered the house at dawn.

'Nothing, there is nothing here, nothing of value, some paintings I know that were here, are gone, most of the furniture, gone, several vases, gone, but more importantly, all the jewellery, gone... and where did Father Dominic disappear to?'

The young man, Nikolai, also a Wenschelburg, wisely not saying a word as he looked across the table at his aunt.

'You checked the coffins?' she asked, finally looking up at him, her face still showing fury and a shade of almost purple.

'Definitely uncle and aunt, not having seen the little girl..'

'But there was a body?'

'Yes'

Several moments of silence. Alexandria was suddenly feeling drained and tired, they had travelled, some distance, from Trieste, to reach Florence, to get to the little girl. Someone in her family had advised of the death, through this plague thing, of her sister and her husband, there had been no mention that the girl too had died.

She was suspicious.

Even more so, now that, having searched throughout the big, house, and discovering many items of value not present, that along with the vast amount of jewellery that she knew her sister had, plus the fact, that this, Father Dominic, whom she had heard about, so suddenly and mysteriously, vanished.

As the sun had almost reached the zenith on this warm day, Father Dominic sat inside a carriage, drawn by two horses, his personal belongings, and the painted Triptych, was with him. He was travelling to Rome.

He was going to stay a while with a distant cousin, Cardinal Farnese.

Smiling, he praised the Lord for good timing. Glancing down at his leather satchel, his smile broadened as he knew he had all the legal documents and paperwork with him which would ensure that madam Wenschelburg could make no claim on the property.

Meanwhile, around 120 miles to the north-east, in Genoa

Viana Vanetti leaned on the wooden railing of the schooner. Standing near the bow she was watching the goings on in the port. She had already placed all her luggage on board, having been giving one of the officer's cabins.

Three months.

She had arrived here early in the month of February, remembering the early morning ride by horse and carriage from Rome to the port of Civitavecchia. on her way, she had hoped, to the city of Antwerp. However, upon arrival in Genoa, staying with one of the Cardinal's cousins, she had been told of the turmoil and danger and had not been permitted, to travel any further at that time.

Viana smiled to herself, recalling how, at first, she thought it might have been a ploy, concocted by the Cardinal and her mother, to keep her from going further with this quest she had, to locate her, most probable, father.

But having seen the expression of the man that evening around the dinner table, she had seen the genuine concern for her welfare, and understanding the responsibility he had for her, she complied to his wishes.

Viana moved away from where she had been leaning and walked towards the stern. Twenty-four years old, she was tall, around five foot ten inches, and a breeze played with her long dark hair. Her vivid blue eyes continuing to take in the activities dockside, in preparation for the ship to leave.

She had recently received a letter, from another of the Cardinal's wide-spread cousins, it was from Monaco, would she like to come and stay with them.

An offer she gladly accepted. It would take her a step closer.

She then noticed the arrival of a monk.

He seemed a little out of place. He wore a long cloak, a grey green sort of colour, made from wool she thought, noticed his bare feet were tucked into leather sandals, carried a stick, around five foot in length and across one shoulder a type of satchel.

Someone approached him, spoke briefly, then gestured for the monk to follow him.

He looked up, noticed her. She gave a nod and a brief smile.

Her mother had been in charge of the servants and was also a confidante to the Cardinal. For Viana it had been a good upbringing in the Farnese household.

By the time she was sixteen, as well as Latin and Italian, she could also speak French fluently. She was looking forward to using that when reaching Monaco.

Viana, setting off to walk along the deck, stopped, looked up at the April sky and felt the breeze getting a little cooler.

Three months.

She was glad to be on the move again, though she had been well looked after, even been given her own maid, she longed for more social occasions.

Back in Rome she had often accompanied the cardinal to functions and knew on these occasions that he felt almost like a proud father.

Viana had enjoyed those events as she relished making conversations with people from a huge variety of backgrounds. These past months had not afforded her the opportunities for such events. She hoped for more social interactions when reaching Monaco. Deciding to go inside as it was now threatening to rain, she would find this monk, looking to hear his story, where he had come from, where was he going. Her ability to speak Latin, though not a huge difference from Italian, would surely be of help, he would surely notice and appreciate that.

Late afternoon, with the light already beginning to fade and the rain having set in, the two masted schooner departed. Viana returned to her cabin, it wouldn't be long before dinner time now, she was getting hungry. Sitting herself on the bed, she took out the leather pouch from a pocket in her long skirt. She would often hold it, take out its contents and admire it.

The very item, that had been bequeathed to her, the lovely miniature, painted on ivory, the very item that had prompted her quest, her longing, to travel and to seek out the person who had so beautifully made it. More importantly however, the person who, she was in no doubt, was her father.

Viana smiled to herself, recalling the conversation she had just had with the monk. She had sought him out, finding him the narrow galley of the ship, tucking into a bowl of soup. At first, he was incredibly shy, would hardly look at her.

But she was good at putting people at ease, spoke to him, in Latin, telling him all about the Cardinal, her mother, the many people she had met and that she was on her way to Monaco, to stay with some relations of the Cardinal.

She did not tell him the reason of her journey, but as she spoke, he became more and more relaxed, could see her genuine interest in him and started to talk.

Viana looked at the item she had slipped from the pouch, held it, felt it, then kissed it and put it back into the black leather pouch. In one of her leather bags, were five other pieces of art by the same artist, given to her by fellow artist, upon his death, a good friend of the Cardinal's, Giulio Clovio.

Standing up from the bunk, Viana checked herself in the mirror that hung above a wooden dresser, tucked the pouch back in the pocket of her skirt and thought back to the story the monk had told.

His name was Bonifatius, he was from Florence, and once he had overcome his shyness and could see the real interest of the striking woman that stood there by him in the galley, he told her the quest he was on. He, along with two others, had been given an assignment, a challenge of sorts, each of them chosen for this task.

He himself had to make his way to the Cathedral in Santiago de Compostela, in the west, a pilgrim journey. His brother Monk, whose name was Flavius, was sent to the north, to the Cathedral in Cologne and the third brother, Ignatius, to the southeast, to a Cathedral in Izmir. As the Romans had thus far already travelled well throughout Europe, they were each given a rudimentary map, featuring some highlights here and there, towns and landmark features that would guide them on their way.

Viana wished him well in his pilgrimage and left him to finish his soup. Quite a journey to undertake, with more or less just the clothes on his back, she was thinking, as she prepared herself to go to dinner, enjoying the motion of the ship as it sailed towards Monaco.

THE PRESENT; San Francisco

Friday 24th April

Terri Hudson swigged a little water from the bottle she carried around with her practically everywhere. As with so many places, the museum was closed.

Though many people had been asked if they could possibly, work from home, this, in Terri's case was just not feasible. She had decided to use the time, and the pleasure of not being disturbed, to do some cataloguing.

She was the assistant curator of the Museum of art.

Terri had changed her name back again, to that of her mother, her biological mother, from whom she had been kidnapped when only seven years old.

Having then lived and being schooled in a private girl's school for the next ten years, believing her to be the daughter of Julian and Sandra Pentegrass.

Julien was indeed her real father, but his name was Rozzini, Sandra was his new wife, and they chose her name to register her as he was wanted by the police in Oregon. Over the years she had made several friends at school but had only seen her father twice a year if that. The woman, whom she believed to be her mother, had not been there on those occasions. She had grown accustomed to being alone, had for herself created a back stop story that her folks were world travellers and so on..

To find out what had really happened, had taken her by surprise, to be reunited with her real mother, was fantastic, though a little awkward.

She was told of the whole story, mainly through a letter, a letter written in guilt, by the woman called Sandra, who had since fled, had flown to Hawaii and had not been heard of again.

Terri had, slowly, bonded with her mother and was pleased about that.

Also pleased that she had not been suffocated, by lost love, but, able to continue her schooling, coming away with a couple of degrees and had subsequently landed a job at the museum, working toward her aim of one day being a curator, especially in the field of art. Already, after less than a year, she had been made assistant curator.

Terri was very happy about that and could see that her mother, Alison, was too.

Taking another sip of water, she thought about her mother, and it just occurred to her, that since being reunited with her, she had not once referred to her, not once called her, mother.

Screwing the cap back on the bottle, she sighed, then carried on with her work.

She also, with a large amount of money paid out to her through the courts, was able to get herself into a lovely apartment, only a stone's throw from the museum.

This had been a little hard for her mother at first, but she had understood.

She loved her mother, knew the heartache and the struggle she had lived through over the period on ten years, even to the point of almost having been killed in her pursuit of finding her.

She knew of Sam, the man who had come to the rescue, she had heard her mother speak of him, sensing the emotion in her voice every time and looked forward to one day meeting him.

She would be forever grateful to him.

With the museum closed, due to the pandemic, she had the run of the place, only a couple of colleagues had come in earlier in the day. But she was now alone.

In the large room, inaccessible to the public, which housed racks and racks of paintings which, either had yet to be authenticated, or some who had been put aside to make room for other acquisitions, she had set up a workstation.

Laptop, clipboard, pens, and a folder to hand, she was checking the contents of this room, which, according to the notes in the folder, had not been done for three years.

The lock down situation was an ideal time, no disturbance.

The now nineteen-year-old stood up, arched her back, took another swig of water, going through the third bottle that day, then checked her watch.

Five o'clock. She ought to think about going home, getting changed and, she had just remembered, had promised to see her mother in the evening.

About to close her computer and getting ready to leave, she heard a noise.

A clinking sound. Someone was in the building.

One of her colleagues coming back?

Her boss, perhaps?

She closed her laptop, exited the archive room, then crossed through a room, which on occasions, was used as a training facility. But the tables had been folded and stacked away as had the chairs and her heels echoed around the walls as she walked across the wooden floor.

She headed for the door at the far end, which, as she got closer, opened.

THE PAST; Period 2

the year 1579- Cologne- Germany

Of the three monks, chosen by Father Dominic, Flavius was, by far, the eldest, almost twice the age of the other two. Also, he, most of all, had the look about him, that folks would expect a monk to look like. He was shortish, stout, had a balding head with a trim of hair around the back, in what is referred to as a tonsure style.

His green-brown cloak was several shades darker than those worn by the other two, and it almost touched the ground. The staff he carried was shorter and thicker and rather than a satchel of sorts, Flavius carried a small cask around his neck. He too also had adorned around his neck, a cross and a key. Though the key, made of silver, had a longer chain, and was kept from view.

He was almost there. From the old farm building, where he had slept overnight in a loft area, he could see the imposing towers of the cathedral.

As he set off on this, the final part, of his pilgrim journey, he thought back to when Father Dominic had gathered the three of them, he had collected them from the monastery personally, had asked them to bring what little personal belonging they might have which they wanted to take with them, then, had taken them to the house in the centre of the city. Here they would stay until it was time to go.

An imposing house, on the edge of the river Arno...

..there he had taken them into the large dining room, where now there were only a few pieces of furniture, the large oak dining table, one chair on one side, three chairs on the opposite. On the table there lay some letters, and gleaming in the light by the table lamp, there were three keys, three silver keys attached to silver chains.

Flavius noted that each key was different. Father Dominic then, after they had been asked to sit down, had sat himself opposite them, and told them all about baby Anna..

..The autumn sun rose from the horizon and having been given some food and drink by the farmer and his wife, Flavius walked through the countryside, the cathedral towers a beacon in the early morning light..

..After the discussion and the assignment he had given them, Father Dominic took them to another room in the house, on the first floor, and there, in a room which had three window facing the river, was a man.

There was an array of painting equipment, three easels had been erected and three wood panels placed on each one, all were the same height, but two were narrower, in fact half the width of the centre panel.

The man was introduced, and Father Dominic, having brought along the keys, gave one to each of them, and explained about the importance of the painting to be done.

Flavius, being the most senior, would be portrayed on the centre piece..

..As he made his way along a narrow dirt road, he smiled a little, thinking how uncomfortable he had felt, being painted by this artist, who, apparently had travelled up from Rome.

He would be glad when he reached his destination.

With just a roughly sketched paper map in hand, he had set out from Florence.

He had reached the lower region of the Alps in a matter of days, going over would be too hazardous, and so began a journey around the foothills that eventually took him to the upper reaches of the Rhine.

Seeing this mighty river drawn on the map he had been given, Flavius looked for and found, an opportunity to travel by barge.

Sadly, he wasn't able to travel a vast distance, but nevertheless he figured to have cut his journey time by at least three days.

Flavius also had, in the beginning of his journey, thought deeply about the opportunity he had been given, this trek, this journey, was very much, he felt, an adventure, and one which he and his fellow brother monks were humbled to be given. He also thought about the choice he had, whether or not, after having safely delivered the important silver key, he would return to Florence, travel elsewhere, or stay in Cologne. Seeing the imposing towers of the cathedral drawing nearer and nearer, feeling his body ache in many places, Flavius had decided that he would stay.

Whilst near Izmir

With the rain beating down, the wind howling, coming in from the sea, Ignatius was thankful that he had found shelter. The old barn wasn't totally wind or rainproof, but he had found a spot that was dry and listened as the wind beat the rain against the wooden structure. The sea, not far away from where he was, was also audible, he heard the waves crashing on the shore.

He knew he wasn't far away now from his destination and thought back to the time he was in one of the upper rooms of the big house, standing as still as he could, whilst the artist was painting..

..Flavius, the eldest, had been first, the artist, who spoke very little, took only little time, to bring up an outline, then spent time focusing on the cloth of the cloak, the short staff that his fellow monk had, and, the key, the silver key..

...As the rain lashed down, the wind not seemingly ready to calm down yet, Ignatius remembered as he had waited, all that Father Dominic had told them, their instructions, their destination, the importance of that key, looking at the one he himself had around his neck..

...He knew all their destinations, Bonifatius, to the West, destination the Cathedral in Santiago de Compostela, a fair distance to travel. Flavius, currently trying hard to stand still, would be going north, to Cologne, perhaps not the same distance, but not easy, mountain ranges to overcome. He was given Izmir, to the southeast.

At least it should be warmer, he had thought at the time.

As the youngest of the three, he was the last to be painted, thinking at the time, as he had seen the portraits done of his two brothers, how quickly and masterfully the artist had captured them..

The light grew a little brighter, the dark clouds began to lighten and the wind, at last, dwindled from a loud roar to a whisper.

There would still be enough daylight left to travel a little further, prior to practically running towards the barn when the storm had started, he had seen a village of sorts not far away. Coming away from his sheltered spot, he was happy to continue.

He was hungry and for sure he would get some food somewhere.

Reaching the dirt road upon which he been travelling, with the coastline on his right, he again saw the settlement ahead.

Father Dominic, after giving each of them such detailed instructions, imparting to them the importance of their mission, he told them at the end, this after having spent four days in the big house, that it was up to them, to find a new home at their respective destinations, or come back, or go anywhere else that perhaps God might be leading them to. With his stomach rumbling, Ignatius walked towards the small settlement and looked around him. Already he had taken in so much beautiful scenery, had in wonder appreciated God's creation and as he looked at the still somewhat turbulent sea to his right, he wondered if this was the area that he would stay in. First things first though, he thought, something to eat. He had eaten a little not long after the sun had risen, it was now mid-afternoon. He figured that he should reach Izmir the following day.

THE PRESENT; Paris

Saturday 25th April

Sophie had decided to involve two men. Two men who meant very much to her, two men, whom she trusted and cared for.

One was Sam, Sam Price, now living in Boston and about to, hopefully, due to these pandemic restrictions, get married in the new year to Chrissie.

She had, at one point, fallen for Sam, had, perhaps hoped even, certainly longed for, a relationship, but it just wasn't to be. She considered him to be a great and trusted friend, after all, he had come to her rescue once.

Then there was Martijn Vogel, he was a Dutch policeman, Sam had called on him to help her, and, lo and behold a relationship, a courtship, had developed, both working together on research at the time, but the distance apart, was too much of a distance apart, but she cared for him, liked him, a lot.

Sam was good at his research, especially when it came to pieces of art, Martijn, being a policeman, could hopefully help with what she had learned from the letter Roberto had written her. It was very early Saturday morning. Sophie made herself some breakfast, a light breakfast, two slices of toast, topped with a lashing of jam, a glass of orange juice and a cup of tea. Looking out of the kitchen window in her apartment, she took her mind back to the previous day.

Having spent some considerable time in researching the painting that had arrived on her doorstep, having read the letter from Roberto, over and over again, and being none the wiser, she had then made the decision to involve both Sam and Martijn.

She sent Sam an e-mail, along with a couple of photos she had taken of the painting and having asked him what he could find out, she would await his reply.

She had, late afternoon, contacted Martijn, briefly spoke about the parcel she had received, informed him of the circumstances in which the painting had come to Roberto and could he find out anything surrounding that time and place, back in 1963. She had wanted to speak longer, but realising her heart was beating quite a bit faster and rather than not being able to control her voice, had made an excuse quickly, and had ended the call.

No doubt about it. She still had feelings for him.

Meanwhile it was ten o'clock Friday evening in San Francisco,

Alison Hudson stood in her kitchen and knew she had feelings for him.

What a day it had been, or more precisely, she thought, as she took the dishes out of the dishwasher, what a few hours.

Automatically placing the crockery and cutlery in their right places, she took her mind back, to only hours earlier, when he had stood in her kitchen, preparing the meal, which he had insisted he would like to do..

..'Still nothing?' he had asked, looking concerned as he could see that she was worried.

'No' Alison answered, 'It's so unlike her..'

'You know that she was going to the museum, was going to do some cataloguing' he said, turning the oven off and walking towards her, deciding to take charge.

'Yes, 'Alison answered, then looking up from her phone as he approached, asked 'Why?'

'Then we go there, it can't be that far, see if her car is there, knock on windows and doors, 'he answered, then stopping right before her, he took hold of her shoulders, looked into her eyes, 'break the door down if we have to' smiling.

Alison briefly smiled back at him.

'Okay, thank you, can we take your rental?'

'Of course'.

Releasing her shoulders, he watched her turn and head for the hallway.

He followed, recalling a time, not that long ago, when he had first met her.

She had arrived by taxi, at the police station, in Albuquerque, he had arrived on his trusty Indian motorcycle. She assumed that he was with the police, ordered him to take her to the bus station. She had been commanding and confident.

He had fallen for her that day.

He had flown from his hometown, to spend a weekend with her, they had been talking on the phone regularly for the past eight or so months.

She invited him. He accepted. He arrived in a rental he had picked up from the airport to find her a little upset and worried.

She had tried on several occasions to reach her daughter, had invited her over to meet the man she had spoken to her about.

To meet Simon Lightfoot.

Three minutes later, holding the passenger door open for her, Alison got into the car and gave instructions as to where to go.

He looked across at her, smiling, saying' This is the, you, I remember, giving instructions!'

She smiled back at him, feeling relaxed to be with him, but something was bothering her, she sensed that something was wrong.

Was Terri alright?

Two hours earlier

It was unusual for anyone to be here, it had just gone five o'clock and when the door opened, Terri was first surprised, but was then the first to react.

One of the things she had learned, particularly in an all-girls school and being prepared for the outside world, was self-defence.

Two people suddenly appeared. A man and a woman.

They were as startled as she was but reacted slower.

Terri, a very fit nineteen-year-old, moved forward quickly, then kicked out her left foot, catching the man just below the knee on his left leg, then in quick succession, shot her other leg out, connecting right on target.

The man gasped, cried out in pain, and buckled to the floor, clutching where Terri's foot had connected hard. But by this time, the woman had reacted, had taken several steps away and when Terri turned to face her, noticed the gun in her hand.

No amount of speed and momentum she might have, would not match that of a bullet. Terri stepped away from the man, still groaning softly, and struggling to get up.

He would be in his late twenties she figured, was slightly stocky in build, already showed sign of hair loss and his face was somewhere between a deep red and purple. Terri looked steadily into the eyes of the woman holding the gun, thinking it was perhaps her she should have attacked first.

She was about the same age as the man, had short blond hair, blue eyes that returned her gaze steadily, and was obviously contemplating as to what to do next.

The gun, a small handgun, was held firmly with both hands.

Terri was in no doubt, that the woman would shoot, if provoked.

Hands by her side, she stood and waited.

Just under two hours later.

'That's her car' Alison said, spotting it as they came around the corner and into the rear car parking area of the museum that was used for staff.

Simon drove the car right up to it.

Just then a blue coloured van, drove around a far corner of the building, picking up speed quickly it drove past as both Simon and Alison were getting out, and sped away. Alison was running towards the staff entrance of the museum.

Simon focused on the van, noted the number, grabbed his phone, and pressed the emergency code. Then following Alison who was by now trying the door handle, he repeated the number softly to himself, waiting for the call to be answered.

Alison ran away from the door, heading around the corner of the building where the van had emerged from. Simon followed, answered the woman who spoke and said he wanted the police..

He was also aware that Alison had gone from view and ran to catch up with her.

He then, whilst running, told of a suspected crime having taken place at the museum, told of a blue coloured van speeding away and recited the number.

Alison had reached another door, tried the handle and it opened.

'In here 'she called out, sensing that Simon wasn't far behind her, faintly registering that he was on the phone to someone.

'Terri, Terri! she called out, her voice echoing inside the empty building.

'Where would she have been, what was she going to do today' Simon asked, right beside Alison now.

Alison stopped, looked at him, thought for a second, 'Cataloguing!'

'This way'

She had been here before, her daughter had proudly shown her around, showed her the office, which was hers to work from, and the various rooms and ante rooms of the art museum. She knew where her daughter was going to be today.

Simon followed, impressed at the turn of speed Alison had.

He had fallen for her on that first encounter, he knew now, that he was very much falling in love with this woman.

Alison opened a door, a stairway before them, she strode down, two steps at a time. Simon now having to move fast to keep pace. Then a door, and she called out again as she opened it.

'Terri!'

'Mother?' 'In here! The blue door! '

Relieved to hear her voice, it didn't register then, that she had called her, mother.

The door was locked as she tried the knob.

Simon could see that it was a store cupboard of sorts, not a door that needed a secure lock. 'Let me' he said, stepping in front of Alison.

Then, producing some sort of tool from his jeans pocket, inserted it and with a few wiggles and prods, heard the click. The door opened.

Terri blinked from the sudden burst of light coming into the room.

She was tied, wrist behind her, to a steel rack that held copious volumes of books.

They had shoved her inside, secured her and left, closing the door, locking it and throwing the key across the room, she heard it slide across the wooden floor.

Alison, reached her first, took hold of her daughter's face and kissed her forehead and Simon, having found a light switch, turned it on and made his way to untie the girl's wrists.

When her arms were free, she embraced her mother, kissed her on the cheek, then said, 'I must check something, we need to call the police, 'then slipped past them both, out of the cupboard and ran towards the next door, this she opened and entered. Alison, throwing a look at Simon, followed.

'The police are on the way' Simon said, I hear sirens, I'll meet them, I take it the main doors are this way?' Indicating with his hand.

Alison turned, took in what he had said, then quickly walked up to him, planted a kiss on his lips, then said, 'Yes, go!'

Simon smiled, the relief on her face was plain for him to see.

Alison went through the door where Terri had disappeared through and found her, at the far end of the room, there was a small table, upon which were several, what looked to be ring-binder folders, a small laptop, and various sheets of paper.

Terri had one of the ring-binders open and walking towards a passageway. There were four such passageways, each with racks on either side that could slide in and out, each rack containing a piece of art.

Alison had not remembered entering this room, perhaps Terri

hadn't shown her, she was amazed at how many paintings there were as she walked down the passage following her daughter.

Terri had pulled out a rack.

'This is the one' she said, looking around at her approaching mother, 'I have just been here, this one is out of place, it is also empty.'

'Fingerprints' Alison called out, reaching her daughters side.

'Of course,' Terri said, blushing a little' well done mother'.

Alison felt her heartbeat loudly in her chest. This was not just from the exertion, the running, the calling out, the finding. This was because, she now realised, that she had called her, mother, twice now.

'Come here a minute' she said, stopping in front of Terri, her face had coloured too.

They hugged for several moments.

Voices were heard.

'In here Simon' Alison said, turning around.

Moments later he appeared.

'Meet my lovely daughter Terri, 'she said, then turning, 'Terri, this is Simon'.

Two police officers were right behind Simon.

Terri nodded a friendly hello to Simon, said, 'Hi' then walked past them both and spoke directly to the officers.

' I'm Terri Hudson, assistant curator of the museum, a painting has been stolen, I was held at gun point' hearing her mother's gasp, ' then put into a cupboard' turning to her mother, she added, ' I wasn't hurt,' then back to the officer she had been addressing, ' They came for a specific painting, they knew it was here, but, it must have taken them some time to find it, I heard them leave not that long ago.'

The second officer then asked, 'Can you describe them ma'am?'

'Oh absolutely!' Terri answered.

THE PAST; Period 3

The year 1593- Florence

It was time. Gina Romano had set everything up, the room, overlooking the piazza, was the living room of the modest dwelling where they lived.

Upon entry to the house from the piazza, a set of stairs led to the upstairs dwelling. Two bedrooms, a kitchen, and a dining room were on the first floor, then a narrow staircase led to another bedroom, at the back of the house, overlooking a garden below, and a living room at the front, a roomy space, even though the roof slanted down at little. It was on this floor that she had placed the girl, though not at first, but, since the child had turned ten years old, this upper level had been hers to live in. It was here, where two scrolls of paper, rolled and bound with a ribbon, lay on a low table, it was here, in one of four chairs, that Gina sat, waiting.

She heard footsteps, then, bounding into the room, she came.

Her long red hair flowing, her face shiny and bright, her dark green eyes full of life and excitement. The dress was made of a dark green material.

She smiled broadly, happily.

It was her birthday.

'Hello mother' she said, quickly coming over to Gina, who was now standing up, and the girl, already the same height as Gina, flung herself into her arms.

She then looked at the scrolls on the table and looked back at Gina.

'Do tell me mother' she said, holding Gina's hands, 'what is the surprise you told me about this morning, that I had to wait all day for!' throwing a mock scowl.

'There will be a lot to take in Anna' Gina said, her voice a little husky, a little emotional, 'please, I would like you to sit down, and please listen carefully, I am going to tell you a story, and it's important, that you listen, okay?'

'Yes Mother,' the girl answered, 'are you okay mother? 'Sensing the emotion in her voice.

'Yes, 'Gina answered, 'Yes, I am, so, now, listen, okay?'

Anna sat herself down, sensed the importance of the moment, and paid attention.

Gina stood by the window, looked down to the piazza below, watching people, a few horses and carts, a wagon, for a moment, lost in time.

She then sighed, and turned, looked at Anna, sighed again, and began,

'Dearest Anna, I love you very much, and what I have to say, is not easy, but very important, 'looking directly into Anna's green eyes, who was focused, nodded, and said nothing. 'I am Gina, ..Gina Romano, and I am not your real mother, sadly, when you were three years old, your mother and your father, died, from a type of sickness that affected many people here.'

Pausing for a moment, Gina then continued' Your father was Petrus Kastanje, now he was a Baron, from a royal family, in the north of Europe, a long way from here.

He fell in love, with your mother, a beautiful lady, you look so much like her, she too had red hair. But she was not from royal blood, in fact, she was, a gypsy, a traveller, moved with her family over many miles and many countries.

Your father met her, her name was Odette. 'Gina paused again for a moment, threw a quick look out of the window, then turned to Anna, who sat, having paled a little, but with eyes open and very attentive, not speaking, but wondering what else would be told.

Your father was not to be denied. He had fallen in love with her, and she had fallen in love with him. Her family was not happy, his family even less so.

But Petrus, being the eldest male child, had a plan, he would take his Odette and leave, travel far away. But, not without taking some of his belongings.

So, one day, they made their plan complete, they left.

There were three wagons, each pulled by two horses, then your father sat on his horse and your mother rode beside him on her horse, then there were six servants, four young men and two young woman. They left very early one day, travelled for three days in one direction, heading to the west.

Then, they turned and headed south, this they did for two weeks, before then again turning east. Eventually they came to Florence.

Nearly three months had passed.

They settled here in this city. They were financially well to do, your father knew how to do business, how to be in charge, how to lead people. He bought a large house, and they were soon part of the new inhabitants.

Then, the sickness came, there had been a sickness, called a plague, earlier, nearly two hundred years earlier, killing more than half of the population of the city. This one was not as bad, but, many people, did die, sadly, including your mother and father, you were almost three years old.

Again, Gina paused, walked up to Anna, knelt before her, took hold of her hands, 'there is a lot to still tell you, I know this must be so much for you, but I made a promise to tell you today, on your birthday, you have to know'.

Anna, her eyes a little moist, nodded, but before Gina could continue, spoke, her voice barely above a whisper, 'I love you, and for me, you are my mother'.

Gina nodded, her eyes welling up now, she stood up quickly, walked over to the window and again looked down onto the daily activities below.

'Your father had enemies. Your mother had enemies. Your father was in danger of being found by his younger brother, who was looking for the family fortunes that your father had taken, as he had a right to do, and your mother was being looked for by her younger sister,

Alexandria, who was jealous and wanted the riches that she knew her sister had.' saying all this whilst still looking out the window. The sky was getting darker.

Then turned, and continued, 'A very important man, came into your father and mother's life, he became a dear friend, a trusted friend, a loyal friend.

His name was Father Dominic.

He knew of the danger, from the brother and from the sister. Knew that they would come, after your mother and father had so suddenly died from the disease. Someone would surely come, so, Father Dominic felt he needed to make a plan, quickly, but carefully.

He himself was a simple man, he had no need for wealth, he was a man of God.

But he loved your father and your mother, they had brought many people together, they were influential in the city, and worked for the good.

He needed to ensure, that, first of all, Anna, you were safe, he was very worried about your safety. That's when he came and spoke with me.

I had just entered a convent, here, in the city, the one that's just over the river.

I was young, I felt I too, needed to follow God, to be a servant for Him.

Father Dominic called me, took me to the big house, and there he told me the story of your father and mother, and of the need, to look after you, to bring you up, to protect you, teach you,' Gina paused, smiled at Anna, ' I was very privileged to have you in my life, it was wonderful to see you grown and to see now, who you have become, you are not my daughter, and yet, you are my daughter'

Anna got up from her chair, she didn't speak but took her mother in her arms and hugged her.

'Goodness Anna,' Gina said, pulling herself out of Anna's grasp, 'there is so much more to tell, please, sit down again'.

Then, 'thank you' and retrieving a lace handkerchief from

somewhere within her garments, she blew her nose, wiped her eyes and again taking a deep breath, continued with what she needed to tell Anna.

'So, Father Dominic explained the situation, he then took me out of the convent, set me up in this house, and you were given to me.

A few days later he brought me the documents that you see on that table there, more on that soon, also I was given the finances to clothe and feed you, and to school you, using, as you know, several private tutors, you needed to be kept a secret, and as far as the people knew, you were my daughter...'

'Which I am' Anna interjected,

'Father Dominic, 'Gina went on, throwing the girl a quick smile, 'made plans. He first had some folks come to the big house and take away many of the things, like furniture, painting, ornaments and so on.

He then had someone come to make a big chest, I have seen this chest, Father Dominic showed it to me, it was a big, strong chest, with many bands across, and it had three locks, also of course, three keys.

Now, there is more to tell on this chest, but these are written in the scrolls for you only to know. Father Dominic then selected three monks, three men whom he knew and trusted.

He gave each a key.

Then sent them out, each to a different location, a different cathedral, somewhere, these details are also in the scrolls for you.

Then, he had an artist, come in, who painted these three monks, Father Dominic explained as to the reason why he had them portrayed, each of them on a wooden panel, I saw them. He showed them to me, there were two smaller panels, narrower, these were connected to the bigger panel, and could close, like a book.' Gina said and demonstrated with her hands.

'Father Dominic took these with him when he went to Rome.

There is more detailed information about them in those scrolls.

I remember their names' Gina said, recalling the day she had come to see Father Dominic and had been taken upstairs to where the artist, a man from Rome, was busy painting.

'There was the elder brother, he was Flavius, then there were Bonifatius and Ignatius'

'I wonder where they went?' Anna whispered.

'Father Dominic has written it all down' Gina answered, then' Now, the last part of the story, from me anyway, I know nothing more, so, you, my dear Anna, are a princess, you are royal. The scrolls will help you understand further, in order to claim your inheritance, again, making sure it doesn't fall into the wrong hands, you must read the scrolls carefully, as to what Father Dominic has written.

The paintings were made so you know what keys to look for, the scroll themselves will help you where to look. You are the rightful heir to a kingdom, and all that represent, how exactly that works, I don't know. You, now being eighteen years of age, must read and decide for yourself.

Only you, with the help of God, will know what to do.

THE PRESENT; New York

Sunday 26th April

'Seriously?!' Tammy exclaimed, then read it again.
'Unbelievable!'

It was mid-afternoon. Though her apartment was quite large, Tamara Wilson was beginning to get cabin fever. She could go out for exercise, but used her own equipment instead, having set up one of the bedrooms as a gym of sorts, with an exercycle, a rowing machine and a punching bag suspended from the ceiling.

This virus was everywhere, it didn't seem to be getter any better, but rather the opposite. Record numbers were being admitted into hospitals around the world, there were shortages of space, as well as shortages of equipment, particularly breathing apparatus as many patients had to be put onto ventilators.

Tammy once more got up from the dining table where she had stationed herself and made into her research centre, already having discovered much of her family lineage these past months.

She, and her best friend Chrissie in Boston, both having decided to spend the time they had now, being in a lock down situation, to delve into the past, to research ancestry in her case and for Chrissie, she was looking into the life of Sam's, the man she was due to marry, great grandfather, who had been an ambassador with an eye for art. Her own research had gone well so far, having traced her family back over seven generations, having discovered that her ancestors on her mother's side had come from France, and that it had been her six times grandfather who had been the first to get to the United States.

She had also discovered that their current wealth, or rather, her current wealth, the fabulous apartment overlooking Central Park in New York not to mention the substantial funds in the bank, had been due to her family having owned several industries in the past, a flour and syrup factory and a large bakery producing cakes.

Tammy had still to find out how all of that had started, following the trail of a William Quinton who had been the one that had left Plymouth in England and had travelled to Philadelphia, way back in around seventeen sixty-three.

He had, she discovered, travelled to find out about the fate of his cousin, who had been murdered and who's killer had travelled on his cousin's ticket.

Tammy stood, arms folded, by the window and thought about what she had just learned, went back to the table, read again what she had read twice already, and picked up her phone.

It had only been the previous evening, that she and Chrissie had spoken at length. It had been only then, that her friend had mentioned that Sam had received a call from Sophie in Paris. She knew Sophie, had met her, had stayed with her a while back, during the time that Sam had gone missing, and Chrissie and a woman called Alison, were in search of him. She had flown to Paris, to help.

Sophie had called to ask Sam for his assistance in the search of an old painting, Sam was good at research. Chrissie had mentioned that Sophie had received a painting, from a known forger, that it was very old, not a forgery and probably painted around the mid fifteen hundreds. She had also said that it was the painting of a monk.

It was this information that had brought the exclamation from her lips.

She had been trying to find out more about her ancestor William, had discovered that he had married, but she had been side-tracked when reading some information about the trading post in Philadelphia, where William had arrived.

She found a little history about it when discovering that young William had landed there.

Zecheriah Strauss ran the Trading Post for almost forty years.

He, together with his brother, who had sadly passed away due an accident only a year after they had set up the post, began small, but over time this turned into quite some emporium. In the history of the life of the Trading Post, Tammy read about the mention of a ledger, called 'The Zecheriah Ledger'.

This intrigued her, so, she searched for, and found it.

This ledger contained all the transactions that Zecheriah had made, over that period, both purchases and sales, often with descriptions and details as to where the sellers or buyer had come from or were going to.

In the month of April 1770, two hundred and fifty years ago, Tammy mused as she calculated the time difference, a painting was bought, described as, a painting of a monk, presumably Italian, wearing brown cloak, carrying a staff and wearing a crucifix and a silver key around his neck. Zecheriah, obviously, was a man who liked details, for he also mentioned that he had purchased it from a Captain Pique, who had just arrived from Plymouth, which was uncanny, Tammy thought, as her ancestor William had sailed from that very port, and that it was oil painted on wood.

'Hi, you are not going to believe this' Tammy said, as Christina Small answered the phone.

'No, no, not more about my family, listen, ..'

In Boston

'Sam!' Chrissie called out, still listening to Tammy, then, when he arrived, Tammy, say all that again to Sam, please,' handing the phone to him...

'Unbelievable!' Sam said, after a few moments, then, 'That just sounds very much like what I am looking for, you say this Zecheriah purchased it from Captain Pique, in April 1770, now, I don't suppose there is any entry as to when it was sold?'

In New York

'Silly me,' Tammy said, scrolling on her laptop, 'got too excited to even think about that, 'a few moments later, 'Still scrolling through, 'she said, then more moments of silence, ' Wooo, yes, here it is, '

Tammy said, ' this is in May, goodness, the year 1803, that's, that's over thirty years later! Sold it to, a Rudolph Meyer, came in from Spain, but is listed as German.

In Boston

'You, my dear Tammy, are a star! Thank you very much, I'll pass you back to Chrissie..' Sam said, then heading back upstairs to the room he had set up as a study, sat down behind his laptop, he typed in the names and dates she had given him.

'Only in your heart', the song by the band 'America', was playing on Sam's sound system which he had set up in the smallest of the four upstairs bedrooms.

With this lock down, he wanted to set up a place where he could do his research, and play music, as he loved to work whilst the music was on. This was not exactly Chrissie's way of doing her research, she preferred quiet and was happy in the living room with the kitchen close at hand.

After the call from Tammy, Sam immediately set about to follow up on what she had discovered, in the Zecheriah Ledger.

A painting of a monk. It was what Sophie had asked him to help her investigate.

A painting of a monk, that she now had in her possession. She had sent him an e-mail with a couple of photographs attached. But surely this was not the same monk, Sam pondered, as mentioned in Zecheriah's Ledger, looking at the prints he had copied from the photos she had sent.

Sophie had said, about the painting received from the forger Roberto Solari, that it was a panel, which at one time had two side panels, one on each side.

Sam studied the prints, one was a straight on shot, the second was from the side, showing clearly, where at one time, something had been attached.

She had the centre piece, he could see what Sophie had meant, about the lines that revealed where two panels would have closed in upon it.

Could it be, that this Captain Pique, from France, had been in possession of this centre piece, or one of those side panels, and who was this Rudolph Meyer who had purchased it? A German, had he taken it back to Europe?

Sam sat himself behind the desk, a wonderful bureau really that he had picked up a while back, purchased at an auction, this was now in the small bedroom, along with a comfy desk chair, a lamp, one bookcase and on a low table his sound system.

Meanwhile Chrissie, having finished her chat with Tammy, was back to doing her research.

A while ago, she discovered in one of the journals belonging to Sam's great grandfather, who was an ambassador, a picture of a painting he had once owned.

It was titled 'The lovesick Maiden', by the artist Jan Steen, and in the painting, placed on a dressing table of sorts, was an ornate box. A box that looked remarkably like the one she had found in a cupboard under the stairs when her father had died, and the house had come to her. She subsequently found out that it had been purchased by her grandfather, Eddie, in an auction here in Boston.

Chrissie was now trying to find out more on this painting, where was it now, and, how the ornate box had become part of that painting.

With coffee by her side, reading glasses on her forehead, she was scrolling the screen on her laptop, pen and paper nearby.

Back upstairs, Sam discovered a name, as he felt he needed a starting point, he had begun with where the painting had been sent from, this he knew from Sophie, was Cannes, this forger, Roberto had acquired it, according to the letter that had accompanied the painting, from a woman, in 1963, a woman by the name of Natalie Umbrego.

So, now having the names of the man who sold it in Philadelphia, a Frenchman named Captain Pique, who had arrived from Plymouth, and the name of the man who subsequently purchased it, though over thirty years later, whose name was Rudolph Meyer, along with the information from the letter that had accompanied the painting, a woman named Natalie Umbrego, and the geographical information of Cannes, he set about his search.

He decided to begin with the most recent date, that of 1963 and the name of the woman from Cannes. It didn't take long before he discovered something, he found a connection in Monaco. Vianetti Vineyards.

Making some notes, he then searched for a Captain Pique and the year 1770.

THE PAST; Period 4

the year 1770- Plymouth

Evonie Dupois Quinton was laid to rest.

For some moments, Rene and his wife Virginia, stood by the graveside.

Other mourners, and the officiating vicar, moved away.

They held on to each other on a chilly April morning. Then, when they at last turned to head back home, they noticed the man.

As they passed him, he nodded a greeting, but said nothing. Rene and Virginia headed for their home, passing by the docks of the port city, Rene thought back to when he had first arrived here, all those years ago.

He and his mother had landed here, from Le Havre in France, in the year 1729. Sadly, his father had been imprisoned as the catholic and protestant war had been raging in mainland Europe. Fights, skirmishes, destructions of buildings, destruction of churches, chaos. They had managed to flee, had reached Plymouth safely. Years passed. His father had never reached them, though no official news, it was without doubt, his mother had accepted, that her husband had perished.

He and Virginia walked hand in hand by the dockyard, heading for their cottage not far away, each with his and her own thoughts. Seven years earlier, they had waved goodbye to their only son, to William, as he had set off to find the man who had so brutally killed his cousin and had taken his travel documents to sail to Philadelphia.

A letter they had received two months later, informed them that he had not been successful to find this man, whom the police had referred to as the Oxman, but that he had met a lovely young girl and was getting married.

Sadly, they had not received any more letters since.

Virginia looked across at her husband as they walked up the path to their cottage, then thought about the man they had seen at the cemetery, he did look sort of familiar.

Anton Pique, after having nodded to the passing man and woman, he knew to be Evonie's son and wife, waited a few more moments, then walked over to the graveside. He had been in love with her. But, although she knew her husband had most likely been killed, she honoured his name and her vows and would not consider any other relationship, but that of friends.

He stood there for some time, then hearing the town's church clock chime the hour, he closed his eyes briefly, then bowed, put his cap back on and walked to the port.

He was the captain of a two master and due to sail later that day.

Whilst in that same year in Cologne

Rudolph Meyer was a scholar. He was a gangly figure that stood well over six foot, had poor eyesight, and his skin was a pasty creamy colour at the best of times.

He was, due to the very nature of his appearance, a lonely man.

Shunned by the men for being at least a head and shoulders taller than anyone around him. He was sullen in his manner, had a stammer on top of that which didn't help in even trying to establish a communication with anyone.

The women would step well to the side as they found him most undesirable.

He studied, he read books, he would spend his days mainly indoor. The sun causing his skin to get blotchy and irritable.

Rudolph was born in Cologne. As well as often to be found in an old library that lay adjacent the river, he would also spend time in the Cathedral.

Then, only three years ago, he discovered a letter. An old letter.

It was tucked inside a Latin volume of a book of legions.

The letter, hand scribed, was written in that language, but Rudolph was well versed in several languages, his native Germanic tongue, as well as French, Spanish and Italian, and the older version of that, Latin.

The letter changed his life.

He became more confident in himself, he became more distant to his fellow men, and women, and felt he now had a new direction, a challenge, and one, he told himself, that he only, would be able to accomplish.

He became a treasure hunter.

The letter had been written, in the year 1593, by a senior monk, simply named Flavius, who was seventy-five years of age. In it, and quite a lengthy letter it was, he tells the story of how, and why, he had come from Florence.

It was three years ago now when he made this discovery.

Since that day, everything changed.

Rudolph knew a number of things, from the detailed letter.

Firstly, there was a key, the key that Flavius had brought from Florence to Cologne, it needed to be found. Secondly, he had the destinations of the other two Monks, being Santiago de Compostela and Izmir. And thirdly, he knew that the paintings that had been made of the three monks would, together, give a code, a secret of where, a large chest filled with riches, could be found.

Rudolph needed three keys, then needed the three paintings, in order to solve the clues as to where this chest was. A treasure hunt.

How that letter had found its way into that Latin book, was a mystery in itself, but Rudolph thought it might have been placed there on purpose, for someone with the knowledge of Latin, to find it. He had found it.

He alone, could do this. He would search and find. He would then, be popular.

Often to be found in the large cathedral, Rudolph was no stranger and an accepted visitor. He searched the various nooks and crannies, searched the vaults below and the various little chambers dotted around the vast building.

He found the key.

In an old cupboard, housing a few other keys, as well as some dusty books, some loose sheets of music, two brass bells, a box of candles and two torn sheets of a dark red material. He knew this was the key he was looking for the moment he saw it.

His heart leapt into his throat. He took it home.

Rudolph lived with his ageing mother. His father having passed many years ago. She lived downstairs, not able to manage to very steep steps that led to the next floor where there were two small rooms.

Rudolph began to set one of those rooms up as his treasure hunt room.

A small table, upon which were several books, and the very letter written by Flavius. Then a simple wooden chair behind that and a bookcase.

The letter and a key.

In the following days, he looked to find out any more about this monk called Flavius. Discovered the very Monastery where he had lived since his arrival from Florence and was granted a visit.

He was welcomed, was asked how he knew about brother Flavius and created a story about some records he had found in the cathedral.

Whilst there he was shown some belongings, in the form of letters, that he had received and of some that he had written, a journal of sorts.

Would he like to read them, he was asked.

He would indeed.

Whilst he was somewhat disappointed, he did find out an important clue, Father Dominic had been the writer of several letter to Flavius, in one of them, an earlier one written in the year 1580, he tells Flavius that the set of paintings had been sent to a person known by the cardinal, to a woman, named Viana Vanetti, in Monaco.

Coming away that day and heading home he came across three women heading towards him. Rudolph smiled briefly at them as they passed.

They hadn't crossed the street, they hadn't avoided his stare, they hadn't shied away.

Entering his house that afternoon, he wondered, might he at last have an opportunity for romance. Might he even, fall in love.

THE PRESENT; San Francisco

Sunday 26th April

'I'm in love'

On the other end of the line, Chrissie smiled, 'In love Alison?'

'Yes, do you remember last year, when I was helping Terri's teacher, Millie, and about the man, Barbara's brother, who was presumed dead and turned up?' Alison asked.

It was early evening. Simon was on his way back to the airport to fly home.

'Yes, I remember' Chrissie in Boston replied,' he was the man, or really a boy at the time, who killed the teacher's mother, at that archaeological site, some thirty years ago?'

'Yes, exactly,' Alison replied, 'well, I had travelled, had flown from here to Albuquerque, then arrived at the police station...'

'Then commandeered the guy on the Indian motorcycle...' Chrissie finished, recalling the conversation.

'Good memory Chrissie! yes him, well, we have kept in touch, then, one day, when speaking with him, I said, come over for a weekend.' Alison said, thinking at the time, as she finished the call, how bold she had been.

'I guess that he did?' Chrissie surmised, pleased for her friend, they had, though at first rivals for the affection of Sam, bonded, in their search, when Sam had gone missing.

Alison sat down on the two-seater in the lounge, where earlier they had comfortably sat together and continued her conversation, 'Yes, he came on Friday, but then, well, something else happened.' her tone changing, which Chrissie picked up on.

'Alison, are you okay?'

'Oh, yes, yes, sorry, it was, well, I had invited Terri over, you know, for dinner and to meet Simon...'

'Simon' Chrissie in Boston said to herself inwardly, having been trying hard to recall his name.

'.. anyway, when he arrived, I had been trying to get hold of Terri, but she wouldn't answer, I was worried, I don't know why, just a feeling, you know..'

'Is she alright? Did something happen?' Chrissie asked, concerned, as her friends voice, which had started so upbeat, announcing she was in love, had turned low and softer.

'Oh, yes, I'm sorry Chrissie, I just, well, anyway,' Alison went on, once more with a joyous tone, ' So, Terri works at the art museum, as the place, like everywhere, is in lock-down, she had gone there to do some cataloguing, it being quiet and an opportune time, well, she didn't answer her phone, as I said, Simon, bless him, could see that I was worried, so, he took charge, we drove to the museum, and, would you believe it, Terri had been held at gunpoint!'

'Whaat?!, oh, what happened? 'Chrissie said.

Alison got up from the two- seater, went back into the kitchen and related the story of these two robbers, who had broken into the museum, had locked Terri into a cupboard and had stolen a painting.

'She wasn't hurt?'

'Oh no, in fact she was angry with herself, she had, when confronted with these two, already kicked the man where it hurts, but the other burglar, a woman, had a gun, they locked her up, as I said, but Chrissie, she called me mother!'

In Boston, Chrissie sat herself on her couch, feeling a little emotional, she knew of the circumstance surrounding Ally's daughter's life, Sam had been so instrumental in bringing about a reunion after more than ten years apart, with Terri having been told her mother had died. In previous conversations with Alison, who now was a very close friend, she knew it had been hard to recreate a bond.

'Oh Ally, 'Chrissie said, calling her by her preferred name, 'That's wonderful'.

'Thanks Chrissie, yes, it was good.'

'So, 'Chrissie asked, intrigued by what had happened and with a newfound interest in art since meeting Sam, 'what did they steal?'

'Terri was marvellous, once the police arrived, she took control, showed them exactly where the thieves had been, in the archive room, and, furthermore, knew exactly which painting had been stolen. She told the police that they had to have good information for them to know it was even here, and that it was the only thing stolen. She also gave them clear descriptions of the pair of them.

Also, 'Ally went on, 'when we arrived a blue van was driving away, Simon, quick thinking and suspicious, noted the number, I'm sure they'll be caught soon enough.'

'Sounds intriguing, but what did they take, was it valuable?'

'No, not really what you might call valuable, Terri is going to do some research on it, it was apparently an oil painted on a wooden panel, of a monk!'

'Did you say a monk?' Chrissie asked, her voice full of sudden excitement.

'Yes, what's up, you sound, like..'

'Ally', Chrissie interrupted, 'this is too canny, please, can you get Terri to call Sam, he is helping Sophie in Paris to find out about an oil painted on a wooden panel, that she only received a few days ago...'

'Sam is in Paris?' Alison asked.

'No, no, he's here, but Sophie sent him a photo, of a painting that was sent to her, a portrait of a monk!'

'No way, how strange..' Ally said, having retrieved a bottle a white wine from the kitchen counter and poring herself a glass.

'Even more so, when Tammy, in New York, who I was talking with and was told about the painting that Sophie had received, discovered that a painting of a monk had been sold, way back in 1770!'

'Wow, that is strange, Terri will be very interested, I will call her and ask her to speak to Sam.'

'Thanks Ally, and Ally..'

'Yes?'

'I am so glad that you are in love, isn't that the loveliest feeling?'

Ally smiled broadly, said she would contact Terri, then ring back to tell her all about it.

Chrissie said she wanted all the details.

THE PAST; Period 5 - Part 1

The year 1803- Paris

Sofia Camille Argent could describe every detail.

She had decided to sit down on the grassy bank. The river Seine flowed serenely by. It was a quiet Sunday morning.

She sighed deeply, there were not many people about. The sun was already warm and there were no clouds to be seen in the sky.

Sofia reflected and remembered, bringing to mind every detail, bringing to mind the past year, a year of incredibly mixed emotions. A year of turmoil, of upset.

Sofia was born in Caracas, Venezuela. She was born with one eye blind. It was a lighter shade of blue that her good eye. But her brain had adjusted, had compensated, and her good eye was very good indeed. In fact, she would often be able to see things clearer and further away with the one eye, than most would be able to do with two.

It was that fact, that had been of some help, when they had been attacked.

A bird, sort of grey in colour, with a longish neck, came gliding in and smoothly landed on the water. She was distracted by it for a moment, then, in her mind, decided she would continue with her reflective thoughts, even though, she knew, they would be painful..

..They had sailed from Caracas a little over a year ago. Leaving her father Christoffer, who was ailing rapidly, behind. He had insisted. There was trouble brewing in the city. It was not the safest place to bring up a family.

She had agreed and so, with her husband Rene, and their little baby boy, Christoffer Junior, they set sail. Heading to France, Rene's home country..

Sofia watched the bird for a moment, trying to hold back the tears that were welling up behind her eyes..

She recalled a sad moment, when, after having stopped in a place called Essequibo, in Guyana, where the ship had taken on cargo bound for France, she had suddenly realised that it was gone, lost. The lovely ivory miniature her father had given her.

Devastated, thinking that she must have lost it coming from the house where they had stayed for a couple of days, to the docks. She promised herself to write a letter to the trading post there when she reached Paris.

She would not reach the city for some time.

Taking in a deep breath, Sofia decided to recall her wedding day. It was a wonderful day, her father, so proud, walking her up the aisle.

Her mother, Clara, had died quite some years ago, but Sofia thought of her particularly on that day. Taking in a deep breath, she wondered why her mind had gone off in a different direction, closing her eyes for a mind she tried to re-focus.

Her thoughts then returned to the event at sea.

The ship was only two days out of Essequibo, when she saw them.

It was only just after daybreak, she had been awake a while, decided to get up and dress and was standing on the port side, near the bow. Her husband and the baby were both fast asleep.

The sound of the ship slicing through the waters was soothing. Now and then carving a wave and causing a frothy reaction. She was still angry at herself, for losing that valuable and treasured item her father had given her. Twice, as she looked at the sea, she saw several flying fish, skimming away, just above the surface, then dipping down and into the water, gliding some twenty metres or so.

Then she looked towards the horizon.

She saw the ship. She saw it was heading in their direction...

..On the bank of the river, Sofia could not hold back the tears, she let them roll down both cheeks. How many times had she done this, she wondered, feeling the tears on her skin. Feeling the emptiness inside of her, the heartache.

How long would it be, before that pain would go away.

The bird, she noticed, dove into the water. She frowned as she lost where it was for some time, then it bobbed up again, a little further upstream.

..Sofia turned away from the railing and headed for the wheelhouse and alerted the captain. Pointing.

Moments later, one of the crew escorted her and the baby, through to a part of the ship she had not been to, on a deck just above the water line, she was ushered into a small cabin, there, the crewman, pulled a set of wooden bunks away from the wall, behind which was a small opening, a small door.

He then, as she made her way on hands and knees, through the door, with the baby, gathered a few things.

He gave her a lantern, which he first lit, then a flask with water and some food.

Then closing the door, he replaced the bunks and left the cabin...

..Sofia got up from the grass, brushed her long skirt and started to walk back into the city. She wiped her tears, sniffed a few times, then made herself walk upright and composed. The next memory was a very painful episode in her life.

She had recalled it all before, several times in fact, why did she have to go through it all again, she asked herself, walking back to the house where she had been living for these past four months now, since arriving from Spain.

Why can't she just, move on with her life?..

...The lantern was good thinking. It would have been very dark and most unnerving, not to mention how scared the baby might have been in total darkness.

The space she was in, was actually quite large, it was long, some five metres or so, not very wide though, perhaps two metres, and once through the small door, she could see the height was reasonably, she could almost stand up straight in it. There were some wooden boxes, she spotted a couple of long spears or lances, and a variety of other bit and pieces.

Her son, perhaps sensing that something was amiss, looked steadily into her eyes. He had not cried, nor made a sound, she had bundled him from the cot in their cabin. Such had been the speed of her being ushered out, she had not been able to say anything to her husband, who was dressing and in readiness to do battle.

For the ship that was heading towards them, was, without doubt, a gang of marauders, bandits, pirates...

..Sofia nodded a greeting to some passers-by. Her house not far away now. Her house, she thought. It had belonged to her husband's family. It was now hers. Rene's father had died, presumably so, for he had been a sea captain, and word had come back, that his ship sank, off the coast of North America, no news of any survivors. His wife, Rene's mother, always mentally ready for him to not come home one day, moved on with her life. Sofia wished she could do the same...

..The battle had been short, but violent.

Thanks to Sofia's early warning, the ship and crew were ready.

The captain, a wise man, a man who knew the sea. Did what the advancing pirates had not counted on. He made the call, then turned the ship, directly towards them.

For protection, their ship had four cannons, one near the bow on both port and starboard side, and along midship, either side.

As the captain made the turn towards them, he readied the starboard forward cannon. Then, watching the approaching vessel closely, seeing which way, the smaller, though equally well armed vessel, would turn.

They chose to turn to starboard, as the current and the wind was from the south, it was a move the captain calculated they would make in order to get extra speed for them to come alongside. He called the order, 'Hard Port'.

Immediately that he did so, he gave the order, 'ready..FIRE!'

The pirate ship was in trouble. The unexpected move, then the sudden turn and the firing of a cannon, was not the way it usually worked for them.

They were used to being the ones on the charge more often than not, their target simply giving in to their demands so as to save their lives.

Not this French vessel.

The cannonball struck their ship, a direct hit into their forward section, ripping through part of the bow structure and into the bottom of the wheelhouse, also damaging the forward mast. They fired their midship cannon at the French ship, which had by now made a full turn to port and was heading away from them, full sail and gathering speed.

It was merely by chance that the fired cannonball even hit the fleeing French galleon, but hit it, it did. The port side stern area exploded into splinters..

..How cruel can life be, Sofia thought, once more a few tears rolling down her cheek. One person had died. Just one.

THE PRESENT; Amersfoort

Sunday 26th April – late evening

'One person died' Martijn said, continuing his report to Sophie.

When he called, he had suddenly realised that it was already getting late in the evening. 'Hi Sophie' he began, 'sorry, it's quite late...'

'No, no, that's fine, lovely to hear your voice, I take it you've got information?'

In Paris, wearing a light purple coloured set of pyjamas and sat up in bed, Sophie was surprised at how she felt as she heard his voice. Yes, they had dated, yes, they had spent some lovely moments together, and yes, they had agreed to part as friends. But upon hearing his voice, her stomach muscles had tightened, and her throat was drying up. Getting out of bed, whilst listening to Martijn, she went into her ensuite bathroom and got herself a drink of water.

Martijn, pleased that he had gathered quite a bit of information that he had spent the best part of the day on, had been unaware of the time, until he had pressed the quick dial number for her.

'Okay then, well, to start with, I began by looking into the year 1963 and the region of Cannes, as you suspected, going by what Roberto had written in his letter to you, that there might have been some form of accident.'

Pausing here for a moment, he too realised that the bond they had formed, was stronger that he thought, he could feel his heart beat a little faster.

'And? 'She asked.

'There was. I managed to find a few eye witness accounts, as you know, my French is not very good, it took me a while to translate, but, I have put together, a, well, scenario, if you like, of what happened, one day, just outside Cannes, in the year 1963.

...In her rear view mirror, Natalie saw Roberto walk up the path to where he lived, saw the approaching Jaguar and was relieved. They didn't stop. They hadn't realised that she had stopped.

'Excellent' she whispered to herself, then sped up and headed out of town.

What to do next, she began to think, passing yet another car. The traffic was getting a little heavier. The Jaguar was still a good distance behind, having closed up with her before, she had increased the distance between them since leaving Cannes as she followed the windy coastal road towards Toulon.

The painting was safe. This Roberto fellow would clean and mend it.

They didn't have it.

Passing another car, then seeing an oil tanker in the distance, coming her way, an idea came to mind. The truck came nearer. There were no vehicles behind it, the road empty. Ideal.

Natalie slowed, then, as the truck rumbled past, she braked, used her handbrake and spun the car around. She had seen someone do it once, a guy, showing off his new car, it had not gone well for him that day, but she was told, how the manoeuvre worked. Just a slight wobble, but she was facing the other direction, then sped up a little and tucked herself up behind the tanker.

Keeping to the outer edge of the road, making sure she didn't slip off and down the embankment, she was hidden.

One car passed, then another. The Jaguar had to be coming soon.

Suddenly the tanker braked hard. The rear wheels locking as the large vehicle slithered across the surface.

Natalie reacted instantly...

'Oh my goodness, what happened next?' Sophie said, having been drawn into how Martijn told the story of what happened.

' Oh, I don't know, do I have more to tell?..' he teased, smiling broadly as he paced the lounge of his apartment.

'Martijn!'

The tone of her voice suggested to him, he better tell her the rest, and so still smiling, he continued…

…Natalie heard the crash. It was loud.

She then saw the Jaguar, it had obviously hit the tanker, then bouncing off, it had left the road, a mangled mess, it rolled twice over and stopped, on its wheels. The roof was crushed, the front was severely impacted, the boot of the car had flown open, windows had been broken and the front windscreen was a shattered maze.

Natalie cut her engine, got out of her car. Checking, she noticed she was just a centimetre away from the rear of the tanker.

Looking down the embankment, there was no sign of life from the Jaguar.

The driver of the tanker got out from the cab.

Natalie went over to him. He was shaking and very pale. Thankfully unhurt…

'One person died, ' Martijn said, the passenger of the Jaguar, the driver was seriously hurt, but alive, taken to hospital.

Natalie Umbrego, was one of the witnesses to the accident.'

'Wow, what a detailed account, thank you, well done, I had a feeling that something might have happened…' Sophie replied, relieved to hear, that the woman, this Natalie, had not died..

A ping alerted her, that there was an e-mail awaiting her.

It was from Sam and whilst still chatting to Martijn, she opened it and read it.

'Just had an e-mail from Sam' she said, 'just read it through..'

In his home in Amersfoort Martijn smiled. His work colleague, Froukje, he had observed over the years working with her, had the ability to be doing several things at once, on the phone to one person, responding to an e-mail to someone else, even making a coffee, all at the same time.

He did not have the gift of multi-tasking.

And when he had just missed something of what Sophie was telling him, and asked, 'what was that you said?' he almost laughed out loud, as he realised that not only could he not multitask, but even had trouble focussing on one thing.

'I can hear laughter in your voice?' Sophie said.

'Sorry Soph., I'll explain later, you said something about a holiday?'

'Yes, do you have any days that you can make free? Sam has already found some information that I was seeking, I know that, with this Covid virus, travel is restricted, but I would really like to go to Cologne'.

'You want to go to Koln? (Cologne) what's there?'

A painting, maybe, answers hopefully,' Sophie answered.

'Okay, 'Martijn said, checking his diary, then, 'how about, you travel up to Rotterdam on Tuesday? From there we'll go to Koln? How long do you need?'

In Paris Sophie smiled, realised she was looking forward to seeing him, then said, 'We have to go to the cathedral, with this virus thing, it might be hard to gain entry, but..'

Martijn interrupted, 'I'll make some calls, anywhere else?'

'Yes, the library?' Sophie answered, now quite flushed with excitement and hearing his pleasant voice.

They chatted a little more, Sophie relating the whole e-mail from Sam to him, then both said goodnight.

Sophie was looking forward to holding Martijn in her arms, and with those thoughts, she turned off the light and went to sleep.

THE PAST; Period 5 - Part 2

The year 1803- Paris

Sofia knelt down and opened her arms.

Her little boy, now nearly two years old, left the side of the older woman, and toddled over to where she waited.

She hugged him tightly for a moment, then asked if he and Grandmother had been playing nicely. Sofia threw a quick smile at the woman on the chair.

Rene's mother smiled back.

Sofia picked her son up, once again thinking that he would never remember his father. Putting him down again she headed for the kitchen, she was hungry. She had been out for some time, walking, sitting by the river, more walking.

Some food, she thought, leaving young Christopher Junior toddling back to grandmother and sitting himself on the floor where he had been playing with some wooden figures.

Why did he have to die?..

..Locked into the space behind the bunks, thankful for the lantern, she had felt the sudden movement of the ship, the sharp turn causing her to almost lose her balance, but she held on to her son and regained it quickly.

She then heard the cannon being fired.

It had sounded so loud.

The turn, eventually made, she felt the ship going back to an even keel.

Then another bang, from some distance, she thought. Then a loud crash.

It shook her, it was seemingly very near to where she was hiding. The ship rocked from side to side a few times, Sofia grabbing hold of a wooden beam to steady herself, then, when again back on an even keel she felt the ship was moving at speed. She heard shouting.

After a while, sitting and holding on to her son, in readiness for another hit by a cannon, for she was sure they had been hit once already, she closed her eyes. Her son was very calm, just holding on to her, an occasional chomp with his mouth, but didn't make a sound, or cry.

'Good boy,' she whispered, 'brave boy'.

But there were no more hits, and she heard the bunk being moved and the door opened. A friendly face.

The man who had escorted her here, had placed her here, to safety.

His face, however, showing concern and sadness...

..Sofia re-entered the living room, a piece of bread topped with some home-made jam, on a small plate, one bite having already been taken.

She looked over to the woman on the chair. Rene's mother, she had not known her long, had in fact not met her before arriving in Paris, and the first thing she had to tell her, was that her son had died...

...The explosion shattered part of the stern structure and the lower side of the rear cabins.

Pieces of wood, and many splinters and shards, flew all around.

Rene had gone to the stern, to keep an eye on the pirates and whether or not they had managed to get their ship in pursuit. They had not.

But he heard them fire a cannon.

He was the only man at the stern at the time, two others were making their way there, also to check on the condition of the pirate ship. The explosion rocked them both off their feet. But other than stunned, they were not hurt.

Rene never knew what hit him. A piece of wood, a sliver really, not very long, not very wide, but very sharp. It entered his throat, just beside his Adam's apple.

He collapsed to the floor, already dead...

..She saw the cross that hung on the wall by the door.

Why did he have to die? Taking another bite of bread, she thought about her faith.

It was somewhat shattered, she felt, taking a seat in the second armchair, looking at her son playing ever so nicely on the floor. He was such a contended child. Had not uttered a cry when they had gone into that hiding space on the ship.

Turning to look again that cross on the wall, it reminded her of that moment at the docks..

...Their ship had gathered speed quickly, the captain had been a wily old dog, had out smarted the pirates and was not to be caught. But the ship was damaged. It would not be wise to sail any further than required and so they made way to the nearest port. The following day, with the pirates nowhere in sight, they reached the port of La Coruna, in northern Spain, a port already in use since early Roman times. The old galleon was more damaged than at first thought, the captain made many arrangements. First, and foremost, was to set about arranging a funeral for Rene.

He also managed, with great success, to sell his cargo. Giving him sufficient funds to repair his ship. He then organised for Sofia and the child, to be taken to France, he ordered the young crew man, the one who had placed her in the secure place, to accompany and protect her. Which he was more than willing to do.

It was three days later, when ready to board a small schooner that would take them to Rouen, that she noticed the monks.

Two of them. The day before had been the funeral of her husband, a service held in a large church, his body able to be buried in a cemetery overlooking the ocean, where, according to captain, many seafarers were interred, she had noticed, what she was fairly sure of, the same two monks...

Sofia finished her piece of bread. Come on! She said to herself in her mind. All this mourning and worrying, wasn't doing her, or her son, any good.

It was time to move on. She looked up to see Rene's mother looking at her, she could see the concern in her eyes. The old lady was doing well. She had coped far better than her, and despite not being able to move around much, due to a lame leg, she was usually smiling, and Sofia could see the joy in her eyes as she held her grandson. No doubt seeing her own son in him.

Sofia smiled.

He was a lot like Rene.

THE PRESENT; En-route to Albuquerque

Sunday evening 26th April

She was not at all like Felicity.

Simon looked out of the window as the plane roared along the runway and into the night sky. Leaving the lights of the city below. The plane immediately banked to port, was over the ocean for a moment, then headed back over land.

Yes, he mused to himself, there had been Felicity, or Fliss as she preferred to be addressed. A small bundle of blond excitement, he had once called her.

She had been special.

But this was different. Alison was tall, had long blond hair, she was elegant, more sophisticated in her mannerism, was very much a quieter person.

He felt about her as he had never felt about anyone before.

Smiling to himself as the plane ascended to a cruising height, he was undoubtedly very much in love. Still smiling, he recalled a moment, on the Friday, after they had left the museum and had driven to Alison's apartment. Terri, having finished with the police, locked up and said she wouldn't be too far behind.

It was when both of them were in the kitchen, and he had found himself standing by the doorway and looking at them. Then suddenly realising they were both looking at him.

'Sorry, 'he said sheepishly, 'trying to figure out who is the mother and who is the daughter' smiling.

'You flatter me' Alison responded.

'But not me!' Terri said, throwing him a mock scowl.

Not quite knowing what to do or say next, Simon had retreated into the lounge.

But he had seen the sparkle in her eyes.

The plane levelled out and the seatbelt signs switched off.

Simon sighed. No doubt about it, he was madly in love.

He thought back to the conversation that Terri had with the police. She had been so focused and confident and her account of all that had occurred was very detailed.

These burglars, this young man and woman, had come specifically to steal one item, not one of the very expensive pieces of art that were on display in the museum, not a masterpiece by Rembrandt or Van Gogh, but had made their way to the archives room, had been after this painting of a monk. According to Terri, as he recalled her reading out the description she had from her inventory.5

Study of a monk, circa 1600, oil painted on wood panel, unknown artist, probably Italian and part of a triptych, the left side panel.

Meanwhile in Boston

'You were attracted to her, weren't you?'

Sam looked up from behind his desk. Chrissie stood in the doorway to what was now his study, originally the fourth bedroom.

'Alison, Ally, you were attracted to her.'

Sam leaned back in the comfortable leather desk chair, frowned slightly, then smiled, leaned forward again to turn his music down lower and said, 'Yes, yes I was, why do you ask?'

'It's just, when she called earlier, and, sounding so happy, saying she was in love, it got me thinking, I'm sure she was in love with you, you know.'

Sam got up from the chair, walked around the desk and towards her.

'I was attracted to her, for sure I was, I was also in somewhat of an emotional quandary.'

He reached her, pulled her towards him and hugged her, saying, 'After, well after her death...'

Chrissie lifted her head and looked up at him, 'Say her name Sam...'

Sam nuzzled himself into her, then, his voice a little broken, 'After

Sonja was gone, well Chrissie, so was I, I was so totally lost, then, slowly, as I focused on my work, things gradually eased, but, well, I was sure I would never fall in love again.

Sam pulled himself slightly away from her, looked into her eyes, then re cuddling her, continued, ' There was Sophie, she seemed to like me, but I kept her at a distance, then, of course, there was you, when we went to Genoa, even before that, when I met you, in this house, I had to push any romantic thoughts away, mainly, because I was still uncertain, a little scared if I'm honest...'

Chrissie held him tight, reached up and kissed him on the cheek, knowing there was more to say, she prompted him, 'Go on..' she whispered.

Keeping a firm hold of her, Sam kissed her on the top of her head, then went on, 'I guess I pushed you away, when we were in Italy, anyway, I was determined to focus on following the trail of the ivory, then, yes, there was Canada, there was Moncton and there was Alison.'

A brief pause, Sam continued, ' She was, she is, a beautiful woman, and yes, we spent some time together, and yes, I was attracted to her, but, you know, somewhere deep down, I knew it wouldn't be right, maybe, I was still too afraid of starting a relationship, and, Ally had to go, she had to be with her daughter, I made her go really, it hurt...'

Chrissie, feeling emotional and a little tearful, kissed him again, 'Go on' she whispered again.

'I remember when I came to New York, seeing you again, it was then when something changed in me, it was then, that I began to understand my feelings, it was then, when, my dear Chrissie, I fell in love with you..and yes, I left, I guess I left you hanging there..'

'I thought you were going to say goodbye to me, I thought you were going to say you and Ally...' Chrissie said, her voice low and she felt tears welling up.

'I should have been braver, 'Sam said, 'but I know, I left you and went back to Canada, sorry that I hurt you...'

'No, no,' Chrissie answered, looking up at him.

Sam noticed her tears, leaned down towards her and kissed her.

They kissed for some time, there in the doorway of the fourth bedroom. On a Sunday evening when a city in lock-down, was getting ready to sleep another night.

'Sam, 'Chrissie said, when their lips had parted, her eyes sparkling and with a smile, 'You did the right thing, making sure, and, I am so happy, that you chose me...'

Sam smiled and released her.

'I take it that was Terri?' who called just now.' she asked.

Sam walked over to his desk, answered, ' Yes, it was, actually it was a little strange at first, we had never spoken to each other before and she began by, well, saying thank you really, for, well, you know, but then, she composed herself, was most exact in all the details of the robbery, and the piece that was stolen, most interesting, very intriguing, I wrote it all down.'

THE PAST; Period 6

The year 1816- Cologne

Seventy-one-year-old Rudolph Meyer wrote. He had a lot to write. Head close to the paper, as his eyes, already very poor from an early age, were failing.

When he had, so enthusiastically set out on his treasure hunt, when he so confidently felt that this would change his life, that he would be someone, mean something, he had not considered that he might fail.

Whilst his mind was still sharp, his body was ailing. His gangly frame was weakening by the day. Since his mother passed, some years ago now, he had resettled himself downstairs, no longer very able to climb up the steep steps.

He had paid a few young lads to shift all his belonging to the ground floor and this was where he lived. This was where he would spend his days, rarely even venturing out, with funds he had, his father, by all standards at the time, had been quite wealthy, these funds had helped Rudolph immensely over the years in his search, in his travels. What he had failed to do, was to make notations, record his travels and his findings, clues he had found and followed.

Now he could hardly move, let alone travel, and keep searching.

He felt it now important, for someone else, to follow up, to hopefully be successful where he had failed.

As the first clue, the first scent of a treasure, had been when finding the letters from the monk called Flavius, which had been written in Latin. So, he, Rudolph, would write in Latin, though not too worried if some of it would turn out to be in Italian. Thinking it through, making sure he didn't miss a detail, he slowly and meticulously wrote. Every day, sometimes for four or five hours.

On a small table, placed against the wall of the small sitting room that separated it from the room next to it, which Rudolph had made into his bed chamber, not wanting to sleep in the cupboard affair which had been where his mother had slept, he had placed his treasure.

The letters. Some other personal belongings and, shining brightly, two silver keys.

Above the table, hung on the wall, a painting, on a wooden panel.

Study of a monk. The right-hand side panel of the triptych.

Now and then, Rudolph would get up, walk over and just stand there.

He felt he had done well. He had located two of the three keys. He had located one of the three paintings, though, and this still surprised him, it had not at all been the painting he had expected to find. Having stopped and looked at it regularly over the years since he acquired it, it was one evening, in dimming light, that he spotted it. Grabbing a looking glass from a drawer, he looked at the area on the monk's tunic that had, in the fading light, seemed flawed. The painter of the portrait had all but hidden it within the colour of the monk's garment, but there it was, in Roman numerals, the number IV.

Rudolph wrote.

Every day, for several weeks, until, exhausted and somehow feeling that his life was ebbing away, he finished.

It would be a hundred and forty years later, before someone would find and read the discoveries of Rudolph Meyer.

THE PRESENT; Rotterdam

Tuesday morning- 28th April

Martijn was waiting by the staircase as the train pulled up alongside the platform.

The high-speed connection from Paris, that would continue to Amsterdam.

He spotted her as she left the train, raised his right arm up high and smiled as she spotted him.

They walked towards each other, embraced and Sophie, sliding her mask down and then slipping Martijn's mask down, planted a quick kiss on his lips.

'Come on, we've got about eleven minutes to get to the right platform and get the train to Koln, let me take you case?'

Sophie smiled and relinquished the small cabin case over to him.

It was good to see him, her heart was thumping loudly in her chest.

Martijn, one hand wheeling the case, the other holding Sophie, steered her down the stairs, along the wide passageway and up the stairs to another platform.

He was glad to see her, knew the instant they hugged that his feelings for her had not in any way diminished, in fact, he was sure they were stronger.

Five minutes after disembarking from the train from Paris, Sophie and Martijn then boarded the train to Germany, to Cologne, in search of any information relating to a Rudolph Meyer.

Once settled in a first-class compartment, they both slipped their masks, a mandatory requirement, down, and Sophie, having sat herself next to him, leaned across and they kissed.

'So, tell me again, what did this Roberto say in the letter he sent along with that painting, and what has Sam found out' Martijn asked, both of them again donning their face masks correctly.

Despite the lock-down and restrictions on travel, Rotterdam Central Station had been quite busy. The train had pulled away from the city by now and travelling smoothly through the flat Dutch landscape.

'Okay, well,' Sophie began, speaking in English as Martijn was more fluid in that and struggled with the French language, often having said to Sophie, as she had burst into a flurry of her own language, that she just spoke too rapidly. 'I took a look at the painting first, then, read his letter, by the way, something I haven't told you, nor Sam for that matter, is, that after I had read the letter, I made a call, found out that Roberto had died. The parcel that came to me, had been packaged and ready for two weeks, with instructions to be sent to me, on his death.'

Sophie turned to again look out the window, though he had been a forger, he was a likeable man, recalling when she and Victoria had called on him.. she broke away from her thoughts, looked at Martijn, and said, 'he wrote about the story of this woman, this Natalie Umbrego, he had been to a party, on board a yacht, had seen her there, but had no conversation with her. He found out later, when he started to investigate, after he had mended and cleaned the painting and she had not returned to collect it, that this Natalie had discovered that he was a forger and a good painter, also that he was a creature of habit, frequenting the same cafe for lunch every day. She knew where he would be. Hence arriving when she did, quickly handing the painting over and then disappeared.

He never heard from her again, nor found out more about her, he had been more interested in the painting, figured it to have been painted in the late fifteen hundreds or early sixteen hundreds, and very likely in Rome. He then put it aside and forgot about it, until recently, obviously, he, knowing that he was dying, wanting to set his affairs in order, then came across it, anyway, that's all the information he wrote. So, my dear Martijn, you found out more, tell me again'.

Martijn looked at her, smiled briefly, then spoke, ' Putting together what I believed might have happened, this from the various witnesses and reports I found on this accident, along with what Roberto said, is this, Natalie drove from Monaco to Cannes, in order to give the painting to Roberto, this, she obviously did, then drove on, heading for Toulon, she was followed, by two men in a dark coloured Jaguar, at some point, Natalie must have been able to quickly to a U-turn, for she was heading back to Cannes, when the Jaguar made a move to pass another vehicle, misjudged the distance to the oncoming tanker, and collided, then rolled down the bank.

I have since our talk, also now have their names..' Martijn pulled a sheet of paper from the inside pocket of his jacket, and read them out, 'Kazim Oblensko and Huzar Kaplova, both from Istanbul.'

'Turkey?' Sophie said, thinking, wondering what the connection might be.

'What has Sam discovered, you got that e-mail from him when we spoke, did he find out anything else?'

'Yes, ' that first e-mail, was to say, as you know, that, and it was actually my friend Tammy, who discovered it by chance as she was looking into her family tree, that a painting of a monk, on wood panel, was bought by the operator at the trading post in Philadelphia, a Zecheriah, back in 1770, from a Captain Pique, then sold it, would you believe, over thirty years later, hence our trip today, to a Rudolph Meyer from Germany. When Sam did some further research, he discovered three things, the captain who sold the painting, had come from Plymouth, the man who bought it, Rudolph, Sam discovered had sailed from a port in Spain called La Coruna, but came from Cologne.'

'And the third thing?' Martijn asked as the train sped across the countryside.

'The name I gave him, Natalie Umbrego, is connected to the Vanetti Vineyards in Monaco.' 'But' after a pause, Sophie said, 'that's not all, I had another message from Sam since, this one a bit more troubling'.

'Oh, in what way?' Martijn asked, frowning, and quizzically looking across at Sophie.

'There's a woman, her name is Alison, she is a close friend of Sam and Chrissie, I haven't met her yet, anyway, she has a daughter, there's a whole story about that, but not now, her name is Terri, she works at an art museum in San Francisco, now last Friday, she was working in the museum, like over here, lots of places are closed, she was working in the archives room, burglars came, held her at gun point, forced her into a cupboard, I'm told, but she was alright, anyway, they came for a specific painting, found it in the archives room, so, they had inside knowledge that it was there, they took an oil painted on a wooden panel, and yes, it was titled ' Study of a monk.'

'Really?'

'Yes, and something else, though Terri had not closely studied this painting, she did know, that it was a left-hand side panel of a triptych.'

'You have a centre panel, the left-hand panel was stolen in San Francisco and, what might possibly be the right-hand panel, was bought by Rudolph?'

'Maybe, don't forget, he purchased in in 1803, it could well be the same, it could well be the left-hand side panel.'

'True, it could also be the one that you now have, the centre piece' Martijn suggested. Then looking up, noticing the cabin case he had placed there, asked,

'By the way, you brought luggage?' he asked, not even thinking about this fact earlier.

Sophie turned and smiled, 'Yes, it's called being organised,' she cheekily said, then explained, 'with all these travel restrictions, although I purchased a return ticket, you never know, so, in case we get stuck somewhere...'

'Mm, yes, organised indeed, hadn't even considered that possibility, we'll store it in a locker when we get to Koln'.

'Good idea,' she answered, then, looking out the window as the train sped along the tracks, she pondered almost whispering to herself, what is so important about these monks?'

THE PAST; Period 7

The year 1864 – Monaco

The narrow dirt track sloped up gently towards the old stone building, on either side were rows and rows of grapes.

The Vanetti Vineyards was established nearly two hundred and seventy-five years ago. Viana Vanetti arrived in Monaco in the year 1578, within the first year she had fallen in love and married Alehandro Esposito. Their first born, was a son, he came into the world in the year 1580, they named him Pietro and eventually he became a captain of his own galleon. Six years later they had a baby girl, named her Paola, after Viana's mother. Four years after that, having purchased suitable land, Viana set up the vineyard, naming it after her own name, as her husband had become the manager of the recently opened Casino and had no interest in working on the land.

Two young ladies, both having turned seventeen a few days earlier, had no concept of the history of their vineyard, now owned and run by their father Rodrigues Umbrego, as they walked towards the old house.

The old stone building, which had originally been the main house, situated at one end of the cobbled square with several outbuilding jutting against two other side, was now the only building left standing. The outbuildings had been torn down and the material used elsewhere, and the cobbled square had been taken up to form part of the new square by the new house some two hundred yards away.

It was a little dilapidated now, used mainly for storage of unwanted bit and pieces, along with some old and now rusted tools.

Eva and Isabella were twins. Eva having come into the world full of life and vigour with a strong set of lungs and a healthy weight.

Isabella, on the other hand, was only about half the size of her sister, struggled with breathing and for a few days it was touch and go whether or not she would survive. But survive she did, although it was soon clear, that the girl had been born blind.

'This is where you took the boy?' Isabella, though known just as Bella, asked.

Eva looked across at her twin sister, growing up had been difficult at times, but, unlike her, Bella was extremely quiet, patient, and placid.

She walked alongside her sister, not holding hands, for Bella's hearing and sense of smell was incredible, and she kept pace by listening to the footsteps.

'Carlos, yes, we had some fun,' she answered, but when I was there, I discovered something, that's why we are going there now'.

'Yes,' Bella answered.

Eva smiled, shook her long dark brown hair, and walked on. She liked fun and adventure, got into scrapes, often came home with either small cuts or bruises and was a bundle of energy. She did however look after her sister, would do anything to protect her. As young girls they were so different is size, but as they grew into young ladies, Bella caught up, physically she was now of a same stature.

They looked so much alike now, but their personalities were like day and night, whereas Eva was outgoing, Bella was the opposite. Whilst Eva got on well with her schooling and learning the ins and outs of running the vineyard, Bella excelled in her studies, and though unable to see, she could smell at which stage the grapes were, she could smell the correct measure of the various ingredients that would get the grapes ready for fermenting into wine. Then, on top of that, though she had no vision, she had a photographic memory of everything that she heard.

'Okay, here we are, let me take you Bella, there a scattered stones and bits of wooden beams all over the place.'

'Okay' Bella answered, holding out her left hand.

After carefully negotiating the various items that were somewhat haphazardly thrown into the old building, they reached a spot to where Eva was heading.

'Okay, now, on the floor in front of me, is a large chest, a sort of trunk, it's a bit battered, it has no locks or anything, but, when I was here, I had a quick peek, I think there are carpenters tools in here, so, if you sit over here..' guiding her sister to a space on the wooden floor, ' I'll open it and we'll see what's inside'

Eva opened the flat-topped lid, which squeaked noisily, and making sure it wouldn't fall down again, she then took out the first item.

Fifteen minutes later Eva had taken ten pieces out of the trunk, handing each one over to Bella, pointing out anything that might be sharp or cause injury, for her to feel and describe in her own words.

There had been three different sizes of hand drills, most intricate to touch and feel, four wooden planes of various lengths, two old chisels which were quite rusty and a leather apron.

It was when Eva had taken out the last chisel, which she first dropped and then picked up again, that Bella, having felt the chisel, said,' When you dropped this, it was not the sound it should have been, will you knock on the bottom of the chest Eva?'

Eva frowned, leaned over and into the empty trunk, then knocked on the bottom of it.

'That's not the bottom,' Bella said, her face looking up towards Eva, her eyes, though unseeing, seemed a few shades darker.

Eva thought about what her sister had said, then asked' What do you mean?'

'Help me up please, and guide me to the trunk?' Bella asked.

Eva did so, then her sister leant into the trunk, tapped the bottom a few times, then withdrew and said, 'It's hollow, there is something under there, it's not the bottom of the trunk.'

Eva, now understanding what her sister meant, grabbed one of the old rusty chisels, leant into the trunk and tried to pry the bottom open.

After a few attempts, she succeeded, pulled a wooden panel upwards and gasped.

'There are three scrolls, like parchment scrolls, then,' having taken these out and placed them on the floor, 'a wooden panel, it, it..' struggling to lift it clear, 'it just fits into the bottom, there! got it!

Eva carefully lifted it clear of the trunk, then turned it over and gasped again.

Bella sat and patiently waited for her sister to tell her what had been revealed.

Eva turned it around, 'it's, a painting, quite dirty..'

'Don't use your hand to wipe it' Bella interjected.

'Okay, I won't, it's a painting of a monk!' she then said, followed by, 'It looks very old'.

THE PRESENT; San Francisco

Tuesday 28th- very early, a little before 1 am.

Patricia Eunice Montgomery was pacing up and down in her living room, in her house in an affluent suburb of the sprawling city.

It had not gone to plan. This was only the first stage of a plot she had spent a few months on creating, and it had not gone to plan at the very beginning.

She was tired, frustrated and a little worried too. She was glad they hadn't harmed the girl, that would have been serious, that would not have been at all as she had envisaged. She couldn't sleep, hadn't slept properly since reading the account of the theft in a local newspaper. She hadn't, for one moment, realised that the theft had been noticed, hadn't for one moment even considered that the girl would be there. She had collected the painting as per instructions, had been inwardly pleased as she took the parcel, but had been shocked to read about the theft, about the fact that the girl was held at gun point.

Stopping her pacing for a moment, she thought a few things through. They didn't know her name, she had given them a false one, all they had was a number for the phone she had. It was what was known as a burner phone, according to what she learned, untraceable. That at least was good.

She had the painting, that too was good.

But, what next.

After thirty-eight years of marriage, her husband, a district lawyer, had left her, taken up with someone younger.

Her three children had been sympathetic, but only just. All of them lived elsewhere in the country, Florida, Georgia, and Illinois. 'Poor mum' and, 'get yourself a toy-boy' had been some of the remarks. Then, after thirteen years of working as an administration manager in the museum, and after she had applied for the position as assistant curator, she was passed over.

A young girl, straight from boarding school, got the job. Having a couple of degrees whereas she had none.

Fifty-five years old. No longer a wife. She felt she had been thrown out, put on the scrapheap, and for a while she had felt sorry for herself, even becoming somewhat bitter. But then, something changed.

She came across a letter, an old letter.

Just as two hundred and fifty years ago, a certain Rudolph Meyer, was inspired and revitalised after reading a letter from a monk, which set him on a new course, which had given him renewed confidence and had given him a new challenge and goal, the same happened to Patricia.

She came across an old letter, written by a monk. A letter written in Spanish, by a monk from Northern Spain, dated 1805.

It was in fact, more than just a letter, it was a brief account.

An account of a journey he and a fellow monk made, from Santiago de Compostela to San Francisco, and told of a secret treasure.

Her mind had been awakened. A fire had been lit. This was a chance, a new direction, a new her, no longer a 'poor mum'.

With renewed energy, she digested the account of the letter she had found in an old book that along with a few others, she came across when sorting out some things in the garage. She had no idea where it had come from but didn't care. She had found it, and she would follow whatever trail or whatever journey it would take her on that would lead to this secret treasure.

To her amazement, when she started the investigation of what she had learned from this Spanish monk, who simply went by the name Brother Cristoph, the first clue, led her to the very museum, where she worked. It was providence, she told herself, it was meant to be. It was fate.

Patricia left the living room, walked down the passage to one of the bedrooms which she had transformed into her study. After her husband had left her, she had, first of all, taken all his belongings from the house and placed them in the garage. She had re arranged furniture, moved into the second bedroom, had someone come to take away several pieces of furniture, including their bed, which she donated to a shelter organisation. It was when she had been rummaging through some boxes in the garage, ready for collection, that she had come across the old books and, unsure as to why at the time, kept them.

So glad she had, for it was in one of those books, as one day she was thumbing through them, that she had found the letter. Fate, again, it was meant to be, she was meant to have found this. Entering her study, she switched on the desk lamp, sat behind it in a comfortable leather chair, opened a drawer and took out the sheets of paper. She had painstakingly translated the monks account into English, had then printed them out as well as keeping a copy on her laptop computer.

She held the sheets, noticed the clock on the wall telling her it was now nearly one o'clock in the morning, but suddenly, she no longer felt tired.

Sure, the first phase of her plan had not gone as expected, but she didn't consider that the girl would be there, moreover, that she would be in the archive room..

Still, they didn't hurt her, that was a huge relief.

Much as she was disappointed that she hadn't got the position, the girl, Terri, was friendly and not conceited or smug. In fact, she quite liked her.

Yes, she was very relieved to hear she had not been hurt.

Once again, Patricia began reading the account, she knew every word, had read it times and times again, but she needed to read it through once more. To regain some sort of confidence, in order to progress further.

Though the first stage had not gone as hoped, she did have the painting.

She was soon absorbed again, in the monks account of his journey.

When the clock in the lounge struck the half hour, in the quietness of the night, she heard it clearly, and she checked the clock on the study wall, seeing it was now half past one, she put the sheets of paper down.

Time to go to bed.

As she prepared herself for that, she ran through the thoughts in her mind, assembling them in some sort of order, a synopsis, to comprehend fully what had occurred and why. Going to sleep with those thoughts in her mind, she figured, would help her and wake refreshed in the morning with a clearer understanding, of what needed to be done next.

Two monks, in the northwest of Spain, had been given a task, this in the year 1803.

The task was to bring a painting, painted on a wooden panel, to the Franciscan monks, here in San Francisco. It was a painting of a monk, whose name was Bonifatius, the painting, part of a set of three, held an important clue to the whereabouts of a treasure.

It was at this point, she recalled, that her heart had skipped a beat. The mention of the word, treasure.

These two monks were due to sail from a port called La Coruna.

According to the monk who had written this account, brother Cristoph, their plans had changed upon arrival at the port.

A French ship had arrived in port the previous day, damaged by an attack from pirates. Sadly, brother Cristoph wrote, one person was killed, a passenger, leaving behind a wife and child. He also noted that he and his fellow brother, who name was Jozef, decided to attend the funeral.

A captain of a Spanish schooner, knowing their destination and the plan to originally cross the Atlantic and sail to Philadelphia, to from there travel over land to the west coast, told them that this was far too dangerous a journey.

He said for them to come with him to Cadiz, from there a galleon would take them to the far east, to Surabaya in Java, where they could then sail onwards across the Pacific, to the west coast of America. Though the sea journey would be considerably longer, it would be the safer route to take.

It was a few days later that Patricia, looking into to history of the city she was born and lived in, read about a Spanish Captain, called Ayala, who sailed his vessel named the' San Carlos' through the Golden Gate into the bay for the first time, and subsequently a colony was established.

It was during the long journey to Java that brother Jozef became ill and died.

Brother Cristoph buried him in the port of Surabaya.

Three days later he sailed onwards and reached the Franciscan monks where he handed over the painting.

'The painting holds a secret', Patricia whispered to herself as she pulled the bedsheets open, and she smiled as she climbed into bed and pulled the covers over her, 'and I know what it is'.

Turning off the light, she fell asleep almost instantly.

THE PAST; Period 8 - Part 1

The year 1957- Eastbourne , England

It was a rainy afternoon. The curved street on the waterfront was glistening. The houses adjoining this road were substantial, detached homes three stories high.

The view over the ocean was magnificent. But not so much today.

The cloud cover was low. The rain had set in and looked to be set in for the rest of the day and possibly well into the night.

At number 12 two people, a man, and a woman, huddled down, walked up the path and before even knocking on the door, it opened, and they went inside.

Some moments later, having dealt with the wet coats and having then ushered them into the downstairs front room, where they took up the three-seater couch, he sat down across from them.

'There were these three monks from Florence...'

'Come on Rog, we haven't seen you for weeks, you ask us to come over because you want to share some secret or other, and you want to tell jokes?' it was the woman who had spoken.

'What? no, no, really, there were these three monks from Florence, it's where the story begins, so, listen up..'

Roger Sutherland was an academic. The twenty-four-year-old studied at the Brighton School of Art, which lay some twenty-two miles to the west.

He was a single child, and his parents were currently in Greece, where his father, a structural engineer and co-owner of an engineering firm, were involved in a project to improve the water supply to the city of Athens. He had the big house to himself.

His guest were good friends.

Kim Frederick was twenty-two, she was an airline stewardess working for BOAC and Roger had known her since school days.

Oliver Mantell was the same age as Roger, also a school friend and the two of them had become close friends when they decided to travel to Belgium and northern France to visit the war graves, as both young men had lost family during the second world war conflict.

'Actually, I have just remembered, made a pot of tea, I'll get it, got so excited to tell you..' and with that he stood up and left the room, coming back within a minute with a tray, holding a teapot, a bowl of sugar, a small jug of milk, and what Kim decided would be his mother's best set of China cups and saucers.

'So, three monks from Florence, this is why you are excited? Kim asked, pouring the tea for the three of them.

'Yes, absolutely,' Roger answered, lighting a cigarette, 'I've been working on this for the past weeks, but I must control myself, not get ahead of myself' he said, putting some milk and sugar into his cup.

Both Oliver and Kim now also lit up and as the smoke swirled around the room Roger began, 'Okay, let me go back, to where it all started.' And as Roger spoke, his mind took him back to that day..

..The Jan van Eyck Academie in Maastricht had been founded in the year 1948. Roger Sutherland had been accepted as an exchange student for a month and after a train from his home into London, then another taking him to the port of Harwich, Roger had then boarded the night ferry and duly arrived at the Hoek van Holland port early the following day. Another train journey took him to Rotterdam and from there he boarded a train for the final leg, taking him to the city in the province of Limburg in the southeast of the Netherlands. One of few areas in the country where the horizon wasn't a straight line.

The scenery was pleasant, rivers, forests, and hills.

His digs for the duration was a small houseboat moored on a canal, practically in the heart of the city.

It was on the third Saturday of his stay, that he wandered through a large street market and was fascinated with the vast amount of goods in the stalls and such a variety. He had been told of this monthly market and was advised to come early if he wanted to pick up some bargains before the crowds arrived.

The advice had been valid. It was getting busier and busier. But Roger had already spotted something, two things in fact, an old suitcase, though dirty and somewhat damaged, he recognised it as a Louis Vuitton, a good quality, inside there were several books and sheets and sheets of paper, he noticed as he rummaged through, all written in Italian or possibly Latin, he didn't have any knowledge of either. Then there was a metal box and another cardboard box containing what seemed to be screws, nuts, and bolts. A strange mixture indeed, then, having leaned up against the suitcase, Roger having moved it aside a bit to check the contents, was a painting, it was this that had drawn his attention to begin with, it was an oil, painted on a wooden panel. The subject was unusual, it was of a monk.

It was old, very dirty and had some damage. The owner, still in the process of bringing some more goods from his Citroen van, noticed him, called out thirty guilders.

Twenty-five, the case and the painting. Roger replied. The man nodded.

When he got back to the houseboat that morning, he was extremely pleased with his purchase, he also discovered that the content of the suitcase tied in with the oil painting of the monk. They had both, at one time, belonged to a German man, whose name was neatly written in the inside lid of the case, a Rudolph Meyer and underneath his address in Koln.

The metal box, when Roger opened it, with some effort as it was partly rusted shut, brought more surprises, for it contained, both wrapped in some sort of velvet cloth, two keys. Beautifully crafted, though similar, different. What was even more astounding, and Roger sat back, holding these keys, when he realised that, the monk in the painting, had a key around his neck.

Knowing his way around art and knowing the procedures for cleaning and mending old paintings, time just slipped away as he carefully cleaned the painting, having himself the right cleaning equipment with him.

Looking at the part of the painting he had meticulously cleaned, Roger came to a conclusion.

The key around the monk's neck, whom, according to what he found on the back, was brother Ignatius, though similar, was not the same. Also, he noted, that at some stage the panel had a hinge on the left side, meaning this was a right-hand panel.

As he now had three keys, two in hand and one in the painting, this had to have been a triptych. But what secrets did they hold?

The many sheets of thick paper, all handwritten and, thankfully numbered, would take some time, to translate, but Roger felt sure, that all those notes would relate to the painting of the Monk..

..Roger stubbed out his cigarette, got up and left the room, coming back within a minute carrying the painting. He set it down, leant it against an oak sideboard, then placed two keys in front of them, next to the tea tray, on the table.

'Wow, are they silver?' Kim asked, picking up one of them. Oliver picked up the other, 'They are beautifully made' he commented.

'Yes, they are silver, and yes well crafted, and you can see they are different, and, also different from the one around Ignatius's neck.

'So, three monks, and from Florence?' Kim asked.

'Yes, it took some time, many late nights, and a few headaches from the concentration, but 'Roger said, sitting back and lighting another cigarette, 'let me tell you the story, the story of a hidden treasure.'

'Treasure?' Oliver asked, also again lighting up.

'Okay then Sherlock, I'm all ears, what is it that you have found, it does sound intriguing' Kim added.

'Three monks, from Florence, 'Roger began, 'they each had an assignment, now, first of all, credit had to go to this guy, this Rudolph Meyer, because he searched and followed clues for over forty years!'

'What? Forty years?' Kim said, now lighting her second cigarette.

'But no treasure?' Oliver wanted to know.

'Patience my friend,' Roger said, exhaling smoke through his nostrils, 'so, now, it was in fact, a Father Dominic, who created this scenario.

He sent these three monks away, in different directions, each, with a key. Brother Flavius, the eldest, travelled to Koln, and it was his writings, found by Rudolph, that started his quest, this search to find these keys.

I learned of it this through the writings of Rudolph, having to translate them into English.

Rudolph obviously knew the language for he never translated the monk's letters into German, perhaps feeling it to be safer.'

Roger paused for a moment, threw a look at the painting, then continued, 'the second monk, was called Bonifatius, he journeyed to Spain, to a place called Santiago de Compostela...'

'I've heard of that' Kim interrupted, 'it's a pilgrim destination, I believe there's a road, called the Pilgrim Way'.

'I believe you are correct' Roger replied, then continued, 'Rudolph went there, now, first, he found the key that Flavius had, found it in some storage room in the cathedral at Koln, cleaned it up and it's one of those two, don't know which.

Anyway, having read the letters, learning of the destinations, he set off for Spain, reached the cathedral there, and, according to his very detailed account, he saw it straight away, in a display box containing other items. He then went in search of some place where he could obtain a key, found one similar in size, buffed it up a little to get a shine on it, then boldly went back inside the cathedral, quickly lifted the glass lid, and swapped the keys over. As far as he knows, no one had ever noticed.'

'You say he followed the clues and obviously travelled a lot, he must have had means, also, exactly what time are we talking about?' Oliver, very much into history, asked.

'Of course, should have started with that, Rudolph began his search after he found the monks letters in 1767, he became too ill in 1805 to continue, then began writing this detailed account, he died in 1810'.

'Wow' Kim said, stubbing out her cigarette, 'That's nearly two hundred years ago!'

'Yep',

'So, he now had two keys?' Oliver said.

'Indeed, but what happened next baffled our Rudolph for some time, you see, he was on his way back home, when he came across two monks, this in a port in northern Spain, called La Coruna, they were carrying a parcel. Now, Rudolph didn't speak to them in person, but was talking with the harbour master, as he was looking for a passage up to either Antwerp, Rotterdam or Amsterdam, as the journey across France had not been easy, anyway, he was told that the monks were on a ship sailing to Philadelphia, taking with them a valuable painting to be taken to a monastery on the west coast of America, to San Francisco.

Out of curiosity, Rudolph asked what it might be a painting of, and was told, a monk. This changed his travel arrangements, he boarded the next available passage to Philadelphia, as he could not secure one on the ship that was about to sail.'

Roger paused for a moment, then realised he hadn't answered Oliver's earlier question and said, 'By the way, yes Oliver, he had means, his father, deceased at this time, had been in banking, he was financially very secure.'

'So, he then sets off for America?' Kim asked, totally engrossed in the story.

A flurry of wind swept the rain onto the windows as Roger continued his account, ' Yes, now, this is where he became confused, because, he arrived at the port, then went along to the ports Trading Post, a very large concern he writes, with a huge array of goods, you could even hire a horse and cart there, anyway, he saw the painting, there it was, on display, a painting of a monk. Now we are now in the year 1803, and, preparing to purchase it and asking the proprietor, fellow by the name of Zecheriah, why the monks had sold it to him, he was told it was sold to him by a captain of a French vessel, over thirty years ago, arrived from Plymouth, and he had not seen any monks.

This information totally stumped Rudolph.

In talking with this Zecheriah chap, and with the man searching his ledger, he was shown, that the French vessel had arrived in 1770, from Plymouth.

Thirty-three years ago.

'Wow' Kim commented, 'what are the chances?'

'Indeed, Rudolph realised then, that he had a different panel and was sure that the monks would have had one of the other two panels. This made sense to him. So, once again he stepped up to see the harbour master, in the hope of finding out more about where the monks might have gone from there to get to San Francisco, there he found out, that they hadn't arrived at all.

'Really?' Oliver asked, 'Could they have just slipped ashore, quietly like' he wondered.

'No, the port ran a tight ship, to coin a phrase, they never went there.'

'So, what happens next?'

'For Rudolph, nothing much, his mother died, he became frail himself and for him., the quest was over really, although he did make a couple of notes of interest, one, Rudolph found a clue in the painting that he had purchased, which he had also established as the right-hand panel, very faintly, he writes, he discovered the Roman numerals IV. Then the other bit of information was about Father Dominic, remember him, the orchestrator of it all, he had, according to a letter he had written to brother Flavius, sent the paintings, the whole triptych, to the daughter of a close friend of Cardinal Farnese, a certain Viana Vanetti in Monaco.'

'Well, 'Oliver said, lighting up a cigarette and putting the flame to a cigarette that Roger had just pulled from the packet, 'what now, you have a plan, I'm sure'.

Blowing out a stream of smoke, Roger replied, 'I have been busy in the kitchen, prepared some lunch, how about we get stuck into that shortly.'

'And then?' Kim asked, getting up from the couch.

'Then, my dear Kim, we will talk about how we can follow up on what the good fellow Rudolph started, leading the way into the kitchen.

THE PRESENT; Koln Germany

Tuesday 28th

Martijn's police credentials got them to enter the Cathedral offices, 'Why is it exactly you wanted to come here?' he asked Sophie, as an elderly woman escorted them to the offices.

'The painting I was sent, has no signature, but, on the back it does have a name, very lightly pencilled in, not by the artist, I'm sure, the name of Flavius, which certainly sounds like the name of a monk, this man, this Rudolph Meyer, must have had an interest in monks, the cathedral is a place that has records, going way back, the library also is a source of information, it's where you'll find census records and so on, but you say we can't go there?'

'Afraid not, to do with quarantine regulations, so, hopefully, we'll find something here, 'Martijn said, then, through his face mask, smiled at the woman as she unlocked the door to a very modern looking office with several desk and computers and a wall lined with filing cabinets.

Whilst his French was a notch or two below useful, his German on the other hand, was very good, he spoke to the woman, then handed her a note upon which Sophie had written the names and the dates, explaining that it was in relation to missing works of art, which wasn't a lie' he thought and again smiled at the woman.

She looked at the note, frowned briefly, then sat herself behind one of the tabletop computers, typed at some speed and then looked at the screen, scrolled a few times, then spoke, her voice quite muffled through the medical face mask she wore.

The monastery lay about two kilometres from the cathedral and where, according to records so quickly found by the German lady, brother Flavius had resided. She had no information on a Rudolph Meyer. Sophie and Martijn both thanked her profusely and went on their way.

Once again outside Martijn hailed a taxi to get them there. The journey took less than ten minutes through the quieter than normal streets of the city.

They waited for some time after having been let into the old and cold stone building, that dated back to around the year 1200.

Then a monk appeared, he walked calmly and stopped some six feet away from them, he wore no face mask, he bowed his head slightly and spoke, 'I am Brutus, and, please,' he said looking at each of them in turn, 'Don't say it' smiling at them.

Sophie, deciding it was alright to remove her mask, smiled back, the man's voice was deep and comforting, his attitude serene and he continued to speak to them in English, 'I believe you are coming for information about a brother from long ago, brother Flavius?'

'Yes,' it was Sophie who spoke, then said, 'your English is very good,'

He nodded again, then said as he turned, 'Follow me please'.

They walked down the length of a stone tiled corridor, then turned into another stone tiled corridor, walked silently along and then the monk turned left after opening a large wooden door which led into a dimly lit wooden hallway.

'So' Sophie asked, after the silence had been enough for her, 'how long have you been here?'

The monk turned his head, smiled at her, said, 'fourteen years, I was in England for three years, 'speaking as he continued walking to the end of the hallway, 'near Nottingham'.

Neither Sophie nor Martijn, having now also taken his mask off, who was feeling a little overwhelmed inside this old monastery, his mind conjuring up scenes of being locked up in here forever more, spoke again until the monk, Brutus, stopped by another large door, turned and again smiled at them both, 'I came back here, 'opening the door and reaching his arm around for a light switch. Two rows of fluorescent tubes blinked on, revealing a vast room with several rows of racking containing cardboard boxes.

'Because I did not like vinegar on my chips' he said, gesturing them inside.

'Ha!' Martijn spurted out, understanding the joke, and suddenly feeling very much at ease, 'I do not like vinegar on my chips either' Smiling at Brutus who was every inch as tall as he was.

'You may search, I will find brother Dauphine, he has much knowledge of the past'.

He turned and smoothly left'.

'Thank you' Sophie called out after him, then looking at Martijn, 'Where do we start?'

Searching through the racks, noticing dates and names, Sophie realised that it was all extremely well organised and with Martijn on her tail, she soon found the box they were looking for.

'There's a large table back there' he said, moving past Sophie to grab the box.

'Yes, good idea'

Reaching the long four plank wooden table, he placed the box upon it and as Sophie was about to take the lid off, a voice said, 'Greetings'.

They both turned, startled, not having heard the monk coming at all.

They all seem to just flow so smoothly along the floor, Martijn thought, then looked at Sophie as she spoke.

'Greetings to you, we have come to find out about a fellow monk, Flavius, 'gesturing to the box by her side, 'I see he passed away in the year 1810'.

Speaking in French now, having no doubt been made of aware of where these visitors were from, the newcomer, who was ancient, at least he looked to be about a hundred, Martijn thought to himself, was barely over five foot in height and very slight in build, also not wearing a face mask, said, 'Yes, brother Flavius, I know about him madam'.

'Mademoiselle,' Sophie corrected, blushing slightly, and giving Martijn a look, 'I have come into possession of a painting of him'.

The short monk frowned for a moment, then produced a folder he had held behind his back, and said, 'Ah, yes, the paintings, my, my.' Then stepping forward he handed the folder to Sophie who took it, questioning with her eyes.

Brother Dauphine slipped past Sophie and opened the lid of the cardboard box, then spoke, 'All that is in here, is written in old Italian, I have translated it into French'.

Sophie looked into the opened box, then frowned, picking up a letter that was at the very top. Turning it over, she noticed it was sealed, a wax seal, it had not been opened. Turning to the monk, she showed it to him, saying nothing.

He took it, frowned, then said, 'This came, later, after brother Flavius passed, someone has placed it in here, I have not seen this, I shall open it?' he asked.

Sophie nodded and she and Martijn waited, watching him read.

After a moment, he said, 'This came from Father Dominic, the only one to correspond to Flavius, it came in 1811, almost a year after Flavius passed, it is very brief, I can translate?'

'Yes please' Sophie replied, again throwing a brief look at Martijn who smiled at her and raised his eyebrows, only barely keeping up with the conversation they were having in French.

'Dear brother Flavius, greetings from Rome. The princess has come of age and has all the instructions, my task and my promise, is fulfilled.

Yours in Christ.

Dominic'

There was silence in the room. It was the monk who broke it, ' Please, take this folder, it is, from memory, very interesting, I translated it more than ten years ago, that last letter, this one, must have been lost or misplaced for quite some time, please, have this also, and may the Lord be with you' he said, handing the letter to Sophie, then nodding to them both, turned and left as quietly as he had come.

'I'll put this box back' Martijn said.

Sophie said nothing, just nodded.

She was eagerly anticipating reading through the thick folder.

What on earth was that all about a princess, she wondered as Martijn returned.

They left the room, switching off the lights, closing the door and Sophie followed him back to the entrance. Hoping they could remember from which direction they had come.

THE PAST; Period 8 - Part2

The year 1957

The train, pulled by two electric diesels engines, slowly rumbled out of the Paris, Gare L'Est station and headed in an easterly direction.

In his first-class sleeper cabin, Roger settled himself down, lit a cigarette and watched the train move through the outer suburbs.

Nearly a month had passed since he had entertained his friends and shared the discovery he had made. Nearly a month since they had discussed and thought about what the best plan of action would be, to follow up on what Rudolph Meyer had started, all those many years ago.

Roger was adamant that he was going in search of the third key. Rudolph had hunted for and located the first key in Koln, had then travelled to Spain and procured the second key from the cathedral at Santiago de Compostela. The third key, he knew, had been entrusted to brother Ignatius, and destined for Izmir, formally known as Smyrna, in Turkey.

Initially Roger had planned for Kim to fly across the Atlantic and, with her connections in the airline industry, secure a flight to San Francisco, however, it was Oliver who was determined to go there, as an engineering student, he wanted to see the Golden Gate Bridge and he wanted to visit an engineering Academy whilst there. Kim agreed, not particularly wanting to travel to the States, so, she had the last target, Monaco. As she had greater opportunities of securing that destination in her work schedule, she was happy to do that and find out what she could about a Viana Vanetti.

As the train had picked up speed once free from the Parisian suburbs and heading for Strasbourg, Kim was serving the passengers on a flight to Monaco.

Meanwhile Oliver, who was given funds by Roger who was, by all accounts, a wealthy young man, was on board a Pan Am flight to

New York.

Staring at the Atlantic Ocean far below, he listened to the engines droning and was rather excited to be going on this journey. He was thankful and grateful for his friendship with Roger, more than happy with the funds he had given him and, in his imagination pondered the various possibilities of the outcome of this treasure hunt. What kind of treasure would it be, what great vault of riches would these three keys open.

Thinking more realistically, he thought about the best way to find out about a painting of a monk, his first stop, once he had arrived safely in San Francisco, and had checked into a hotel, would be to check out the monasteries in the city.

According to research that Roger had already done, they were three possible places where the two monks from Spain might have gone. Although, according to the written account by Rudolph, the monks never arrived in Philadelphia, Roger assumed that somehow these monks would have reached San Francisco as it was their destination.

Oliver was stirred from his thoughts by a lovely stewardess in a powder blue outfit that brought him some lunch.

In Southern France the weather had deteriorated and the airport in the principality of Monaco was closed. The plane was diverted to Cannes.

Kim, having taken some vacation time, whilst, she had hoped, in Monaco, now had to rethink her plans. She was due for another shift on a return flight from Monaco in two days, it didn't give her much time to investigate, now having to find a way to get from Cannes to Monte Carlo.

Making sure the passengers were securely strapped in, she took her own seat as the plane was buffeting in the strong winds. She wasn't worried, had flown in even worse conditions before and had faith in the expertise of the pilots. She gave a broad smile at a young boy who sat on the front seats alongside his mother.

He smiled back.

The rain eased up for a moment, there was a break in the clouds and suddenly the plane was below the bad weather and heading directly for the glistening runway.

The engines changed their tune, flaps were operated, the landing gear was activated and moments later, after an initial little bump, the wheels settled on the tarmac and the plane reduced speed quickly. Sighs of reliefs escaping from the mouths of many of the passengers.

Whilst the plane was taxiing towards the terminal, Kim got up and through the intercom system announced that a coach had already been despatched and would be arriving shortly to take everyone to Monte Carlo, information she had only moments ago received from the co-pilot.

Twenty-three minutes later Kim sat in the very front seat of the coach, having ensured that all the passengers were accounted for, and the luggage loaded, and looked through the large windscreen of the bus as the wipers easily dealt with the rain which had once again started to fall. I'm not that far behind schedule, she thought to herself. She would, once all the passengers had safely disembarked, check into her own hotel, have dinner and speak to the concierge, who, in most hotels, would be the person with the best local knowledge, and ask if the name Viana Vanetti meant anything.

Meanwhile, far to the north, Roger was anticipating his dinner as the train smoothly slipped through the countryside, now heading for Munich. He was also wondering how his friends were getting on. Looking at his watch he calculated that Kim would be in Monte Carlo now, and his good friend Oliver should be on the descend to New York.

THE PRESENT; New York

Tuesday 28th April

Tammy sat on the edge of the end of her bed. Her sizeable bedroom easily accommodated the king size bed, furthermore there was room enough for a comfortable couch, a dainty desk and chair, a dressing table and stool, two bedside tables and a low table that was placed in front of the couch. One door led to a well- appointed bathroom, which held a jacuzzi style bath, a separate shower, a washbasin, two electric towel dryers, and toilet tucked away on the far side of the shower cubicle. A large mirror was hung above the basin and there were two glass doored cabinets either side. The last piece of furniture was a tall shelves rack holding a variety of towels.

A second door led to the walk-in wardrobe, with racks and shelves on three of the walls, housing her clothes and shoes.

A third door led into the wide corridor off which were four more bedrooms.

Sitting on the bed, she looked into the walk-in wardrobe where she had, moments ago, just been, the door was open.

She felt as she hadn't felt at all ever before as far as she could remember, normally priding herself for being upbeat and optimistic, she felt low right now. A small clock on her bedside table showed it to be just after eleven in the morning.

Not only did she feel low, but emotional as well. She had been tearful.

Tammy sniffed, then wiped her eyes, took a deep breath, then mentally gave herself a talking to. To snap out of it, to get a grip, to not be so silly!

It must be all this being cooped up inside, she told herself, getting up from the bed and running through her mind the things that she had discovered this morning that had brought about how she felt.

She closed the wardrobe door, she had been in there to see her outfit, the one she had worn that day, fifteen years ago, when she had received that letter, the letter that had taken her, in her old, battered VW Beetle car, to Yonkers. To visit the law firm of Stratford, Strauss and Helpin. The day she found out about her grandmother Rosemary Quinton, and the journey that she had subsequently been on.

That day, when driving ever so carefully, back to her Hoboken fourth floor apartment. What a world of difference, she thought, moving to the large window of her 28th floor Central Park apartment, which not only had five great bedrooms, three of which had an ensuite, there was also a large dining room, this now her tracing room, as she referred to it in her mind. Genealogy brought about such a range of emotions, feelings for people, though related, that you've never met. Frustrations of not quite finding all the information that you had hoped for. Anger for the injustices that may crop up in delving into the past, sadness for the many discoveries of children who had died at birth or very young. Shocked at the revelations of the ravages of war, and surprised, perhaps, at the skeletons found in the proverbial cupboard.

She had received an e-mail, from the secretary at Stratford, Strauss and Helpin. Over the years, Tammy, grateful for their help, support and, who were now her lawyers as well, had been in touch regularly. She was informed of the sad passing of Robert Stratford, one of so many, who had succumbed to the deadly virus. He was sixty-five and had planned to retire this year. This news had been what had tipped her over the edge emotionally. He was such a nice man.

She had tearfully gone to her wardrobe, where, protected by a clear plastic covering, she had hung the very outfit that she had worn that day. A memory of what once was. Strangely, as she thought back to that very day, she vaguely recalls a young smartly dressed black man, opening the door for her as she left the premises, giving her a broad smile. As she sat herself on the bed, she was puzzled a little as to why she had not remembered that before.

Prior to that, she had been a little angry at a discovery that brought about other questions. One thing Tammy knew, in her recent delving into her family history, including a journey that led her to find out about Evonie Dupois Quinton, who had come over from France to Plymouth, that not all might be as it seemed. For one, she finally took a look at her own birth certificate and realised she had a second name, Monique, how had she not known that before, but most of all, this very strange morning, she had wanted to find out, why Percivald, her great grandfather, Rosemary's father, had insisted that Bastiaan Bouten return to Belgium.

Bastiaan had been her grandmother's lover, more than that, had every intention of marrying her and was the father of a child she was carrying.

Tammy dug up the letter she had found, this was after a dream had awakened her at four o'clock in the morning. A dream about a handbag. She had then retrieved this bag and discovered the letter. A letter from 1946, which contained a brief handwritten note. Standing by the window of the dining room, overlooking Central Park, and noticing that it was lightly raining, she held the note, reading it again. *'Chap you came back with from Belgium, Bastiaan Bouten, had him checked out. Bounder is married, dealt with him, sent him packing back to his homeland.'*

It was just signed PQ.

Tammy knew that this information was incorrect, she knew that he was not married, knew in her heart that his intentions were good and though her grandmother did not mention him at all in her letters, she felt that it was likely to painful. But why had Percivald done this? This she had hoped to find out. What she did find out however, that his marriage to Rosemary's mother had been short and that he was quite a rogue and a bounder, this according to an article she had found.

Looking into the past was surely quite the emotional roller coaster. To then hear of the death of Robert Stratford had been more than she could handle at that point. After rushing to her wardrobe, seeing that outfit and sitting herself on the edge of her bed, she cried.

At the beginning of her research, at the beginning of the Covid

Virus that was spreading all over the world, at the beginning of all the measures taken to help protect the people, to stay indoors, to wash hands, to keep a certain distance when in public spaces, in those early days, having decided to use this time to delve into her past, her family history, Tammy had researched and gathered information as to how best to do this. This had also given her some contacts, some links to others who, also having decided to use this opportunity for research, were posting their finds and their hints online.

One such person was Cornelia O'Hara, seventy years of age from Yonkers, New York. It was the township of Yonkers that had drawn her attention, not knowing that less than two hours later, she would receive that e-mail about Mr. Stratford.

This woman posted her findings, feeling she wanted to share how so very interesting it could be, digging into one's past. You're not wrong there, Tammy thought to herself, remembering the journey that her grandmother's letter had taken her on. This was also a story about a grandmother, and as Tammy began reading, she came across a name, a name that drew a gasp from her mouth.

Percivald Quinton. As with her own grandmother's letter, she was drawn into the story she was reading on her laptop screen...

...to those who may read this in the future. My name is Charlotte Pasveer, my parents immigrated to America from Delft in Holland. I want to share the following story as I believe it may help someone in the future, not to throw caution to the wind.. '

At this point Tammy was hooked, deciding on this Tuesday morning to get herself a coffee and immerse herself into this tale, wondering where it might lead to...

..when I was twenty years of age, I met a man. He was tall, he was handsome, he was the perfect gentleman, or so I thought. His name was Percivald Quinton..

When coming across that name, Tammy nearly choked on her coffee, had to put her mug down, cough several times and rush over to the kitchen to get a drink of water, before returning to take up the story, a perfect gentleman, or so I thought? Tammy mused, as she continued reading...

..you were working as a waitress in a cocktail bar, these words, an opening line from the Human League song, 'Don't you want me', from 1982, came to my mind as I was reading my grandmothers diary for the year 1924... Cornelia wrote.

She was indeed a waitress, and worked in a bar, not just any bar, a posh gentleman's club bar, just off 5th Avenue. It was there, one evening, when Percivald came into her life. He was sure of himself, he was confident, and after ordering a drink that evening, he asked her if she wanted to go to Monte Carlo with him.

At first, she though he was just making small talk, but as the evening went on, he stayed by the bar and in between her serving drinks, kept chatting to her.

'My name is Percivald' he said, distinctly pronouncing the letter 'd' at the end, saying that a mistake on his birth certificate was a sign that he was just different..

...at this point Tammy, after having recovered from her coughing fit, and once more engrossed in the story, made a mental note to check his birth certificate later..

.. I am going to fly to Monaco, in a few days' time, have you ever been on an aeroplane?' he asked her, now on his second drink and keeping the conversation flowing and taking the opportunity, when, in between serving, she would look at him, to smile and look her in the eye. 'A chance not to be missed,' he had said, 'You have really beautiful eyes,' he commented. Then, after a pause, when she was really busy, he said, 'Look, I know you like your job, you are really good at it, now, I can assure you, that if you come with me, only a week away from here, you will not lose your job.'

'You can guarantee that?' she asked.

He knew then that he had her hooked...

It was at that point that a 'ping' alerted her to an incoming e-mail. It was then that Tammy found out about Robert's death, it was then when it all became too much for her and she was emotionally overwhelmed.

THE PAST; Period 8 - Part 3

the year 1957

Oliver Mantell was emotionally stricken. He stood frozen on the spot, his throat was dry, he felt his legs tremble and it seemed he couldn't move.

The boy lay dead at his feet. And he was a boy, ten, maybe twelve years old. And he was dead, of that he was certain. He came bounding, actually, more like stumbling, out of the alleyway, had collided with him, and Oliver, being of stout built and a regular rugby player, a forward prop usually, was to the boy an unmoveable object, he bounced off and landed hard on the sidewalk.

He was dead, the breath went out of him, and he went limp. There was blood, Oliver then noticed, as he also sensed people come rushing towards him. The young lad had been stabbed, in the abdomen, and several times he could see. Then someone blocked his view and examined the boy.

'You're not from here' a voice enquired, the voice of a woman, he heard it, understood it, but was still frozen to the spot. He had never seen a dead body before. Just a boy.

'He's just a kid' he managed to say, his voice soft and broken.

'What are you doing in this neighbourhood? It's not where tourist come' the voice said, and this time Oliver turned to the woman who was standing beside him and had taken hold of his left arm, just above the elbow.

'You must go, come with me, you don't want to get involved, do you understand me?' she said, her face close to his, her eyes, dark brown he noted, giving him a piercing look. He recovered a little, still feeling quite weak and his legs moved, only, he realised, because she had firmed her grip on his arm and was steering him away.

Several people were milling around now. He saw them, but didn't notice them, and then, just as suddenly as he was there, he wasn't, they had turned a corner, it was quieter, two people came running toward them, but passed by and went around the corner. Oliver, now having more control of his legs, walked quickly, was in fact more or less forced, to walk quickly, and he threw a sideways glance at the woman, a young woman, maybe about twenty, he thought, his mind still quite clouded. She was almost as tall as he, and despite his muscular stature, she had no trouble in steering him, moving him along the street. They turned another corner, an even quieter street. It was, after all, he thought, some clarity at last returning to his senses, quite early in the morning. She had very dark hair, done in a ponytail, he saw, taking another quick look at her. She sensed him looking, returned a gaze and smiled.

'Come on' she said, her voice still only just above a whisper, 'a little further'.

Then, she began to slow down a little, still grasping his arm, and asked, 'So, mister, what are you doing around here?' then, not waiting for any sort of response, said, 'lost, are you? Did you come in on a ship, here for a day, thought you'd be smart and come away from the normal tourist attractions, maybe thinking, the rumours you heard aren't true? Thought you were brave?' Tough?'

He took it all in, what she was saying, her voice no longer soft, but with an edge to it. He realised he had been breathing heavily, he controlled it, began to feel less dizzy, more coherent, stronger.

'I came here to visit the monastery' he said.

She stopped walking. 'The monastery? You mean the Franciscan Brothers?' looking at him, puzzled now.

'Yes, I guess they would be called that, I have the address' he answered, glad they had stopped, and he was able to catch a breath. He was normally very fit, but this had shaken him up in a way he couldn't have even imagined. Trying to clear the image of the dead boy from his mind, he fished out a piece of paper, showed it to her. As she took it and read, he said, 'Oliver, Oliver Mantell, thank you for whisking me away, however, shouldn't I be speaking to the police?'

She looked up at him, noticed his blue eyes, noticed his smile, and, though still quite pale from shock, she figured, before her stood a rather good-looking man.

'No, it wouldn't be of help, the boy was already badly wounded, nothing you did, or could do, talking with the police would not be of any help, in fact...' but she broke off her thoughts, then said, ' come on, the place you want is only a few blocks from here, and, we are even going the right way, so, come on' Again steering him by the arm and leading the way.

'Mercedes, 'she said, when they had turned yet another corner, walking at a normal pace, throwing him a look, 'Mercedes Juarez'.

Meanwhile on the other side of the Atlantic

It was early evening in Monte Carlo and Kim sat in the lounge and foyer area of her hotel. It was the end of her second day, and she would be on duty in her flight back to England the following morning. She had been partially successful. With only the name Viana Vanetti to go by, she had done well. Though in fairness, the name Vanetti was well known in the area as they were one of the oldest established vineyards in the region. She had taken a taxi earlier in the day, had spent a little time, but, alas, had found no-one that could even remember the woman, Viana, who had been the one to set up the business all that time ago. Mind you, she said to herself, drawing many blanks when asking in her somewhat broken French, that had been the late fifteen hundreds.

She could find no older person, someone perhaps in their sixties or seventies, who might know some history, nor could she locate any of the current owners, a family by the name of Umbrego. She accepted defeat, there was no point in asking anything about a painting of a monk, if no one there knew any of the vineyard's history. Having asked the taxi to wait, she decided she wasn't getting anywhere here, and that the local library might prove more helpful. She was about to get in and give the driver new instructions when a voice called out, a woman's voice, well, young woman, Kim noted as she strode towards her, her long red hair flowing like a mane, late teens, eighteen maybe.

'You stay in the city?' she asked, speaking broken English.

Kim nodded and gave her the name of the hotel.

'Tonight, about seven, in, what you say, foyer?' she girl asked.

Kim nodded again, 'in the foyer, at seven'.

'Oui'

and with that she turned and left, striding back towards the reception area and store where one could sample and purchase their goods.

Kim checked her watch, two minutes after seven. Then she came breezing in, it seemed like this girl could only do one speed, fast! Her hair once more flowing she looked around, her face smiling, her eyes sparkling. She was just so exuberant, Kim thought as she raised her arm, but the girl had already seen her and came bounding over. 'Bonjour' she said as Kim was getting to her feet, then grabbed her shoulders and planted a kiss on either cheek, before sitting herself down in the comfortable leather lounge chair.

'Err, would you like a drink?' Kim asked, not quite sure what to make of this extravert type.

'Oui, white wine please' she said as Kim drew the attention of a passing waiter.

'Natalie, 'she said leaning forward, extending her hand, 'Natalie Umbrego'

Kim grasped her hand and at the same time ordered two white wines.

'You ask about Viana' she said, 'Why?'

Straight question, Kim was thinking, to the point, it needed a straight answer, 'I am looking for a painting of a monk, that was sent to Viana, about four hundred years ago'.

This momentarily stumped the red-haired girl, who looked at Kim for some moments, wheels seemingly turning in her mind.

The drinks came and Kim signed a docket, then handed her a glass, held one herself and raised it as in a toast.

'Salut' she said, taking a sip, then, 'placing the glass on the table that was between them, said, 'In the library, there is a book, all about Viana Vanetti and the vineyard, I think we must also have one in the house somewhere, I think I saw it once, but you say a painting of, a monk?'

'Yes' Kim answered, 'it was sent from Rome, by a Father Dominic'.

'Why?' the girl asked, a puzzled expression on her face as she picked up the glass of wine and took a few more sips.

Without hesitation, for it was a question that she had anticipated, Kim said, ' My friend has a painting of a monk, painted on a wood panel, this panel is part of three, he has the right hand panel, he is looking for the centre and the left panel, knowing that the three together, were sent to this Viana woman' then after a quick sip, added, 'are you related to her, in any way?'

'Oui, 'she answered, 'on my mother's side, but I know little,' then frowning and pausing a moment, said, 'I should know more' admonishing herself.

'When you're young you think you'll live forever, the past often is not important then' Kim answered, thinking how little she herself knew about her own family.

'I did go to the library, earlier, but found nothing, only a little booklet about the history of vineyards in this region and the Vanetti Vineyards were listed in there, no personal information though, and nothing about any paintings of monks.'

'I will look for you' Natalie said, then drinking the rest of the wine, put the glass down, stood up, 'you tell me your address, I write, I will go now, party to go to' she said, smiling broadly. Kim rummaged around in her handbag, took out a card, her airline business card, stood up and gave it to her.

Natalie took it, 'Merci' she said, then leant forward, kissed Kim on the lips and turned and left. Like a whirlwind she moved through the foyer and was gone.

Kim sat herself down, sat back and slowly sipped her wine. What a bundle of energy that girl was, and wondered if she would ever hear from her.

At the same time

About seventeen hundred kilometres to the east, Roger was having dinner.

He had arrived in Izmir mid-morning, this after he had crossed over by ferry from Istanbul and took the train from Bandirma. The station at Izmir was old and small. Entering the main hall, of the building, he walked over to where there was a board holding several leaflets and cards. There was also a map of the town stuck on the wall, two of the corners were peeling away and at some stage it looked as if some liquid had spilled on it, but it was legible. On the board were several advertisements for hotels and working in conjunction with the map, Roger picked one that, if the photo was anything to go by, looked good, moreover, it was just across from the cathedral.

Reaching into his trouser pocket, he retrieved the paper train ticket, turned it over and with the pen from the top pocket of his jacket, wrote down the details.

Visualizing the map, he set off and not once making a wrong turn reached the hotel. He was pleasantly surprised as he entered through the doors, stuffing the train ticket back in his pocket he greeted the receptionist and booked himself a room for two nights. Afterwards he meandered around the town, having first walked around the St. John cathedral, which he could see from the window in his room, then, after a light lunch in a rather charming cafe, he went back there.

An imposing frontage, like a colonnade, inside it was magnificent, paintings, high arches, a lot of gilding, statues, several banners, and the fabulous high ceiling. He walked quietly down the main isle, taking it all in.

There were several visitors milling around. Giving a friendly nod to some as they passed him by, Roger began to wonder where the key might be kept. He had learnt from Rudolph's detailed writings, that the German had found the first key, having belonged to Flavius, in an old storeroom in the depths of the cathedral. Then, having travelled to Santiago de Compostela, the key there had been one of several keys and items on display in a glass case. Rudolph had purchased a similar key and had then quickly and boldly replaced it. Where would this third key be, Roger pondered, realising the cathedral was vast, there would be many rooms and chambers. Taking it all in in wondered as to where to start, and when.

Roger carefully noted everything he saw in his mind. Then, having now a general knowledge of the layout, he knew two things, one, he knew where to go to avoid the three cameras which were in a static position, and two, he would need to purchase a torch.

Finishing his dinner, he checked the time, then decided to put his plan into action. After having visited the cathedral, Roger purchased a torch and had checked out the timetable for return trains. Purchasing a ticket for the very first scheduled departure, seven minutes after 6am, he came away thinking he would have one chance only, to search and find the key. He had booked and paid for two nights as that seemed to be a sensible thing to do, a touristy thing to do.

Roger paid for the meal, walked back to his hotel, entered his room, and rummaged in the holdall for the black rolled collar pullover he had brought along. as he had anticipated that he would need to attempt to do this at night. As he got ready, he was a little cross with himself, for although he had anticipated it to be a night job, why hadn't he brought a torch with him?

Checking himself in the full-length mirror on the wardrobe door, he blew out his cheeks and left the room, wondering what the penalty might be for breaking and entering a cathedral.

Even though it was still early evening, the streets were quiet. The night sky was dark with clouds and the forecast, he had picked up, was for rain.

Be bold, he told himself, do as if you own the place, as if you have a right to be there. Easier said than done, he thought, as he approached the large building, feeling a tightness in his stomach muscles and a dryness in his throat.

Having also observed the outside of the building, he had spotted a door, on the far end and to the side. Moreover, he had watched someone enter by that door. Would it be locked yet, or at all? He did have a plan B but strode along the path as confidently as he could muster, reached the door, turned the ring iron handle, and pulled.

It opened, with just the slightest of squeaks.

Roger, feeling his heart now thumping in his throat, softly closed the door and let his eyes adjust to the dimness. Taking several steps along a short stone paved corridor towards another door, in his mind, he visualized where this would come out.

He hadn't needed his torch yet, beyond this door was the main part of the church, he closed his eyes briefly to picture the exact whereabouts of the cameras, then grabbed the handle and slowly pushed it down, then pulled the door towards him.

He noted that several lights were on, he noted that by the altar, many candles were lit, and he noted, that, at the far end from where he stood, one of the front doors of the cathedral was open. But as he slipped through the door, he also noted that there was no-one about. He needed to cross over to the other side where he knew were several ante rooms. Checking in the sufficient light that several lit lamps threw, he saw the cameras were in the same position as earlier, he wondered if they were even working. Taking a breath, he moved quickly and quietly across the front of the altar, reached the other side, and decided to pick the first door he came to. It was unlocked, it opened and inside was darkness. Roger stepped inside, closed the door, pulled the torch from his pocket, switched it on.

It was much larger than he had visualised in his mind and as he shone the beam of light around, he noted that there were racks of robes, several bookcases which held what looked like sheet music, a desk and chair was tucked away in a far corner, and he then saw another door. Making his way there he was momentarily taken aback when the light from his torch caught a reflection in a wall mounted mirror.

Blowing out his cheeks and getting his heart rate down again, Roger headed for the door he had seen. Switching the torch off first, he carefully opened it.

More darkness. Turning the light back on he saw that he was in a corridor, very similar to the one where he had entered, a stone slab floor. Three doors on the left, one door on the right. To the left, he felt, would lead back towards the main hall of the church, the door on the right, he noted, had an old-style iron ring handle, whereas the three on the left had modern fixings.

To the right, he thought, he was looking for something that had been brought here, by Brother Ignatius, well over four hundred years ago, providing of course that the monk had made it this far, the door on the right, was an old door. He shrugged and smiled at his own reasoning and walked up to this door.

He tried the ring handle and pushed and pulled. But it didn't budge. Shining his torch around the frame, he noticed a short iron turnkey, a bit like a butterfly wing nut in shape, but of flat iron. Reaching up, he turned it.

Trying the door again, this time it opened as he pulled the heavy door towards him.

It hardly made a sound.

Closing it behind him, Roger now found himself in a space that looked very much like an old cellar. There were two rows of wooden racks, bottle racks, here and there he noticed an old bottle, covered in dust.

No-one had been in here for some time. That was a good sign, maybe, he thought, walking around the racks.

There were no other doors, there was nowhere else to go from here. Shining the torch light around the walls he noticed three wooden shelves and then, a small cupboard. It had a wooden door. Walking up to it, Roger estimated that it would be about two inches deep, no more than ten inches wide and probably around a foot in height.

There was a key. Heart again thumping loudly, though this time in his chest, Roger turned the key and opened the door.

He gasped. There were three rows of keys. All sorts of sizes, mostly quite rusty, and as he felt along these keys, he felt the rust come off into his hand.

There it was. He had found it. Taking it off the hook, he studied it in the light of his torch. No doubt, this was the one. It was badly tarnished, but as he rubbed his thumb on the crafted handle, it began to gleam a little.

Blowing out a sigh of relief, he pocketed the key, closed and locked the cabinet, and made his way back to the old door. What he hadn't realised, was that as he shoved the key into his pocket and withdrew his hand, the train ticket, upon which he had written the hotels address, came out as well and fell to the floor.

He made his way back to the old door, listening for a moment, he then pushed the door open. Nobody around. Softly closing the door remembering to also turn the small butterfly shaped wing nut.

Going back the same way, forcing himself to walk calmly and not to rush, he reached the outside door. Putting his hand on the handle, and his torch in his pocket he briefly wondered if he might have triggered some silent alarm and that there would be the Turkish police awaiting him on the other side.

But there weren't.

Once back in his hotel room, he took out the key, using some bathroom soap, he cleaned it as best he could. It began to shine.

Smiling to himself as he sat on the bed, looking at it, he knew.

He had found the third key.

THE PRESENT; Rotterdam

Tuesday 28th - early evening

'I wonder if Rudolph ever went to find the third key?' Sophie asked, putting down the translation in French that brother Dauphine had, obviously, meticulously translated from brother Flavius's Latin account. The train was approaching the Central Station of Rotterdam.

Martijn, sitting across from her, had been watching her read, practically the whole journey from Koln, caught her eye and said, 'We should stay at Sam's place'.

The suggestion brought a little colour to her face, she could feel it. It also quickened her heartbeat. She could feel that too. 'You still have a key?'

'Sam wanted to keep the apartment, an ideal base, if, and when, he and Chrissie might find themselves on this side of the Atlantic. We sorted out his stuff, his books and music and so on, but the furniture is all there, also kitchen equipment, bathroom equipment, towels, sheets, all there, Sam said for me to hang on to the keys, and, to use the place whenever.'

Sophie looked at her watch, thought about her return ticket to Paris, was secretly pleased she had packed an overnight case, then looked at him, 'That's a good idea, I need to change my ticket though'.

Martijn was pleased. He too felt rather excited at the prospect of being with her again, it had been a successful day, and though Sophie had not given much away as she had read the account, he was sure that it contained a lot of information.

'Yes, sure, we can do that at the station, you said something about a key?'

'Aha, oui, wondering if Rudolph ever ventured to Turkey'.

'Turkey? so you have found the connection to Turkey?' Sam asked.

'Of course, silly me, I have been reading this translation, you have no idea, oh Martijn, I should have spoken to you as I read...

'It's okay, it was lovely just to see you so totally engrossed, you even showed your ticket to the conductor without looking up'.

'Oh shut up!' she admonished him, 'Okay, well, the brief version, we'll go through the whole account later, we are slowing down, must be getting closer to Rotterdam. 'It turns out, that Rudolph, oh yes, you didn't see, but I noticed, that on the inside lid of the box, was a sheet of paper, it was faint, but I saw the name, Rudolph Meyer, written there, so, he definitely went to the monastery, must have followed up on what he learned from the writings of brother Flavius, after all he went to Philadelphia and bought that painting, he also had the information, that we now have, the destinations of the three monks. Flavius, the name on the painting I have, came to Cologne, it is likely, that Rudolph found the key he had, why else go to the trouble of travelling across the Atlantic, it is also possible, that he went to Santiago de Compostela, that is where the second monk, his name was Bonifatius, went, actually I'm sure he did, because Tammy discovered, in that Zecheriah ledger, that Rudolph had travelled from Spain. '

The train slowed down further.

Sophie stood up, started to grab her gear, then taking her jacket off the hook, ' Thank you kind sir,' as he helped her put it on, ' So, ' she continued as the train stopped and they made for the door, Martijn taking her cabin case from the luggage rack,' By my thinking, he could well have had two keys, and one painting, which made me wonder, if he knew where the third key was, did he ever try and go there?'

They both put their face masks back on.

'Mm, maybe,' Martijn answered, 'if he thought he had a painting, with the third key, if indeed he had the other two, he might have thought it would be enough,' helping Sophie from the train onto the platform, 'also, that region was pretty volatile at that time, maybe felt it was too dangerous, maybe we'll never know.'

'What I do know, is this, 'Sophie said, managing to hold on to her handbag and folder with one arm whilst grabbing him by his arm with the other, whilst he trundled her case along.' First, get my ticket sorted, then we'll head for Sam's place and sort out something to eat, I'm hungry!'

Twenty- five minutes later they boarded a tram heading for the suburb of Schiebroek, and as they sat down, Sophie said, 'I have been organised, my dear Martijn, brought along some overnight gear', patting her case that was on the floor beside her 'but, what about you?' smiling behind her daisy patterned face mask.

'I'll pick up a few bits from the store across the road from Sam's 'Martijn replied.

'So, tell me again, 'he asked turning toward her, 'you believe, this Rudolph, had two keys?'

'Yes, I do, two keys, and, one painting, plus, he knew all the information that we now have..'Sophie stopped speaking, stared past Sam out the window of the tram and suddenly focused on him, saying,' I have been so slow, ' Then breaking into her own language for a bit, before again focusing on him, 'I didn't think about it, until just now, I know that Rudolph found a clue, in the painting...'

'Really?.. ' Martijn interrupted.

'Sorry, yes, so much to tell, soon, anyway, he found a clue on the monks garment, the Roman numerals IV, now, on the painting that Roberto sent me, there is a crest, of sorts, on the cloak he was wearing, on his chest, just above his heart, it is very faint, but I thought it was , well, like a monogram of the monastery or something, never gave it another thought, until just now, it is a clue...'

'I am still somewhat lost in this whole story, you'll have to explain all to me, 'Martijn said, looking at the French woman beside him and thinking how lovely she was, 'but, 'he continued, getting his mind back on the story, 'Rudolph didn't know about that last letter, did he? About the princess?'

'Of course!' she answered, turning to look at him. Then smiled, thinking she couldn't wait to get to Sam's place, take those damn masks off and kiss him properly.' He did not have that information, it's something we will have to look into'.

They rode on in silence for a while. Martijn keeping an eye out for the correct stop.

He too was thinking of that final letter, sent to brother Flavius, mentioning the coming of age, of a princess! Who was this royal highness, he wondered. Three monks, from Florence, each with a key, three portraits, each with a clue. The whole thing was certainly quite perplexing he thought, pressing the button for the next stop.

THE PAST; Period 9 - Part 1

The year 1963: Eastbourne

Roger Sutherland was rather perplexed. He hadn't thought about it for simply ages.   He wandered around the house, checking every room. A house, that, as his parents had decided several years ago now, to remain in Greece, was now his. After a careful check, he sat himself down on the leather two-seater in the lounge.

There was no doubt about it. Somebody knew. There was no doubt about it, for they, whoever they are, knew what they were looking for. It was all they took.

They had not made a mess, not turned everything upside down, not taken anything else. They must have taken the time, were not in any rush, which meant, they also knew he wasn't at home, nor would be for some time to come.

He had gone to Maastricht, a reunion with a few guys and girls that he had studied with, whilst spending that month in the Dutch city, six years ago.

Sitting on the couch, Roger played a scenario through in his mind. Had the invitation been a ruse? A plan to get him away from the house? But the friends he met, they knew nothing, he was sure of that, none of them had been aware of what he had purchased at the market, none of them could have known what he had in his possession and his subsequent plans. No, he said to himself, getting up from the couch he walked through the house, no, he again said to himself, they, whoever they were, must have been watching the house, waiting for an opportune moment, perhaps even following him to the airport two days ago, seeing him depart on a flight to Amsterdam. This all sounded very well in his head, but the question remained, who were they and how did they know about the keys and the painting?

For that was all that had been taken, he had placed all those items, the keys, the wood panelled painting and all the documents that he had that day purchased, along with the painting of brother Ignatius. It had been out of sight. He hadn't thought about any of it for a long time.

He would check with the neighbours, ask if they had seen anything. Should he go to the police? He felt it better not to, this had been a professional job, no damage, no clues left, no fingerprints to be seen.

Making himself a fresh pot of tea and lighting a cigarette, Roger pondered as to what to do next. He thought back.

The treasure hunt, for that is what he called it, had started so well, the excitement in this very house that evening as he discussed his finds with Kim and Oliver. The planning they construed, each with their own task, their own challenge. Working together and the dreams of finding this, what had to surely be, quite some treasure.

But it had not gone quite to plan, the excitement had soon petered out. He himself, had been elated, had felt quite the adrenalin rush, wandering around that big cathedral, finding that old door, the old cellar, and the pure joy when he found the key. That had been great. The excitement had been there then and all the way back home.

Kim had not been at all successful, having found out next to nothing about this Viana Vanetti, other than that she had been the one who had set up the vineyard business.

Oliver was a little more successful, he had found the painting that had travelled all the way from Spain, delivered by a monk, a brother Cristoph, sadly his companion, a brother Jozef, had perished on the journey. There was an account of the whole tale, and a friendly brother had, with enthusiasm, told him the full story. There was no way he could take the painting, but, having a camera with him, he took practically a whole roll of film, also taking shots of the monk, and of a rather pretty young girl, whose name was Mercedes and Oliver, in a letter accompanying the film, had told of the story of the dead young boy, and that he was staying in the States.

He had fallen madly deeply in love, he wrote.

Roger, suddenly recalling, raced up to his bedroom, he rummaged in a couple of drawers.

There! He found it. The letter from Oliver, the photographs, it was there, he hadn't put it with the other stuff. Why, he didn't know, but a sigh of relief that he still had something.

His joy, however, after feeling quite perplexed and angry earlier, turned to deep sorrow the following day.

THE PRESENT; San Francisco

Tuesday 28th

Whilst Martijn and Sophie were tucking in a Chinese take-out meal in Rotterdam, the police knocked on the door of Patricia's house in San Francisco and any joy that she had felt upon the success of acquiring the painting, was instantly gone when she opened the door.

She lost all colour, tried, but failed to speak, and only barely registered the document that was shown to her.

A search warrant. What had gone wrong? She wondered as she stood aside to let them in, two of them, a young man and a woman. Closing the door behind them, she was still in shock as to how it was that she had been found.

'What is it you are looking for?' she asked, finding a voice of sorts, though it was broken and croaky.

'Best you just tell us where the painting is' the policewoman said, 'we needn't turn your house upside down' having turned and looking directly at Mrs. Montgomery.

Five minutes later she was ushered into the car. The policeman carrying the painting, which he carefully placed in the trunk, having taken a towel from the bathroom to wrap it in, then got into the passenger seat. and the policewoman started the engine and drove away.

What Patricia Eunice Montgomery didn't notice that it was not a police car.

It wasn't until they had been driving for five minutes or so, that, registering where they were and in what direction, that she suddenly felt ill at ease.

Pushing those thoughts of doubt away for a moment, she tried to think as to how the police had come knocking on her door, when she had been so careful. The girl she had hired for the job, did not have her real name, nor, she was sure, would she be able to recognise her as she really was, as with her one and only meeting with her and the young man who had accompanied her, she had changed her appearance quite dramatically.

This not only to keep her identity hidden from the young woman, but in case of being caught on any of the many security cameras that these days are just about everywhere. This, together with the masks that so many were wearing now, she felt secure in the knowledge that she was well disguised.

She had given the girl instructions, to leave it at this particular dry-cleaning service, making sure it was wrapped in brown paper, tied with string and with the further instruction that it was for a Mrs. Trapp. Patricia had, again wearing her disguise, arranged this with the dry cleaners she had found, one of few that were still operating during this pandemic where so many businesses had to be closed. With a handsome payment, she had told them it was for a special surprise gift for her husband. The brown paper and the string and calling herself Mrs Trapp was her for her own amusement and the girl she hired would likely not understand the connection. Her search for this young lady, had taken the longest. As her ex-husband was a lawyer and having dealt with many cases over the years, Patricia had found, not only the letter from the monk, but, in that same afternoon as a plan began to formulate, came across some old case files. Once again, she told herself it was fate, this was all meant to be.

But as she looked out of the window of the car, it seemed fate had turned its back on her. She was confused. They didn't seem to be taking her to the central police station. A feeling in the pit of her stomach turned a little doubt, into fear. Finally, she dared ask, 'Hey, where are we actually going?'

She saw the policewoman's eyes as she looked into her rear vision mirror, then the policeman turned around in his seat and spoke,' It's okay Mrs. Montgomery, we are going to see someone who might prove very helpful to you' then turning back around again.

Prove helpful? Patricia thought, beginning to watch careful as to where they were taking her, then she saw. They were heading for the museum.

Stopping by the rear door entrance, the same one where Alison and Simon had entered through the previous Friday, the policeman opened the car door for Patricia to get out. As they approached the door, it opened.

'Terri?' Patricia said, stopping in her tracks.

'Come on in Patricia, 'Terri said, nodding to the policeman and woman, noticed that they had the painting with them, then closing the door, she turned, passed by them, and walked ahead of them, 'Follow me' she said, then added as she walked on,' As none of us are wearing a mask, let's keep a distance from each other, please.'

Terri entered a door that led into as small room, there were several tables and chairs, a coffee machine, a drinks machine, and a small kitchen. The staff cafeteria.

'Okay' Terri said, totally taking command of the situation, looking at Patricia, 'now, sit down, and listen, okay? ' and before any response was forthcoming, she went on to say,' two options, one, you tell me everything, everything you know about this painting, why it is of interest to you, and, you tell these lovely police people, who the woman and man were that you hired' Terri let that sink in for a second, then continued, ' option two, you say nothing and you'll be taken straight to the police station and charged.'

Patricia looked at Terri, then said, ' I...I saw in the newspaper, that they.. that you were held at gun point, ...Terri, I am so sorry, I had no idea that it would be like that, I am so grateful you weren't.. anyway, are you saying then, that she didn't talk and lead to the police to me?, so, how...'

'It was Miss Hudson who worked it out, that it could only have been you, she approached me, spoke to me and my colleague about the deal, the museum won't press charges, nor will Miss Hudson, option one is a good one.' the policewoman said.

'Yes, I.. I can see that, but, I only know the girl, the young woman, yes, I will give you all the details, I didn't know about the young man, yes, he was there when I met her, but I don't know his name..but, ' looking at Terri, ' why are you doing this, I don't understand, well, maybe, but still, you were held at gunpoint, you have every right to be angry with me..'

Terri stepped over to where the policeman had placed the painting against the wall, picked it up, took the towel away from it, and turned again to face Patricia, who by now had some colour back in her face.

There's more to this painting, more than you know, more than I know, it's important we work together on this, so, are you in? Or will they take you away'.

'No, no, I mean, yes, I'm in,..'

'Alright Mrs. Montgomery, this is how it will go,' sitting down at the same table and producing a notepad, 'We want to know who you hired, we want to know how you found her, we want to know the instructions you gave her, we don't need to or want to know anything about the painting, the news will be that an anonymous person returned the painting. 'Pushing the notepad and a pen towards Patricia, 'what you and Miss Hudson then do about it, is up to you, our job will be done'.

Patricia looked at her, then looked up at Terri who, still holding the painting and studying it, said, 'There will be no mention of you Patricia, none at all'.

Patricia began writing.

THE PAST; Period 9 - Part 2

The year 1963 Cannes

Natalie Umbrego was writing. She was sitting in the same cafe where only hours earlier Roberto had eaten his lunch. She had ordered coffee, had asked for a sheet of paper, and had then sat down, taking a pen from her handbag and when taking her first sip of the drink, she realised she was shaking slightly. Shock setting in, she figured. Carefully placing the cup back onto the saucer, she took a deep breath and began writing. So many things were on her mind. One thing she was glad of, the painting was safe, and they would not have any idea where it was.

Taking a few more deep breaths, she finally let her shoulder down and tried to relax. Another sip of coffee, this time her hand was steady. She felt relieved.

They had chased her, they had come after her, one of them was dead, the other seriously injured. But there could be more, probably would be more, she had to protect her family, herself. She had to go somewhere, and figure this all out.

As a freelance journalist, she could do this, she could investigate, she could ask questions. She could smile at the men. They were usually very forthcoming. She continued to write for some moments, then sat back, finished her coffee, ordered another one and chose a bun to eat, she needed some sustenance.

Getting out her journalist note pad, she flicked through the pages, the pad was practically full, hence her asking for a sheet of paper, she would need to put all her notes in order, she was sure, that something she had said, maybe some time ago, or someone she had spoken to, must have triggered this sequence of events. Events triggered by a single phone call.

Natalie then thought of something, she remembered the airline stewardess, who came and was asking about Viana Vanetti, yes, what was her name... She had given her a card. Rummaging around in her capacious bag, she found it. Goodness, she thought, how long ago was that? Three or four years? She needed to sort out her handbag more often, no wait, it was, yes, six years ago!

Feeling positive that this woman, as she was looking at the card she had been given, this Kim Frederick, knew something, for she had mentioned the painting of a monk, Natalie made up her mind, that was going to be her first port of call. Eating the bun and drinking her second coffee, she was beginning to feel stronger and more relaxed. She would also need to know the names of the men in that accident, the ones that had risked their lives trying to get to her, trying to get to the painting.

What was more puzzling to her though, who was it that had called, who was it that had warned her and had set all this in motion.

Hastings, England, two days later.

Kim was taken aback, she put the phone down and frowned. The young lady she had met whilst in Monte Carlo, whilst at the Vanetti Vineyards, Natalie something or other, had called. Wanted to meet, important. Moreover, she was close, in the vicinity, for she suggested a pub not two blocks from where she lived. And, even more confusing, she had moved house, had married, had a new name, different telephone number, how had she found out? Her husband was at work. Their first child was at nursery, she was carrying their second child. What was going on?

Not to be deterred and rather inquisitive, Kim checked her make up, then got ready to go out. Would it have anything to do with why she had gone to Monaco in the first place? She wondered, as she walked towards the pub.

'Goodness, congratulations!' a voice said and Kim turned around to come face to face with the young lady. Her red hair was long, her face was vibrant, her eyes were sparkling, she was astonishingly beautiful, Kim observed.

Natalie moved forward, planting a kiss on either cheek whilst taking holds of Kim's shoulders and said, 'come on, over here, I have a seat, you have questions' it was a statement not a question.

'Yes, how..? 'Kim began, still somewhat overwhelmed by the exuberance of the red head, she remembered she was the same, what, six years ago? She thought, taking her coat off and sitting in the booth.

'How I found you?' Natalie asked, smiling and then' what would you like to drink?'

'I'll have an orange juice please,' Kim replied.

'Relax, I will explain everything, back soon.' and off she went to the bar.

Kim watched her go. Though still a little wary, she did begin to feel more relaxed.

Natalie came back with the drinks, then said, 'right, well, I am a freelance journalist, so, I am good at getting information, and, well, if I ask a man nicely, and smile, I can get all the information I need' smiling and raising her glass of white wine.

Kim couldn't help but smile in return, knowing that she was right, she would get any man to talk.

'So, Natalie went on, 'I had your card, you give me, remember?'

'You said you would call' Kim reminded her.

'Yes, I did, but, other things happened, anyway, my first question to you, is this, did you come to find out about Viana Vanetti because of a painting of a monk? I remember you saying?

But before Kim could answer, 'No, sorry, I am not polite, your baby, your first? how long?'

Kim smiled, then said, 'Six months, and no, we have a three-year-old son.'

Two days earlier in San Francisco

Oliver lay bleeding on the shop floor.

His three-year-old son was being comforted and hugged tightly by his mother, who in turned was being hugged and comforted by two people.

The small convenience store, around the corner from where they lived, was the scene of chaotic madness that lasted all of thirty seconds.

About to place their groceries on the counter, two young men had burst in, one waving a gun. Oliver had instantly reacted, his main goal was to protect his wife and child, he placed himself between them and the shouting intruders. Then, seeing the gun pointing directly at him, he simple charged, feeling there was no other option open to him at that moment. Without a word he was upon the intruder with the gun, he used to play rugby, he was solid, his weight and his momentum stopped the intruder, and they both went down. Oliver had hold of the gun, twisting and ramming his elbow into the young man's face. Then a shot rang out, it was muffled, then another shot, which echoed loudly throughout the store, heard above the screams of two other customers.

The second intruder also had a gun, he had fired it into Oliver. The first shot, the muffled sound, had been the first intruder's gun, Oliver having managed to turn it inward. The second intruder fled the scene, ran out of the store, jumped into a waiting car and with screeching tyres, the vehicle sped off.

The storekeeper had come around from behind his counter as he saw Oliver charging into the young man. He now knelt and turned him over, and could see that both he, and the first intruder, were dead.

He turned to the woman holding her child. He knew them, knew them quite well, Mercedes and the little boy was Roger, just three years old.

'Please, go into the back, wait there' he said, his voice only just above a whisper.

Mercedes looked, her eyes wide open, her colour drained, and her gaze was met by a negative shake of the head. The two women who had come to comfort her, now escorted her to the back of the store. Sirens could be heard. Someone had phoned the police.

Oliver Mantell was dead.

THE PRESENT; San Francisco

Tuesday 28th

On the other side of town to where Terri was talking with Patricia Montgomery, her mother Alison, received a call.

'Hello?' 'Roger, yes, of course, you know my address? Okay, about twenty minutes, sure..okay'

Alison ended the call and looked around the house. A few things to sort and tidy, she thought, setting about clearing a few dishes and getting the coffee machine going. What was this all about? She wondered, checking herself in the hallway mirror to make sure she was presentable. Not that she was interested, but a woman always liked to look her best, she thought, heading for the bedroom to run a brush through her long hair.

Twenty-three minutes later the doorbell rang.

'Detective Inspector' Alison said, opening the door, 'A nice surprise'.

'Thank you for seeing me Miss Hudson..'

'Oh for goodness sake, call me Ally!' she said, closing the door, 'come on in, I'm sure you'd like a coffee?'

'Ahh, okay, Ally, yes, that would be nice, then as a sudden afterthought, 'goodness, I took my mask off in the car, should..

'No, it's fine, these masks, I guess they must be effective, but sure are a nuisance, please...' Alison pointed her guest in the direction of the lounge, then prepared the drink, calling out from the kitchen, 'I'm curious as to why you want to see me'.

Roger Mantell sat himself down on the two-seater and waited until Alison appeared, then answered, 'We have identified the third person in that satellite surveyance film, on the dig site that following evening.' Referring to an incident that occurred over thirty years ago when a tornado struck an archaeological dig-site near silver city in New Mexico.

'Really? Who?' Alison, placing the drinks on the table, asked, being fully aware of that event and the subsequent investigation which led her to meet Simon.

'The Dean of the university'

'What?'

'Yes, that is, the dean at the time, I think I may have mentioned, that this whole case, was just not investigated properly, everything seemed to have been blamed on the tornado and nothing more came of it. Thankfully there were some people who were suspicious, like Simon, then we have of course those findings from Mr. Raphael Morton, mostly it was when Robert Pentegrass was asked to investigate the disappearance of Eddie Philpot, that things began to be uncovered, by now of course, as I know you are aware, we are talking some thirty years later. Anyway, all of that was, thankfully finally resolved, thanks to you and Miss Parker, and, also because of Eddie, who uncovered a part of the puzzle we didn't know existed, the exact number of gold coins that had been buried. So, 'Detective Inspector Mantell taking a break here and sipping some coffee, before continuing, 'so, having then re-opened the case again, I went through everything, it was then, checking on everyone involved, that I discovered, the dean at the time, was having an affair with, yes, Mrs. Shelton. .This made me dig deeper, though Mrs. Constance Shelton carried on her life in the same manner as always, thus not creating any suspicion, and if it had not been for that sketch drawn by Professor Emily Parker, she may well not have been caught at all, anyway, turns out, about five months after the tornado strike, the then dean, resigned and left, his name, by the way, is Malcolm Lynch, and all we know so far, it that he travelled to Spain.' Taking another sip, then looking across at Alison who had been intently listening, he then said to her, 'But that is not why I am here, it's not why I called'.

'Really?' Ally asked, holding her cup, raising her eyebrows, and looking at him questioningly.

'No, as a law enforcement officer, I get more detailed news of crimes that have happened, I read about the theft from the museum, your daughter being held at gun point, she is alright, isn't she?'

'Yes, she a tough cookie, she's fine, angrier with herself I think, actually, she did some sleuthing herself, figured out that it could have been only one person, who knew where this particular painting was..' Alison paused for a moment, thinking about how much she could reveal'.

'Miss Hudson? .. I mean Ally? what's going on, she's not going to do anything silly..'

'Oh, no, she has a friend in the police force, she called her and together they made a plan, just not sure if I am breaking a confidence here.. oh, it's nothing illegal, I assure you..'

'You have my word, please trust me, I have an interest in this case, which is really why I called, because I wanted to speak with your daughter...'

'With Terri?' Ally asked, putting her cup down, then studying the inspector for a moment said, ' Alright, at this very moment, the woman who was responsible for arranging the theft, is speaking with Terri, the deal was, or is, that this woman would give all the details to the police about the persons she hired, how she had found them and so on, oh, and the painting has been retrieved, back in the museum, in return she would not be charged as long as she told Terri all she knew about the painting and why it had been so important for her to steal it.'

Roger Mantell, finishing his drink, took something from the inside pocket of his jacket and placed it on the table for Alison to look at. It was a photo. He said nothing and looked across at her.

She looked at it, then picked it up and looked at it closely. Two people, two young people, a couple, they were standing in what looked to be a crypt of sorts, stone walls, stone tiles, arches, dim lighting. They stood in front of an alcove, and on the wall in that alcove, hung a painting.

'Is that the painting that was stolen?' He asked, when she finally looked up at him.

'I, I don't know, I've not seen it, Terri would know for sure, but it very well could be'.

'The monk in that painting' Roger began, ' 'Is brother Bonifatius, it is the left hand side panel of a triptych, ' Seeing that he had her full attention, he went on, ' you see, there were three monks, from Florence, they each travelled to a destination, each with a key, also, as well as that, a painting had been made, of all three of them, the centre panel was brother Flavius, the eldest of the three, the right hand side, was brother Ignatius, he was the youngest, and this one, ' pointing at the photo which Alison had placed back on the table, ' was Bonifatius'

After a moment of silence, Ally asked, 'so, how do you know all this?'

'When I read the police report, regarding the theft, what I learned, which was not public knowledge, was that it was a painting of a monk, this, well, stirred some memories.. you see, the people in that photo, are my mum and dad.'

'Wow,' Ally said, picking the photo up again, 'when was this taken?'

'In 1963'

'I need to make a call' she said, standing up, I'll explain soon, okay, if you want another coffee? Please, help yourself, actually, pour one for me'.

Alison located her phone and pressed some numbers.

'Chrissie? Can I speak with Sam please?.. Hi, that painting, the one that Sophie received, you know a little about it? Oh, and by the way, the one stolen from the museum here, it is back, Terri knows much more, and she will call you soon, but, about the one that was sent to Sophie, what can you tell me...

Several minutes later she ended the call, placed her phone on the table, said, 'Thank you' to Roger, who had returned from the kitchen with refreshed cups and was looking up at her from the two-seater.

'Right' Ally began, sitting down, ' you mentioned this triptych, well, the centre panel was sent to a friend of our in Paris, well, I consider her a friend, though I've not met her, she received this painting, from this forger she knew, he died and left it to her, along with a story of how he got it, though a well accomplished forger, this painting was real, and he was given it to clean and repair, in 1963.'

'The same year' Roger said.

'Sophie is at this time, working with another friend, a colleague of yours in a way, he is a Dutch policeman, to find out more, because they discovered who had purchased the right-hand hand side panel, way, way, back in 1803. I will give Terri a call next, you need to indeed, speak with her, and how are your mum and dad involved?'

After a moment of reflection, Roger said, 'My father was Oliver, and he along with his good friend Roger Sutherland, by the way I am named after this Roger, and a woman, Kim, were in search of the mystery surrounding these three monks.'

After a quick sip, Roger then continued, 'When I was three years old, my father was shot and killed in an armed robbery, he made sure mum and I were safe, then, 'Roger's voice trailed off and he fell silent.

'I am so sorry' Alison whispered.

'You see,' Roger said, clearing his throat, then went on,' My father had come over from England, to specifically find this painting, which he did, but he met this young woman, my mother to be, fell in love, took a bunch of pictures, which he sent to Roger.'

The detective picked up the photograph, then said,' back in those days, the photos were on film, had to be developed. Later Roger sent this one back, I am glad I have it..'

'A lovely photo' Alison began, her phone rang, interrupting, 'Hey, yes, okay, I'll be there soon, and Terri, I will be bringing a friend...' looking at the detective,' no, just trust me, this is very important.. okay, see you soon'.

'Terri asked me to come to the museum as you heard, okay?' Ally asked, giving the detective a smile, 'you are an interesting piece of the puzzle.'

'Absolutely, 'Roger said, standing up, then, taking the cups back into the kitchen, said, 'It would be nice to see this painting, compare it to the photo, we'll take my rental, is that okay?' then, fully registering what she had said, 'Interesting piece of the puzzle?'

Alison smiled as she opened the front door, then as he walked past her, said, 'You have no idea..'

$$\mathcal{O}\!\mathcal{G}\!\mathbin{\blacklozenge}\!\mathcal{O}\!\mathcal{O}$$

THE PAST; Period 9 - Part3

the year 1963: Istanbul

The room was large, situated on the first floor, it had five windows, all overlooking the Bosporus from the European side of the city. A massive Persian rug covered the entire room in colours that ranged from muted oranges and reds, through to soft shades of green and yellow. A set of double doors, in a dark wood gave entry to this room from the hallway. A single wooden door of the same wood was at the far end. The three walls completing the rectangular shape were covered in a dark green wallpaper and adorned with several paintings. The drapes that hung from a high ceiling flanking each of the five windows were a dark maroon in colour and made of heavy velvet. The most unusual feature of this room was that there was no furniture.

The woman that stood by the middle window, looking out and observing the sun dazzling its light upon the waters, was angry. Much like her ancestor had been, over four hundred years ago. An ancestor she had only learnt about, six years ago.

One of the double doors opened and closed, a man had entered.

Alexa, though only a very few people knew her name, and none called her by it, spoke without turning, 'Yes?'

The man, elderly, late sixties, stopped about ten feet away and observed the woman for a moment. Her stance upright, her chin slightly upward showing her lovely neckline. Her hair was dark, almost black, and cut quite short. He noticed her simple pearl drop earrings, and said, 'It is confirmed, Kazim died in the accident, Huzar is very badly injured, in hospital, his condition is bad'.

'And the painting?' she asked, still not turning to face the man.

'The girl had it, took it away. 'He answered.

For a moment all was silent. The man observed the woman by the window, the woman was only to be addressed as Madam X, or simply

Madam. He, one of very few, knew her to be Alexa, though he had no idea of her full name.

'Get someone to follow up, find the girl, any news from England?'

'Yes Madam, happy to report all items were secured, on their way here.'

'And the States?'

'No word Madam, as yet' the man answered.

Finally, she turned, he could see her face showed anger, yet her voice had been calm, authoritative, without emotion. 'Carry on'

'Yes Madam' he replied, turned and left as quietly as he had come.

Alexa once more turned to look out of the window.

Six years ago, she was on a small private aeroplane, flying out of Trieste, heading for Venice. An air-pocket accompanied by a sudden squall of heavy rain buffeted the light craft and the pilot, a young man with a severe lack of flying hours and even more severe lack of flying in difficult conditions, lost control.

The light plane twisted, then turned upside down. In a struggle for control the pilot did, to his credit, manage to get the plane the right side up again, but then, as suddenly the rain, which had been so severe, stopped altogether, he noticed to his horror that they were almost on the ground. There wasn't anything more he could do, he failed to lift the aircraft higher, ploughed into a field of corn and slithered along until a large oak tree at the far end of the field halted all progress.

He was killed instantly.

She was injured, having been first thrown from her seat onto the ceiling of the plane as it turned, then upon landing back down her hip was broken, finally as the plane came to that abrupt stop, she was flung forward, collided with the door to the cockpit and lay unconscious. A broken leg and fractured arm, adding to her injury, along with concussion and several cuts.

Three weeks in hospital, then, at her grandmother's insistence, she stayed with her for a further three months. Slowly getting better.

It was during this time, in the beginning so bored living in the tiny cottage in the countryside, far removed from the partying lifestyle she had been leading, that she heard stories, her grandmother was often telling her stories, of their heritage, their family line, their ancestors. At first Alexa had just smiled and suffered the lengthy accounts, but then she picked up something about jewels. Lots of jewels.

Her mind was awakened, her curiosity stirred. No longer bored, but, with a new goal, a new direction. What was the story about jewels all about, was it real, was it hearsay. She needed to know. Nothing else to do, she set about on a journey of discovery.

A journey that led to her so many times generation ago, ancestor, called Alexandria

Wenschelburg. Immediately liking this woman, she had the same name, it was highly probable that she had been named after her and, she was the one with the story of the jewels. It had been a frustrating time of patience as she needed to recuperate before being able to travel and follow up on the information she had gathered whilst in her grandmother's care.

Alexa smiled at the memory, when, finally, with the aid of crutches, she was allowed to travel, has first gone back to her small apartment in Trieste, then nearly five months after the accident, she moved to Venice, took an apartment there, and whereas before she would sleep in till noon and then go to parties or clubs until the small hours of the morning, Alexa now rose early, and every day for nearly two months, she would walk, still with the aid of one walking stick, to the library.

The old library, the Marciana Library, also referred to as the St, Mark Library, after the patron saint of Venice, was now a museum, all the books, maps and documents had been transferred to the building next door, the Zecca. Here she spent hours and hours. Here she found out so much more, about her family, her heritage, her ancestry. But, for weeks, though it was all rather fascinating, she could find nothing about jewels. Until, one day, deciding to follow a name she had come across in her research, that of a cousin of Cardinal Farnese, a certain Father Dominic, that she almost shouted out of a discovery, remembering in time that she was in a library.

It was a children's book, titled, 'The secret princess' written in

Italian, by twins Eva and Bella Umbrego. It was on the back of this little book, a short biography of the twins, having been born and raised on the Vanetti Vineyards in Monaco, that had drawn Alexa's attention. The connection with Father Dominic

Sitting back after having read it through twice, Alexa knew. The stories were real, the jewels were real, the treasure existed. She painstakingly copied the words, feeling elated, feeling her heart beating faster.

Standing for several moments longer looking out of the window, Alexa then turned and crossed to where the single door was and left the room.

Whereas the large room was plush, an expensive rug covering the entire floor, wallpaper that would practically cost and arm and a leg per roll, the velvet drapes were of the highest quality and made to measure. From the high ceiling three ornate crystal chandeliers brought light into the room and above each painting, and there were ten in all, was a soft tube light set into a brass covering. The room which she had just entered was a lifetime away. It was well lit, had just one window that overlooked the Bosporus, a basic carpet on the floor, there were two metal filing cabinets against a wall, there was large wooden desk, behind which a leather chair, there was an area where a coffee machine had been placed along with a low table, two chairs and an old-style standard lamp. On the desk, which was rather sparse, there was a metal tray, a telephone, a large daily diary and some type of ledger which was open.

From one of the drawers, she took out a stick of gum and chewing it with vigour she sat herself behind the desk and made some notations in this ledger, then closed it and got up to leave.

Not long after having fully recovered from her injuries, her grandmother, who had been such a source of information as well as a lovely companion and had nursed her back to fitness, suddenly died. She was devastated. She was also angry with herself, for prior to her accident she had little time for her family, had only a few friends, and lived her life by her own rules and for her own pleasure.

Yet she knew, how she was inside, her character, would surely resurface, for, she often said, standing in front of the tall mirror in her bedroom, I am what I am, and I live for me, beholden to no-one. She knew, in her heart, that this was also why she had so few friends, she was selfish. Selfish, proud and arrogant, she had heard other speak of her, and so, that who she would be.

What did astound her at the time, that after the funeral she was told of her inheritance. The cottage in the countryside was now hers, the one where at first was the last place on earth she wanted to be, and yet, it was the place where she had learned of her past, of her ancestry, her lineage. She was drawn into the world of Alexandria Wenschelburg, was sure that she was named after this woman, it being a family name, discovered the gypsy routes and set out to find out all she could, again, standing to admire herself in the mirror and smilingly thought to herself that she was no doubt a gypsy beauty.

It was time for lunch.

She put on a short leather jacket, then left the office, entering a small lobby area. From here you could head for a modest kitchen in one direction, or down a corridor to where there were two bedrooms, both with ensuite. Alexa had purchased the whole first floor of the old building which in times gone by had been the residence of an ambassador. For along with the cottage, she inherited a vast amount of money. Though had no idea, where it had come from, not that it worried her, she wanted more, plenty was never enough for her, or ever would be.

Fools! She thought to herself, descending the stairs to the ground level, an easy task, get the painting, they had clear instructions, knew who had it, where it was, simple, what, she wondered, as she opened the door to the outside, had gone wrong? Taking the car keys from her pocket, she walked up to her modified Corvette and unlocked the driver's door.

Spitting her gum out, she got in, fired up the engine and roared away. Her information was good, her research had been meticulous, it had taken time, too much time, but she had persevered, changing gear and almost drifting around the corner and onto the main road. They must have blundered somehow, she almost said to herself, changing gear again and ignoring speed restrictions, she felt no remorse, no sorrow, no compassion that one of them had died, the other badly injured, not her fault.! They blundered.

Ignoring a couple of beeps from other traffic, Alexa headed toward the bay where she regularly ate in a well-known restaurant there.

She briefly wondered about the twins, who, between them had uncovered much of the history of the secret jewels, nearly a hundred years ago, she mused, and smiled as she sped through the streets, because she figured as she screeched around a sharp bend, that she was going to be the one, to find them.

Meanwhile, back on the first floor in his office, just outside of the two big wooden doors to the large room, Youseff had heard the powerful engine of the corvette, looked out of his window and saw her speed away. He sighed. Then returned to his desk, there was paperwork to sort out, the arrangement had to be made for Kazim's body to be returned and, if possible, if he was well enough, for Huzar to be transported to a local hospital. Also, the costs of the car to be recovered. Though he did not agree with the coldness in which his employer, Madam, had shown with regard to the death and injury of these men, he was of the same mind as to how they could have blundered. Grabbing a folder that lay on his desk, he opened it, flicked through the notes, and thought about who to contact to complete the task in which these two had failed.

Whilst Alexa was shown to her regular table at the restaurant on the bay, a KLM DC9 was flying over the Swiss Alps. Hugo Visser was on the flight from Amsterdam to Rome. He looked out the window at the snow-covered peaks below and for a moment or two admired the beauty of the scenic panorama bathed in sunlight. Smiling to himself he then sat back and felt good. He had easily accomplished his assignment. She would be pleased.

Coffee was offered and he accepted the beverage as the plane flew through the very blue sky, as he looked, Hugo could not see a cloud anywhere.

Sipping carefully, he thought about the conversation he would have with her. He smiled again to himself as he could picture her face.

Closing his eyes briefly, he thought about his life, about his journey to this point.

His mother was Italian, his father Dutch. His mother was volatile, animated, passionate. His father was placid, yet stern, quiet, yet commanding.

When he was five and feeling quite excited to be going to the big school soon, in Roosendaal where they lived, his mother took him away. He recalled the journey, to some degree, remembering that they had travelled on several trains, that his mother spoke very little, smiled a lot and many times kissing him on his forehead.

She had left to go back to her hometown. He didn't understand, he had been wanting to go to school, now, he was going to another school, but they all spoke a different language. For several days, he remembers hiding in his room, recalls being angry with his mother, wanted so badly to see his father.

Three years passed, seemingly quite quickly Hugo thought, then his father was there, one day, as he came out of school. He was overjoyed to see him, excited, and speaking in a sudden mixture of Italian and Dutch as he clutched his father's hand.

On board the flight, Hugo finished his coffee, threw a look out of the window.

His father had bundled him into a car, they had driven some way, and then were at an airfield and getting into a helicopter. Whilst this was all very exciting, Hugo recalled, he suddenly felt most peculiar. Was he not going home to his mother? Would he now not see her again? As an eight-year-old, it was all rather unsettling.

Finally at the school he had been looking forward to going, needing to relearn the Dutch language, it took quite some time before he felt settled. But five years on, finishing lower school and preparing for the next stage of his education, his father left. Over the years, other than the first few months, he had not grown close to him. He left with another woman and flew to South Africa, leaving him in the house and with his grandmother who had come to stay.

His grandmother was sweet, cooked and cleaned the house, but Hugo realised that though she spoke very little, she drank quite a lot. Her condition and ability to keep house diminished over the months.

Hugo noticed, he started to plan on his fourteenth birthday and the day after he had turned fifteen, he left.

Throwing another look out the window, Hugo noticed some cloud cover appearing as the plane started its descent towards Rome.

Events in his life had made him who he was. He smiled again at the thought of telling her.

Closing his eyes again briefly, he again thought back.

With funds saved and obtained, Hugo, armed with a passport he had applied for, forging a few signatures here and there, took a train to Rome. The very place he was approaching this day.

From there he travelled by train and bus and went home. His mother was overjoyed.

But, although it was good to see her, Hugo was determined to live his life according to his own rules, all for one, he would recite, and not one for all.

It had been by chance, four days after his sixteenth birthday, that he had decided to go for a walk around the town where he now lived, Eraclia, a little to the east of Venice, with a large pinewood forest and a long beach upon he frequently walked and daydreamt.

This day was wild, the storm was crashing the waves onto the beach, the wind was howling through the trees and the rain would come down from one direction and then change to come in from another direction, making it hard to know which way to turn away from it. Hugo reached the corn field. Saw the big oak tree, he had often climbed into it, he did so again. He felt secure perched halfway up, was to some degree sheltered and settled himself down to watch the scene around him through the leaves of the old oak.

He picked up a sound. The noise of an engine. Peering in the direction, he then saw the little plane, it was weaving all over the place, then seemed to glide into the corn field, and Hugo watched as it approached with some speed, slicing through the corn and coming directly at him.

The crash was loud. The old oak shook, but only briefly, below him, the plane was a crumpled mess.

A bump shook him from his thoughts. The plane had landed.

Hugo took in a deep breath, stretched, then, once again with a smile on his face, prepared to disembark when the craft had stopped.

Yes, he thought, he couldn't wait to tell her. It was the right time now, to do so.

Alexa finished her lunch and looked out over the Bay. She was pleased that Hugo had been successful and that the acquired items were on their way. She smiled as she anticipated meeting him when he arrived, looking at her watch and calculating that he would have arrived in Rome by now. His transfer flight was just over an hour away. Yes, she was looking forward to that moment and thought back at how she had discovered all about a man named Roger Sutherland.

Sipping her white wine, she recalled the first major clue she came across, the writings of the twins from Monaco. This in turn led her once again to this Father Dominic, but with newly found information details in the manuscript by the twins, and after several more days of research, discovered about three keys and three clues. Three keys held by three monks, three clues within the paintings on wood panels of those three monks.

She was in Istanbul, so, it seemed natural for her to visit Izmir first. She talked her way into having a good search in the cathedral, then eventually came to the old door. Despite a little protestation by the man who was guiding her around, saying this room had not been used for many, many, years, she insisted, and he agreed, twisting the lock near the top of the door, then opened the large wooden door that led into the cellar.

There is no light in here, he said, but left and came back with a torch, which she promptly took.

Here she discovered the little wooden cabinet on the wall after running the torch light around the various wine racks and old bottles and stood in front of it, opened it and knew, this was where the key would be, but though rummaging through the few keys that were there, she also knew, it wasn't here.

Shining the torch around some more, she then saw the ticket. The train ticket, on the floor at her feet.

Picking it up, she studied it in the light, turned it over, then again looked at the ticket. In the dimness of the cellar, and away from her guide who had remained by the door, she smiled. Someone had been here. Someone, she was sure, had the key that ought to have been here, the train ticket was from 1957, six years ago!

Thanking her guide, she had then taken herself over to the address written on the ticket, a hotel, just across the road.

It didn't take long, and she charmed her way into seeing the guestbooks, so, she thought, when she made the discovery, who are you Mr. Sutherland from Eastbourne, England.

Alexa got up from her regular table, nodded to the door manager, knowing her man would regularly come and pay the bill. Got into her corvette and sped away in the same way she a had arrived. She was pleased, thankful for this Mister Sutherland, who, she had discovered after Hugo had informed her, having telephoned her from the airport in Amsterdam, had done quite the research, all of it hers now. Thankful to Hugo, for so professionally obtaining it all.

Yes, she thought, once again racing through the narrow streets, she was looking forward to seeing Hugo.

It was four and a half hours later, when she walked from her office back into the large room. Lights were lit above each painting. The three chandeliers from the ceiling were lit. It was dark outside as Alexa walked over to the centre window, her favourite spot. Hugo was right behind her.

On her desk, in her office, neatly in a row, were three keys, all polished and shiny. Hugo had, with a little ceremony, placed them there. Behind her desk, leaning up against the wall, stood the panel, the right-hand panel of the triptych, delivered by first class same day courier from England, along with a bundle of type written notes, in English, that, according to Hugo, who had read through them, explained Mr. Sutherland's findings and research.

Three keys, one painting holding a clue, two to find. Alexa thought, looking into the darkness at the Bosporus, then turned and smiled.

She walked up to Hugo, placed her left hand behind his neck, drew them closer to her, then, whilst kissing him on the lips, her right hand had pulled a small revolver from within her garment, pressed it against his chest and pulled the trigger.

Hugo stumbled back, one pace, then collapsed onto his knees, his face registering shock, but briefly, as he began to fall backwards, his left arm reached behind his back, then looked up at her, smiling, he said, 'I pulled you from the plane that day'.

It was Alexa's turn to register shock as she took in what he had said, always having believed that she herself had crawled from the plane. Her jaw dropped and her eyes widened, for she could see now, that he had pulled a gun from behind his back. He pulled the trigger with the last breath he had, then went limp and died.

The bullet, in an upward trajectory entered her chest just below her heart, the power of the shot almost lifting her off her feet, tearing through her, the bullet exited her back and embedded in one of the heavy velvet curtains. The sound of the shot still reverberating around the room as Alexa hit the floor and died only seconds later.

EPILOGUE; Boston

Tuesday afternoon 28th April

'The task is so much harder, with all these restrictions' Sam observed, having just come of a lengthy conversation with Terri, 'difficult to travel, borders are closing, several countries in Europe are closed, nobody in or out, practically'.

'This is not an easy time' Chrissie agreed, 'so many people still being admitted into hospitals all over the world. Still thousands dying, still no vaccinations ready, I am so glad that you weren't badly affected' approaching her husband to be and they hugged for a while.

'No, indeed, we must not forget the enormous grief that so many are going through, got a bit selfish there, and you are right, the vaccinations are being frantically worked on, but from what I hear, maybe by December'.

Sam kissed the top of Chrissie's head, then said, 'but, we must not get into a slump either, and whilst we can't travel, we have people in various places around the world, and working together, we may unravel the mystery of the three monks.

'That was Ally's girl, Terri?'

'Yes, interesting development, the painting that was stolen, is back'.

'Really? How?'

'Well, I can't possibly relate and explain the whole thing..'

'Without your music?' she teased.

'Without coffee' Sam answered, smiling, then planting a kiss on her lips, said, 'I'll make us a cup, and then,'

'Yes, then, let's run through everything we know, it's rather complicated I feel, need to refresh my memory as to what is what and who is who..'

'Good idea, that means I'll need a biscuit or two as well'.

'Ready?' Sam asked, having sat himself in his now favourite chair, the single chair in front of the front room window. The very chair he had been asked to sit in when he first came here, first visited Boston and had come to this address, where the search for the ivory item had led him. The very chair he had first really observed her, recalling her enthusiasm of that day.

A coffee was steaming hot on the table before him, he had already eaten a biscuit and having finished that, was now ready to run through what they knew.

'Ready' Chrissie answered, smiling at him, knowing he was in his element with all this research, despite being housebound with all this lock down business, having healed from catching the virus himself.

'Okay then, 'Sam said, then slightly frowning, he concentrated, 'must be sure I have everything together, all the ducks in a row, much as those one in the park here, ...'

'Yes, ' Chrissie interrupted, smiling at the mention of her local history, ' the ones in the Boston Public Gardens, do you know, I remember this from my school days, it was all because of a book, by.. let me think, yes, Robert McCloskey, called, 'Make way for ducklings, then, a sculptress, Nancy..Nancy Shon, or something like that, created the bronze statues, Mrs. Mallard and her eight ducklings, so cute, I didn't know you knew about them..'

'Saw them once in passing through, yes, like I said, getting our ducks in a row,'

giving her a smile, then, clearing his throat, he started, 'First, where it all begins, for us, today, in the present, is with Sophie..'

'You mean the delectable Sophie' Chrissie teased as he often referred to the Parisian woman that way, teasing her.

'Indeed, the delectable Sophie, 'Sam replied, threw Chrissie a mock scowl, then continued, 'she receives a painting, from a known forger, Roberto, the painting is genuine, it portrays a monk, and we know this monk to be brother Flavius, Sophie's original thoughts were that it was painted in Rome around the sixteen hundreds. The other information we have, was from the letter that accompanied the painting, stating that he, Roberto, had received it from a Natalie Umbrego'

'Right' Chrissie interjected, 'clear on that part, then sipping her drink, 'go on'.

Sam took a sip of his coffee as well, then carried on, 'So, delving into this mystery, we have found out the following, this Natalie woman was part of a family that operated and owned the Vanetti vineyards in Monaco and Martijn discovered that there had been an accident back in 1963, when Natalie had given the painting to Roberto, one man died, the other seriously injured, and they had been the ones chasing Natalie, for the painting.' taking another sip, Sam then said, 'In comes Tammy, bless her, who discovered, quite by chance and if you hadn't mentioned the fact about a monk, probably never would have taken a second look, found out about a painting of a monk, bought, this according to a very interesting ledger she discovered, called Zecheriah's ledger, I would..'

'Don't get side-tracked now..' Chrissie interrupted.

'Of course, well, she discovered the painting was bought from a French captain, named Pique, in 1770, then it was purchased over thirty years later, in 1803, by a Rudolph Meyer, who had sailed from Spain, but was a German. Subsequent search found out he came from Cologne.'

'This then sent Sophie and Martijn there' Chrissie filled in, feeling she had to remind him that she did have some of the facts straight.

'And that, my dear Chrissie,' is where they hit the jackpot, thanks to a French monk who had translated the writings of this brother Flavius, that there were three monks, from Florence. Sophie and Martijn had hoped to find out more on this Rudolph character, but found nothing, Sophie, having discovered in light pencil, the name Flavius on the back of the panel that Roberto had sent, and believing this to be the name of the monk, decided that the cathedral might prove useful as they keep very good records, and so, struck gold as it were, from there they went to the monastery and struck even more gold, and were given the translated writing of this brother Flavius. Sophie... Sorry, the delectable Sophie, ' Sam teased and smiled at Chrissie who gave him a mock scowl back, ' read this through on the train, now, she and Martijn are staying at my old place tonight, and so, my dear Chrissie, we have all the information that Rudolph had, it obviously sent him in search of the mentioned treasure, we can conclude that he found the key that Flavius had which he had given to the cathedral, we can also conclude, that he had a second key. He sailed from a port in northern Spain to Philadelphia and purchased that panel, so, Sophie thinks he must have gone to Santiago de Compostela, for that's where the second monk, name of brother Bonifatius, went. The third monk, Ignatius, went to Izmir, in Turkey. So, before the summing up, we come to Terri in San Francisco, the panel she has, is the left-hand panel, and she confirmed it has the name Bonifatius, faintly able to be seen, on the back of it. Also, thanks to the woman who had organised to steal it..'

'Yes' Chrissie chirped in 'Ally told me all about Terri's sleuthing and the deal she made with a police friend and how the painting was returned..sorry..'

'No, you're right, the young lass did very well, this deal, as you mentioned, meant she got all the information from this woman, Patricia somebody or other, and why she had wanted this panel, she too, found a letter, or an account of sorts, so, from that, and Terri related it all to me, we know, that two monks, these are Spanish, left Spain, from the same port where Rudolph sailed from, initially intending to cross over the Atlantic to Philadelphia, hence, we believe, is why Rudolph went there, however, they were given a safer option and sailed from there, via Cadiz to the far east, and from there across the Pacific, to San Francisco, sadly only one of the monks, named Cristoph, made it, it was his writings that this Patricia woman found. '

'And then?' Chrissie asked, 'there is one more part to tell'.

'Has the stunning Alison already revealed something to you?' Sam asked smiling.

'Okay, okay, so, now we have the delectable Sophie and the stunning Alison? Where does that leave me?'

'I know that Tammy was always teasing you, so, seeing as she is stuck in New York, I thought I'd take that role over for a bit.'

'You did, did you' Chrissie answered, trying hard not to smile.

'You, Chrissie, are my beautiful Chrissie'.

'Mmmm, alright then, yes, Alison did mention a detective?'

'Indeed, yes, detective inspector Roger Mantell, well, we now come to a whole new set of facts, so, ready?'

'Yes, off you go'.

'Right, well, this Roger, the detective, is the son of Oliver Mantell, sadly, very sadly, Roger was only three years old when his father was shot and killed in an armed robbery,..'

'Yes, this is what Ally told me, we were both almost in tears in relating that story.. sorry..'

'Oliver Mantell had come to San Francisco, specifically to locate the panel of the monk, you see, back in England, was his good friend, Roger Sutherland...'

'Yes, Ally said that the detective was named after him.. sorry again..'

'It's fine, ' Sam replied, smiling, trying to finish his coffee which by now was just lukewarm, he drank it down and continued, ' So, this Roger, in England, he found, or rather, bought at a street market, a panel of a monk, this one, turned out to be the one that Rudolph had purchased in Philadelphia and is that of Ignatius, the right hand side panel, and as well as that, turned out, in a suitcase that he also bought at the market, all of Rudolph's findings. Including, and this confirms our earlier thoughts, two keys.'

'Wow, so, where are we now, where is this Roger and..'

'Wait, there's more..' Sam interrupted, 'then smiling at Chrissie, said, 'So, this Oliver, on his way to the monastery where they believed the painting to be, ran into a young woman, and.,... they fell in love..'

'This tends to happen a lot, it seems' Chrissie replied.

'It does, doesn't it, you and me, Sophie and Martijn and Ally and this Simon guy, anyway, I digress, Oliver found the painting, took pictures with the camera he had, sent it over to England where Roger developed the film and sent Oliver, who had informed him that he was staying in the States, a picture. The detective had this photo and it compares to the painting, now, all this was happening quite some time ago, in 1963,..'

'Yes, so, 'Chrissie said, standing up from the two-seater, she walked over to Sam, sat herself down on his lap and said, 'let me recap then. 'Closing her eyes briefly, she then kissed him lightly on his lips and spoke' Three monks from Florence, each are sent, with a key, to three locations, Cologne, Santiago and Izmir, then three portraits, making up a triptych, these are eventually sent to Monaco, but somehow are separated and sent elsewhere, at least two panels are, the left hand side panel, ends up in San Francisco, Terri has this at the museum, Sophie has the central panel, in Paris, the right hand panel was in the possession of Roger Sutherland in England, he also had two keys, but this was back in 1963, so, my dear Sam, is this what we know?'

'Very good, yes, however, a couple of things to add to that, thanks to detective Mantell, you see, he has a letter, from Roger in England, to say, that he, English Roger, had travelled to Izmir, and.. found the third key!'

'Really?'

'Yes, ' Sam replied, gently rubbing her back as she sat with him, ' and, not only that, but, getting back to Sophie for a moment, when she was on the train reading through the writings, in particular the letter from a Father Dominic, which we'll get to in a moment, something clicked in her mind and knew what the clue was on the painting that Roberto sent her, it was a crest, the crest of a city. And Sophie knew then that this city was Florence.' Then,' now getting back to the information that detective Mantell provided, this Rudolph had also discovered a clue, in the painting he had purchased in Philadelphia, the Englishman, Roger Sutherland, wrote this to Oliver in the States, the clue was the Roman numeral IV, and then, finally, we come to the lady who stole the painting in San Francisco, she had the panel in her house, and she discovered the third clue, Terri confirmed it, faintly to be seen in the painting, three small circles on an arched line, and both Terri and this woman agree that this must represent a three pronged crown, and this is set inside a triangle outline'

Sam stopped speaking and holding her as she sat in his lap, they both fell silent for a few moments, it was then Chrissie who spoke,' don't forget about that last letter from Father Dominic'.

'Yes, of course, 'Sam said, then trying to bring up the exact words of the short note, he then said, 'The princess has come of age and has all the instructions, my task and my promise is fulfilled '

'Well recited' Chrissie said, then, kissing him on the cheek, she got up, then turned and said, 'Three monks and three paintings, three keys and three clues, and a princess, how very intriguing'.

Then her phone, that was on the low table, rang.

BOOK 2
THREE LOCKS
TO CHOOSE.

PROLOGUE; Boston

Tuesday afternoon, 28th April

Chrissie picked up her phone and answered, 'Hi Ally' recognising the caller number.

'Yes, we've been summarising, setting all our ducks in row, so to speak,' smiling and giving Sam a wink, you have a clever daughter.'

'Okay, I'm listening..'

Chrissie paced the lounge, listening, every now and then throwing a look at Sam, and every now and then saying an 'Aha'..or ' Okay'.

After some time, Chrissie, once again having said, 'okay,' then said,' Now listen Ally, that all sounds great, but there are severe restrictions on flights, so, how about this, use a private plane...'

'Oh yes, I know not only someone who can arrange that, but, as she is already involved, can speak French, is a friend of mine and knows Sophie well, she must go along.'

'Oh yes, she would like nothing better than an opportunity to not only get out of the house so to speak, but to get involved in this mystery.'

Listening some more, then, 'I will arrange it, I will call you back later'.

Smiling at Sam, but not revealing anything, Chrissie pressed some numbers on her phone.

THE PAST; Period 1

1578 - Florence

Father Dominic lit the candle lamp in the room which had been his bed chamber for the past couple of months.

It was well before sunup, but he had ears and loyal friends in many places, and he had been informed, they were here, they were in the city and would likely come today.

He put the lamp on a stand, then set about to gather his belongings which he rolled into a bundle and placed in an old leather bag.

Taking another look around, he was satisfied he had everything, picking up the lamp, an ornate looking metal candle holding lantern, and left the room.

He was ready, everything was ready.

He made his way down the staircase, the light of the lamp creating all sorts of strange shadows as he descended. Opening a door, he entered the large foyer area. Beautifully tiled, it was sort of octagonal in shape and there were five doors leading off from it. The double doored front entrance, then, directly to the right would lead to a large dining room, the room, now void of most furniture, which he had been using as an office, using the large oak dining table as a desk. The door directly to the left led to a cloakroom then onto a large lounge area. The second door on the left was the one he had just come from, leading to stairs to the first floor. The second door on the right-hand side led into a narrow corridor and ended up in a narrow kitchen area, the fifth door was the one he was now heading for.

He thought about his good friends, Petrus and Odette, such lovely people, such an important influence they had been for the city and its people.

The illness had gripped them, and quickly. Odette succumbing to it in a matter of hours. Petrus was determined to hang on to life, until he had spoken with him, had sent a servant out to fetch him. He had come at once and spent the last few hours with his friend, listening to the request that was made.

Father Dominic reached the door and opened it towards him, the door that led to a secret.

Placing the bag on the floor, he reached around, found the lever, and pushed it upward. Then, placing the lantern on a shelf there, to the side of this lever, he then went out, entered the door that led to the kitchen and came back with three more lanterns. Once again, he entered the fifth door, used the lantern there to light one of the three that he held, then, also managing to grab the leather bag, he descended the stone steps, being careful as the steps were worn and uneven.

When he had arrived by his friend's bedside, he was told to listen, time was short.

Petrus was pale, perspiring heavily and would occasionally shiver almost uncontrollably. He explained about the lever, and the secret door.

Father Dominic reached the bottom of the steps, the lever at the top, released some form of mechanism, which he didn't quite understand the workings of, this enabled him to push a certain stone in the wall, and smooth as butter, it moved inwards and leaving a narrow gap, through which he entered and the wall kept turning, completely, so that the wall on one side, was now on the other. Identical, in every way. However, there was also no way back the same way, the mechanism had reset itself.

The room he was now in, this inner chamber, was spacious, Father Dominic walked over to where there was a wooden table, placed the lit lantern upon it, set his leather bag on the floor and proceeded to light the other two lanterns, he would need those later.

On the opposite side of the room to where the table was, was another table, though much shorter and lower to the ground. Upon this, stood a big chest.

Walking over with one of the lanterns, he admired it again. It was well crafted, a beautiful chest with a rounded top. Three brass bands were looped around the woodwork, and at the front, three locks. The master craftsman had explained these to him, they had to be opened, in a certain sequence, and each lock would need a slightly different key.

He smiled in the light of the lantern as he recalled seeing those silver keys for the first time, and in talking with the man who had crafted them, made sure he knew which key was which.

Leaving two lanterns burning, Father Dominic headed for a low wooden door, bending down he opened it and entered a corridor, he walked along for about four metres or so, then stopped. The stone corridor ran on to eventually come out at the riverside. But where he had stopped was another secret door, another lever to pull, holding the lantern higher he saw the correct stone, pushed it inwards, heard the click, then turned around to the opposite side, pushed another stone, and lo and behold, the wall moved in and opened, in the same way as the door leading from the crypt.

Having been told of this, he remembered the day he had tried these out, he had been fascinated then, he still was, still having no idea how this all worked.

Walking through, the wall closed, and he made his way up the stone steps, at the top he opened a small door, squeezed himself into the space, closed the door, then opened the one opposite and stepped into the kitchen.

The box like contraption was an elevator that could be pulled up to the floor above by a pulley system, referred to as a dumb waiter.

Perspiring a little from the effort, Father Dominic returned to the foyer area, leaving the third lantern in the kitchen where ha had also made sure that the back door servants entrance was unlocked.

He was ready.

The main concern that Petrus had, still holding the hand of his wife who lay beside him, was the safety of Anna.

He had understood, he prayed over them, whispering a promise that he would fulfil the task that he had been given.

Since that moment he had been going nonstop, ideas and thoughts coming into his head, how to protect the girl, how to deal with the servants, the possession, the transportation, and the plan slowly began to take shape.

His first task was to tend to the bodies of his friends, the couple who he had so quickly bonded with, who meant so much to him. With their status and Father Dominic's connections, the bodies were quickly prepared and taken to the crypt where he performed a small service for them, along with the little girl, her body having been obtained from a small hospital, a girl who was about the same age, and prepared also. Father Dominic had the name plates made by the same man who would craft the locks and keys to the chest.

He sent all bar two of the servants away to start with, two to take care and watch over the three-year-old.

He organised the possessions, the paintings, some of the fine furniture, the clothing and other decorative items, to be packed and shipped out. The special items, he had an idea for, a chest, an intricate chest, with three keys, and this idea formed and began to take shape. He contacted various people, then found four people who would be instrumental in the completion of this task. The young woman, Gina, he knew her family, she would be given the task of bringing the girl up, of raising her. He was in no doubt that he had chosen well. The other three were brothers, monks from the monastery, these three he would send on a journey, each with a key.

As the days went on, and Father Dominic could see that the plans were coming together, he praised the Lord and knew that all would be done in time.

Father Dominic placed himself in the foyer and there he stood and waited.

He smiled as he thought back to a moment, when the painter he had brought up from Rome was getting ready to paint the brothers and he had the three keys in his hand, for a moment he had stopped, had to quickly think, which key was to be for which brother, the sequence, was important, as the clues in the painting would reveal. But he remembered, smiled, and was secretly pleased with the plan he had come up with, a plan written down in detail for the young Anna one day to read.

There was a rattling at the door, through a window above the door Father Dominic could see that the day was just breaking.

They entered.

'Well, figured you would be here Father, where is she?' the woman said, as she saw him standing there.

THE PRESENT;
Friday 1st of May

Tammy looked across and saw that Terri was fast asleep. No wonder, she had been up and about since two o'clock in the morning.

The small private jet flew smoothly over the Atlantic.

Day was breaking and looking out the window she thought, as the sky began to light up into a soft shade of blue, that it would be a good day.

She smiled, it was great to be outside, great to be away from her apartment, but even better was to be involved in this mystery, the mystery of the monks. Chrissie had completely updated her on the chains of events. Looking out the window again, it took her mind back to when she had first flown across this ocean, enroute that day also, to the French capital, to Paris. What an adventure had unfolded that time, and what a complete change of life for her. It would be good to see Sophie again, recalling the last time, when they worked together solving an altogether different mystery.

She again threw a look across the aisle at the sleeping young woman. She also knew her story, and that of her mother who she had yet to meet, but looked forward to the day when that could happen.

The call from her best friend Chrissie, on Tuesday, had set her heart racing, her mind whirling and felt herself blush at the excitement of it all. Hearing the story, hearing about the current state of affairs, hearing the request.

Yes, she had answered immediately, yes, I can sort that out, how thrilling.

Having ended the call with her friend in Boston, Tammy headed for the dining room area, to the table there where she had, these past weeks, spent many hours in ancestry research, sitting down, she pulled a blank sheet of paper towards her, grabbed a nearby pen, then started writing down some details.

A private jet had to be found. The pilot was ready and living in a place called Myrtle Creek, Terri, Alison's daughter, was ready and she lived in San Francisco, she had a painting and needed to get that, and herself, to meet with Sophie in Paris.

Looking at those details written down, she began to do some research on her laptop.

In under half an hour, she had her plane. Would it be able to fly the distance required, yes it would.

Tammy then contacted the pilot, having been given his number by Chrissie later that Tuesday. Speaking with him, knowing a little about him, this again from Chrissie, she found his voice pleasant and after quite a detailed conversation, all was ready. He called back within two hours and gave her detailed information of how this would all work and could she reach a certain airfield he mentioned. She said she could.

Across the aisle, Terri stirred, shifted in the plush seat, then resettled and slept.

Tammy got up, walked over to the cockpit area, opened the door and said hi, asking if he would like a drink or anything to eat..

Thomas Klaassen turned and looked at her, said he would love a coffee, if that was possible.

Tammy smiled at him, assured him it was very possible and set about to prepare it.

Thomas enjoyed flying this fabulous plane. Twin jet engines, it easily and smoothly pushed the craft through the now blue skies.

He had left the house he shared with Claire, his assistant and housekeeper, early on Wednesday morning, sad that he couldn't take Cynthia with him, as she was with her parents in Portland, self-isolating, as they both had caught the virus.

He spoke with her over the phone, giving an outline of what was happening, not wanting to talk too long so as not to give her too much of the story that she would be missing out on. Wished her well, told her he missed her and would she pass on his regards to her folks.

Claire reminded him to take and wear face masks and to be careful.

He drove to a small airfield to the south of Portland, showed his credentials, certificates and passport and was given a brief rundown on the plane.

He lodged the first flight plan, to an airfield on the west side of San Francisco, and in answer to the request of the nature of this flight, this due to the severe restrictions that were being put in place, Thomas informed them that it was in co-operation with the Albuquerque police department and gave the name of a Detective Inspector Mantell as a reference.

Calls were made.

Just after lunchtime Thomas boarded the plane and moments later taxied onto the runway.

Tammy came into the cockpit area and handed him his coffee. Then decided to sit herself in the co-pilots seat for a bit, asking if he minded.

Thomas smiled, sipped his drink and thought about what he had found out about this young woman, this Tamara Wilson, that she is a successful chef and restaurateur, who lives in New York and obviously has funds to finance this operation, was all he had found out. And who was this Detective Mantell, he also wondered, though he felt he knew the name, he couldn't place him.

When he landed in San Francisco he was met by Alison Hudson and her daughter Terri. He had known Alison from his high school days, she was a friend of Cynthia, a woman who had once treated him badly, but who he was now, dare he admit it, in love with.

The young lady, Terri, the assistant curator of the art museum, had a wrapped-up painting with her, and it was this painting that was the reason for this flight to Paris. He was told very little. Was told he would be informed further by Terri along the way.

He knew the destination. Paris. And to whom they were travelling. Sophie, the only person in this equation, that he actually knew and had met.

The next flight plan he lodged was to an airfield near Yonkers in New York State.

Again, he got all the approvals and landed there at a little after midnight.

A smiling petite blond woman greeted them warmly.

Flight plans approved, he accelerated down the runway and took to the sky at a little before two am.

They had sat in the plane awaiting the clearance.

Tammy and Terri in deep conversation and the blond New Yorker was shown the wood panel upon which was painted the image of a monk.

Having then completely and with exuberance and enthusiasm told Tammy the whole story, and not having slept since boarding the plane in San Francisco, young Terri promptly fell asleep before the jet even reaching cruising height.

Looking out the window, having returned to her seat, she thought the whole story through, was looking forward to meeting Sophie, and wondered, who was this princess that was mentioned in a letter from Father Dominic.

THE PAST; Period 2

the year 1593 - Florence.

Gina kissed the top of her head, then quietly slipped from the room, and headed to the floor below.

Anna sat in the chair and stared at the low table in front of her. Her green eyes staring into space for a moment. Taking a deep breath she sighed, realised that she was tearing up, took out a lace handkerchief from within the sleeve of her green dress and blew her nose. So much to take in, her mother had said, much indeed, and though, now knowing that she was not her birth mother, it mattered not to her, she was her mother, no matter what. Her eyes refocused and looked at the scrolls on the table, all neatly rolled up and tied with a ribbon. For some reason Anna wondered if it had been Father Dominic who had so prettily tied a bow on these purple silk ribbons.

She smiled at the thought, then sat back a moment, rethinking, recalling all that her mother had just told her. Particularly the last bit, that she was a princess?

Taking another deep breath, she leant forward and picked up one of the scrolls, she noticed then that there was written up the outside, very neatly and small, the number I, reaching for the other one, she spotted the number II. Well, number one first then, she thought to herself, putting the second one back on the table.

Gina quietly re-entered the room, placed a glass of orange juice on the table along with a narrow slice of what looked like a type of fruit cake.

'Happy birthday Anna' she said, almost a whisper, then gently touching Anna's shoulder, left the room.

'Thank you, mother' Anna called out after her, making sure she spoke loud enough for her to hear.

Gina heard, she smiled as she went down the stairs and a tear had suddenly appeared and rolled down her cheek. She wiped it away and headed for the kitchen, there was an evening meal to prepare.

Again, looking at the neat writing, then, as she undid the ribbon and opened the scroll, she figured by the beautifully written lettering, that it must indeed have been Father Dominic who had tied those ribbons so neatly.

After taking a quick sip of the juice, Anna sat back and began to read.

It was nearly an hour later when Anna reached for the slice of fruit cake, almost without thinking, whilst she took in all that she had read. Each scroll contained two sheets, and having read through them once, she read through them a second time, much slower and making sure she understood what had been so, obviously painstakingly, beautifully scribed.

About her father, Petrus, about her, birth mother, Odette. Their story, their journey, their influence for the good of the people here in Florence. Read about her father's brother and his determination, news of which was received through the grapevine of well-wishers, of reclaiming the family heirlooms, not to mention the royal title. Anna took in what was known about her mother's sister, and her designs on the jewellery that her mother possessed.

She was tearful when she read of her father's last wishes that he asked of Father Dominic. Took in all the plans that he, Father Dominic, had created and executed, was again tearful when she read about the choice he had made in finding Gina, and she surely would be forever grateful for him for that. Reading it through that second time, and fully concentrating, she began to see the intricate nature of his planning. The sending out of the three monks, the making of the chest, the creation of the paintings, the secrets of the crypt and the importance of the silver keys.

Smiling she took another bite of the cake, wondering what kind of man Father Dominic was. A man of the church, sure, a man of God, sure, but she detected a man of intrigue and mystery, romance even. She would ask her mother about him.

She played with her long red hair for several moments, before drinking the last of the juice and remembering the very last lines that had been written on the second page of the second scroll. A riddle of sorts, a challenge, one that she, and she alone, along with the information she had, would need to solve.

Three keys. Three clues. Three locks to choose.

THE PRESENT; Paris

Friday 1st May at an airfield near Paris.

The jet taxied towards the hangar.

Tammy, sitting on the port side of the craft, spotted her friend. 'There she is' she said aloud.

Terri, fully awake, having been stirred from her sleep as the jet was descending and having then refreshed herself in the plush shower facility, moved across the aisle, sat behind Tammy, and asked,' Who's that guy she's with?'

Tammy had noticed him too, standing next to Sophie was a dark-haired guy, clean shaven, broad shouldered and probably just under six foot, and wondered who he might be.

'He's quite the hunk' Terri observed.

'Yes, he is' Tammy agreed, then,' You're too young for him Terri, 'smiling and realising how quickly she had bonded with this young lady.

'And you are probably too old!' Terri responded, very lightly reaching over the back of Tammy's seat and punching her shoulder. Also thinking how she had taken such an instant liking to the blonde New Yorker.

'They are wearing masks, we had better do likewise' Tammy said, reaching into her bag.

The plane stopped, some young chap, also wearing a face mask, had appeared from somewhere to place chocks by the wheels and the engines were winding down.

Thomas moments later came out of the cockpit and proceeded to open the door and place the steps into place, before donning his face mask.

Tammy grabbed her handbag and was the first to descend the metal steps, already she noticed Sophie coming towards her.

They embraced, and though their lower facial features were

covered, in their eyes there was an obvious joy and sparkle. Terri, with Thomas right behind her carrying the again wrapped up painting reached them, as did the dark-haired man.

Sophie relinquished her hold on Tammy, took a few steps to reach Thomas and greeted him in a similar fashion, being careful not to knock the painting from his grasp.

'O, Terri, it's so good to meet you' she then said, speaking English, and giving her a hug also, then, in a flourishing movement, whirled around and said, 'This here, 'indicating the man, 'is my Interpol friend, Walther'.

Meanwhile the young lad who had placed the chocks, obviously knowing his way around aircraft, had opened a hatch on the small jet and had taken the luggage out, placing several small suitcases and a leather holdall onto a trolley.

Sophie turned to Thomas, 'listen, sorry you can't stay, the plane, it has to go back, you, need to rest the required time, there is a room for you here at the airfield, Walther is here to authorise your flight plans for your return,' giving Thomas another hug, who, in the meantime had passed the painting over to Terri, ' Thank you for getting them here safely, and Thomas, so sorry to hear of Cynthia's parents, do wish her and them well for me?'

'Of course, good luck you guys, and keep me informed?' he asked, then nodded to the French Interpol man and followed him.

A blue coloured seven-seater van appeared and stopped by them. The young groundsman opened the side sliding door, the went around the back to open the rear hatch, in order to place the luggage inside.

Sophie led the way, talking, 'Oh Tammy, so much to tell, this is all so very exciting, and Terri' turning to her as she reached the vehicle,' quite the detective I hear, this is going to be fun, yes?'

Not quite knowing what to say, Terri smiled and at the French woman's gesture, got into the van, placing the painting safely next to her. Tammy followed and Sophie, having waved a farewell to Walther and Thomas, then, speaking French, thanked the young man who, after she boarded, closed the door. Then, giving a signal to the driver, sat herself next to Tammy.

Thomas turned to see the van disappear, noticed the young man entering the jet and turned to the man from Interpol, who, sensing his concern, said, 'He is seventeen, young Paul, knows more about aircraft than I ever will, he will secure the jet, it will stay where it is until you leave, very strict rules at present, you will come with me and we will lodge the flight plans you require, then I will show you to quarters, yes?'

'Si, Oui, 'Thomas answered, getting his languages confused, then' Walther, not a particularly French name'.

As they entered a building adjacent to the hangar, holding the door open for Thomas, he answered, 'some of my friends call me PPK'.

Though rather tired and looking forward to getting some sleep before flying back across the Atlantic, he got the joke almost immediately and laughed.

Forty minutes later he entered the room. It was nicely appointed, a good-sized bed, a desk and chair, a comfortable armchair, a flat-screen television on a wall and a well-appointed shower room. Taking his mask off, Thomas stripped and headed for the shower. Once he had taken the required rest, he would fly across to Inverness in North Scotland, take on fuel, then over the North Atlantic to Halifax in Nova Scotia and from there the last leg back to the airfield from where he had started this journey.

Seven minutes later he slipped beneath the sheets and fell asleep in seconds.

THE PAST; Period 3

The year 1595- Monaco

Anna slowed the horse, a white mare, to a gentle trot as she entered through the archway into the Vianetti Vineyards. It was a glorious morning, as she rode up the dirt track towards the homestead, she took in the rows and rows of grapevines that were on either side on the track, in neat rows as the road sloped upwards to where several buildings surrounded a cobbled square on the top of the hill.

Slowing the mare down to a walk she entered the courtyards, the horse's hooves audibly clicking over the cobbled stones.

Three men and a woman turned from their work outside one of the outbuildings and stared at her.

Then a woman appeared, she was tall Anna observed, with long almost black hair and was moments later joined by a boy.

Anna stopped her horse, dismounted in a fluid notion, nodded a greeting to the woman who had come out of the house, then turned to the group that were still standing watching her and held out the reigns of her horse.

The woman at the doorway, gave a nod, then one of them, one of the men, came over, bowed politely and took the reins.

'Merci' Anna said, then stepped up towards the house, taking off her riding gloves which, as she was walking, she put into a cloth bag that was slung across her shoulder and said, speaking Italian, 'Good morning, my name is Anna'.

It took Viana only seconds to register the name, then said, also speaking her native tongue of Italian, 'Welcome to my house Anna, this is my son, Pietro'.

Anna nodded a greeting to the lad, who was, wide eyed, taking her in, she noticed, then smiling offered her hand to who she knew must be Viana Vanetti.

Once inside the house, a little girl came bounding down the stairs, all excited and speaking French, asking about a huge white horse and if it was hers.

'My excitable daughter Paola' Viana explained.

Anna, quite well in her ability to understand and speak French, knelt down and said, 'Actually, no, I borrowed it from a friend, but isn't she a beauty?'

'Oh yes, may I go and pat her?'

'If this is alright with your mother, then yes, of course' Anna answered, standing up again.

The little girl got the nod from her mother and ran through the short corridor to the front door.

'Please, come on through, you have been on quite a journey' Viana said, leading the way into a warmly decorated parlour room. The boy, Pietro, still quite dumbstruck by this beauty that had appeared on her horse, stood by the doorway, then, feeling rather uncomfortable, withdrew and disappeared.

'You have lovely children' Anna said, sitting in a chair that Viana gestured to, who then said, 'Would you like a drink of water?'

Anna said she would and Viana left the room leaving Anna to look around the room.

To the left as she entered, there was a window that overlooked the courtyard. From where she was seated, she noticed that someone had giving the little girl what looked to be a cabbage leaf and she was feeding this to the horse. It reminded her of her childhood years, when she too had been introduced to horses and how utterly thrilled, she felt at the time. The far wall was adorned with a few small paintings, a low dresser upon which stood a lantern, which was to the left of the window that looked out over the vineyard and a glass fronted small cabinet to the right, which held what looked to Anna, like pottery vases and a bowl.

Viana returned, placed two short stemmed glasses on the low table and sat opposite her in a worn leather couch that could seat two and said, once again speaking in Italian, ' You have come, because of the scrolls left to you by Father Dominic?' she asked, then before

Anna could respond, said, 'I was almost going to tell my daughter, that you are a real princess, this would have thrilled her beyond belief, but, would not have been the right thing to do'

Anna reached for the glass, 'I can imagine, when I was a child, I would love to hear stories told of princesses and princes and white horses' then, taking a sip, ' this if refreshing, thank you' taking another sip, Viana meanwhile having picked up her own glass, Anna continued, ' Yes, I have, but not for the reason you may think, I was informed that you now have the three portraits of the monks?'

'Yes, along with a scroll, it was sealed and is with the panels.

Anna reached into her cloth bag, pulled out two scrolls, neatly rolled and tied with a purple silk ribbon, just as they had been when, just over two years ago, she had received them.

'These can go with them,' placing them on the table, 'I came to hopefully see the portraits, see the images of the three monks that were sent out with the keys, I have no further interest in anything else.' Anna said, taking another sip and noticing the quizzical look on the woman who sat opposite her explained, ' much as being a princess sounds all very nice, like in a story, I have a mother, she is not my birth mother, but she brought me up, she taught me, looked after me, cared for me, loved me, she gave up her own life, to take care of me, Father Dominic chose her, and he could not have chosen better. But I don't want to be a princess, I don't want to look for the riches that are mentioned in the scrolls, I don't want to find out about my royal connections. ' Then, taking a breath and sensing Viana was taking it all in, Anna went on, ' I came out of curiosity, to see these monks, who, for my sake, were sent to these places, the scrolls here, belong with the portraits, what you do with them, well, it's up to you, what I know is that some bad people, in my family, want to have these things, they must not have them, I do not want them, I give you these scrolls and I will return home, to be with the woman who, for me, is my mother, and I love her very much, my heart belongs there.

She has taken care of me. I will take care of her'.

Anna took a few more sips, placed the glass on the table and sat back.

Viana nodded, understood. She herself had left home, at an early age, nearly seventeen years ago, she thought, leaving her mother behind never to see her again.

'I have two lovely children' Viana said, my daughter, nine years old now, I named her after my mother, I left home, on my journey, not even considering... I have my mother in my daughter, her hair, her eyes.. I understand,' then standing up, said, 'Come, I will show you, then leading the way, said, 'I met one of them you know, his name was Bonifatius,'

'Really?'

'Come, this way' Viana said and proceeded to go up the stairs, with Anna following she led her to a small attic room, light from the sun streamed in through a window in the roof.

Viana stepped aside and Anna saw the wooden panels. Walking over to them, Viana then opened them up, swinging the panels out to the left and right.

'Here they are' she said, standing to one side for Anna to see.

Anna stood and took them all in.

'This is Bonifatius' Viana said, 'on the left, I met him in Genoa, on board a ship, he was on his way to Santiago de Compostela, in Spain. The older man, in the middle, is Flavius, he went to Cologne, and on the right, we have Ignatius, his destination was a place called Izmir.

'The keys, so beautifully painted,' Anna observed.

'Of course, whether or not they each got to their destinations, is not known' Viana said, recalling her conversation in the galley with Bonifatius, 'though I'm sure that this man, 'indication the monk on the left-hand panel, 'reached Cadiz, in southern Spain, I left the ship here in Monaco, but that's where the ship was heading next.'

'Thank you' Anna said. Then walked over to Viana and gave her a tight hug, 'thank you, I will go home now'.

Having not been able to persuade Anna to stay longer, she stood in the courtyard, her son by her side and watched as her daughter was animatedly chatting to the young woman as she mounted the big white horse.

Anna smiled at the girl, then nodded to the man who had brought her horse from the stable, she then turned and nodded a farewell to Viana and her son.

Not looking back, she trotted off. The sun still shining in a clear sky, and she took in a deep breath as she passed through the archway and headed back to the town. She was pleased she had come, giving those scrolls to Viana had been a release for her. Over these past couple of years, she had often read them, pondered about the contents, about the intricate plan that Father Dominic had conceived. Had often also, thought about the royal connection, the chest of treasures that was hidden somewhere, about the detailed trail that needed to be followed, in order to connect the clues and find the location of the chest.

But after careful consideration, she had made up her mind.

She just wanted to be Anna, just wanted to be a good daughter to Gina, to lead a normal life, find love, have children. The scrolls were no longer in her possession, she felt relieved and gently brought her horse into a trot, leaving the Vianetti Vineyards behind.

'Who was that lady mama?' Paola asked, watching the big white horse ride away, 'she was just like a princess'.

'Yes, she was' Viana answered, then turned to go inside.

Pietro stood next to his sister and watched until they saw her no more.

Later that day Viana walked from the house to one of the outbuildings surrounding the cobbled courtyard and entered. This was a large workshop, here they would build the vat and barrels for the wine, here they would build equipment needed for the distillery, here they would mend broken furniture, or fix rotting windows frames.

Two men worked here, father and son.

Viana saw the young man, now in his early twenties, working at a large wooden bench.

He turned as he heard her coming.

His name was Charles and Viana had a specific job for him to do.

The wooden trunk that he would build, to the dimensions given him by Viana, with the false bottom panel, would one day be discovered and opened by the twin girls, Eva and Isabella Umbrego, over two hundred and seventy years later,

Friday 1st of May

'Oh, it's good to be home, can take this mask off and greet you all properly' Sophie said, in rapid French as she unlocked the door to her apartment and entered, throwing the keys into a wooden bowl that sat on a small narrow table which also had a placement for umbrella's at one end and to the left of it a series of hooks formed the cloakroom. Taking her lightweight jacket off she practically threw this onto one of the hooks and headed for the kitchen area. Taking her mask off as she walked.

Tammy, right behind her and picking up what her friend had said, smiled, placed her cabin bag and that of Terri's which she had been carrying, down, took her jacket off which she hung neatly on the hook, then, taking off her own mask replied, ' For me it's good not to be home, felt so, like a chicken, being cooped up' then turning to throw a friendly smile at Terri behind her, said, 'She hates these masks', then turned again, picked up the cases, and said' follow me Terri, take you to the guest-room'.

Terri, carrying the painting, left her coat on and followed.

The guestroom was a good size, with two single beds, its own ensuite bathroom, two wardrobes, a dressing table, and a small armchair.

Tammy, having stayed here before, chose the bed she had used then and placed her cabin bag upon it, placing Terri's on the other bed, who, right behind her, placed the painting next to it and proceeded to take her coat off.

Moments later, when they entered the lounge, Sophie was there, there were three glasses of white wine on the small table and she said, 'Now, 'let's say hello the French way' speaking in English and stepped forward to embrace Tammy, kisses and hugs. Then turning to Terri, 'when in France' she said, smiling, and more kisses and hugs.

'A drink then ladies,' Sophie said, handing a glass to Tammy and to Terri, to whom she smilingly said, 'you are allowed to drink?'

Terri coloured a little, but smiled back and said, 'Oui, tout alors' dragging this phrase up from the depths of her mind, though not quite knowing if it was the right response.

Tammy! She speaks French! Sophie said, then raising her glass, 'to solving a mystery'.

Terri smiled, relaxed, and knew she had made new friends this day.

Several minutes later, Terri came into the lounge and unwrapped the panel. Sophie had brought out the centre piece and Terri placed it beside it, on the left-hand side.

All three stood and took it all in.

'So, Sophie' Tammy said, 'you and Martijn, what have you two uncovered' grinning at her friend.

'I will punch you again, you know that hurts!' Sophie threatened, but smiled also, then, looking from Tammy to Terri, began to explain their findings.

THE PAST; Period 4

The year 1770 – Somewhere on the Atlantic Ocean

The sky was a vivid blue. Not a cloud to be seen. The swell on the ocean was gentle, there was no wind. It was hot, oppressively so, he thought, a change was coming, a storm was likely. He looked up at the mast, a young lad sat in the crow's nest. Though pirates usually operated along the coastlines, picking on smaller coastal schooners, it would not do to be complacent. A watch must be kept. The two masts were barren of sails, they had been lowered, an opportunity for inspection and repair. Sixty-five-year-old Anton Pique, nodded up to the boy who gave a wave back. Then, taking a last look around the empty ocean, he retreated into his quarters.

Against a wall, secured with some rope, was the panel. He knew it to be the right- hand side panel of a triptych. He didn't much care for it, but he had come by it, all in the quest to win the heart of the woman he loved.

A love that would now never be returned. Captain Pique sat in the wooden armchair. Upon a cushion she had made for him. He thought back, back to when he had first seen her, first had been taken by her beauty. Over forty years ago, he half smiled to himself, thinking back. He was a first mate then, on a small schooner, preparing to set sail, he had been informed of some passenger coming on board, passengers that needed to leave French soil immediately, for they were in danger of being captured by religious zealots, he was told.

The captain was ready, he was ready, the crew was ready, and the tide was right.

Two horses pulling a cart came trotting up.

A woman and a boy emerged. Men quickly escorted her aboard, took care of the luggage they had, took care of the driver of the cart, who promptly turned the horses about turn and left.

When the captain a few moments later introduced them, he could find no words to say, his voice seemed to have completely been lost. Moreover, his feet were firmly anchored to the floor and all he could do, was manage a nod and half a smile.

Evonie Dupois Quinton and her son, Rene.

She spoke in rapid French to the captain, thanking him, then, and he recalled the moment, she turned to him and gave him a smile.

That, he now thought as he sat in the chair, the ship so very gently bobbing on the swell of the ocean, was the moment he fell in love.

He threw another look at the painted wood panel. The monk it portrayed he knew to be a brother Ignatius. It was of no use now, she was gone. He would sell it when they reached the port of Philadelphia.

He had it, because of the search he made, over many years, too many years, perhaps, he was thinking, getting up to find his pipe. That journey, when they had successfully left Le Havre and reached the safety of Plymouth in England, he had inquired of the captain, their story, why it was they had to flee.

It all made no sense to him, to hear that she had a husband who had been arrested and imprisoned, made him want to help, in some way, to comfort her.

During that voyage he had not spoken to her, and though on leaving the ship, she had again thanked the captain, and also said her thanks to him as he stood beside his skipper as they disembarked, he again could find no words, merely nodded.

Anton lit his pipe, puffed several times to get it going and through the haze of smoke threw another look at the painting.

In his mind he figured, that in order to even be able to woo her in some way, he had to find the whereabouts of her husband. If he was still alive, she would be grateful, if he was not, she would be available, possibly. Though whether he even stood a chance of that happening, he thought most unlikely.

The years passed, he worked hard, learned all that he could about mastering a ship and ten years later, was made captain. During those years he had visited Evonie several times, to bring her an update, a promise he made to her, to find out the fate of her husband, for although she accepted that he was very likely no longer alive, she would be true to her vows.

Anton resigned to that fact, and a friendship grew. He was able to speak to her, without fumbling his words, he became confident in her presence and could sense that she was comfortable in being with him.

More years passed and there was a time, quite a few years, when he had not seen her, as he had been sailing to the far east and to the African continent.

Then, a conversation heard whilst in a tavern in his hometown of Rouen, puffing on his pipe, Anton thought about when that was and calculating in his mind, he figured it was the year 1768. two years past already..

Pascal Quinton. His ears had pricked up, he heard the name being spoken, he knew that name. Pascal, it was the name of Evonie's husband.

Without hesitation, he walked over to where three men were talking, introduced himself and said he was looking for information on the person they mentioned.

As they looked up at him, perhaps with a hint of suspicion, he followed up, by saying he was looking on behalf of his wife and son.

They accepted his reason, asked him to sit with them and then, after having ascertained that he indeed knew Pascal's wife and son, told him the story of a battle..

In his quarters Anton felt a change in the swell, threw another look at the painted panel and headed outside.

The wind had picked up, a now stiff breeze had come, and he made orders to get the sails back up. Once satisfied that all was under control, he retreated into his cabin, relit his pipe and continued to reflect how it had been that he now had this painting in his possession...

A battle had raged just to the north of Orleans. One monastic order against another. Sticks and clubs clashing in the fields as the sun was rising. Corn and maize trampled underfoot in a melee of chaotic thrashing. A battle that raged swaying first in one direction, then in another. Bodies falling.

There had been a silence, prior to the attack, a silence as these two orders stood and faced each other, dew on the grass, dew on the maize and corn. The birds, earlier chirping their morning song, had fallen still.

After the battle, that had taken no more than about twenty minutes, there again was silence. The two orders slinked away, each taking their wounded with them.

The trampled field the only sign left of a battle having taken place.

Several had, that day or the next, succumbed to their wounds. A total of fourteen, coincidently, seven from each side. One of those who died, was Pascal Quinton, who had sought refuge from pursuit and had subsequently only been very willing to join the battle.

The three men in the tavern had known Pascal personally and one of them had all the details of where the man was buried.

It was nearly a year later that Anton had the opportunity to visit the monastery and had been able to visit the grave. It was whilst he was there that he was given the painted panel and was told of its history and how Pascal had received it.

It was another year on before he could travel and deliver it to Evonie, but, sadly, by that time, she had passed away.

Anton noticed his pipe had gone out, sighed and left his cabin to take in the fresh air. The ship was gliding smoothly across the waters, heading for Philadelphia.

✦❧

THE PRESENT; Portland – Oregon

Saturday 2nd May

Standing barefoot on the kitchen floor, dressed in light green pyjamas over which she had a lightweight dressing gown in the same colour, Cynthia Barnes held her mug with both hands and slowly sipped the coffee.

It was early, her parents, both still quite unwell, were resting. Her mother, more seriously ill, slept in the master bedroom, Cynthia had, upon arrival five days ago, insisted that her dad should sleep in the main guest room, this in order for them to have a better chance of more quickly regaining their health. She made herself at home in what was once her own bedroom.

She had been quite shocked to see them is such poor health, but such was the huge influx of patients in the hospital, the doctor had advised them to stay at home, if at all possible.

Cynthia agreed on this advice and had set about making them as comfortable as possible, had then organised the delivery of groceries and would stay in isolation with them.

On the Wednesday morning, she had woken in a sweat, had a headache, was hot and cold at intervals and knew she had caught the dreaded virus.

But she was normally very fit, made herself get up and make sure her mum and dad were looked after, drank lots of fluids and kept herself as busy as possible.

Thursday came and went and by Friday she was already much better. Sadly, her mother was still quite ill, but at least her dad was improving.

Taking another sip of coffee, she was relieved to be feeling much better this morning, the coffee tasted good, she had an appetite and no longer had any bouts of shivering.

Looking out of the kitchen window onto the garden, she thought of Thomas, having received a message from him that he was flying back across the Atlantic and would be back in Myrtle Creek later today. She knew he had deliberately not told her too much about his sudden mission of flying to Paris, did know it involved Alison's daughter Terri and some woman from New York, and that he would meet up with Sophie in Paris. But, although knowing he had not wanted her to feel left out, she had heard the excitement in his voice.

Thomas.

What goes around comes around, she was thinking, finishing her drink and decided to check on her parents, then have a shower and dress.

Twenty minutes later she sat on a stool at the kitchen counter-top with her second coffee and some toast and honey.

Her mother was asleep, thankfully her breathing was good. Her father was awake, more colour in his face and smiled as she poked her head around the door.

They were on the mend, thankfully, but still needed to be sensible and careful. The news on the radio was negative. More and more people falling ill, all around the world, further restrictions on travel, hospitals struggling to cope.

Cynthia sighed, then turned the radio off.

Stay positive, she told herself, taking a bite of the toast.

But her mind had other ideas and she found herself reflecting on her first night back home. The Monday, having taking control of organising her folks, making sure they had provisions in the house, she at last had gone to bed.

Her old bedroom. Getting into bed she thought back, back to her school days, back to the day her brother had killed himself, back to how such a bad person she had been. It hadn't taken long for those thoughts to make her cry. It took some time for the sobbing to stop, for her body to stop trembling.

She missed him.

Thomas.

She would make him tell all when he landed. Who was this woman from New York and how was Sophie involved?

Taking another bite of the toast, she felt a pang of jealousy.

She was in love with a man, who, when just a teenager she had been very unkind to.

Getting up from the stool, she admonished herself, keep busy, stay active, get better, help mum and dad.

Cynthia set about to prepare some breakfast for them, though her mind, once again, reverted to the past, to the day of the funeral. Her brother's funeral....

It was overcast, but the wind was soft and warm. Yet occasionally she shivered. Standing a little away from her parents, Cynthia felt uncomfortable, vulnerable and more than a little shaky. Standing as still as she could, she looked at the coffin as it was lowered into the grave, she didn't dare look anywhere else for the moment, felt that many eyes were upon her.

She had cried so much these past days and nights, it seemed there were no tears left.

She could hear her mother sob, being held and comforted by her father.

Only barely could she take in the words the minister spoke. Earlier, in church, she had sat quietly, there had many who had come, fellow students, teachers, Cynthia had, though briefly looked, not been able to maintain eye contact with anyone.

Her brother had died, had thrown himself off the bridge and into the river. He had been bullied at school. Her fault.

The letter, the brief message her younger brother had written, had been read out at school.

It was the letter that had hit home, had hit her like a diesel train, had taken the wind out of her, stunned her, shamed her.

Her fault.

She had, when sitting in the assembly room at her high school, looked across at Barbara, sitting next to her and at Alison, who sat the other side of Barbara, as they made it a thing, to sit, or walk in a line, Alison, Barbara and herself, the ABC girls.

They were mean, arrogant, and bullying.

But as the letter was read out. There was a hush, there was a moment of stunned silence, then the sobs came, it was then that she knew, all eyes were on them, it was then that she was hit with the sad truth of it all.

Her fault, their fault.

Her brother had started school, had not long into the term, being her younger brother, been targeted, bullied. A retaliation, revenge.

Her fault.

It had been her last day at school. She had come home and had hidden away in her room. She had cried and cried.

Her father and mother took a handful of soft dirt, threw it on the coffin. Ashes to ashes, dust to dust, she heard the minister say.

Shivering again, she stood still. No tears would come..

Cynthia sniffed, took a deep breath, then picked up the breakfast tray to take up to her father, then would check out if her mother was awake yet.

Going up the stairs she was thankful that her parents had forgiven her. It had been difficult in the beginning, she had come home that day after the assembly, and had broken down and told them everything, her role, her part in the bullying, they had listened, they had not spoken, but they had hugged her.

The first few weeks had been hard, but slowly she got her life together a bit more, would cry a bit less.

They had forgiven her, had comforted her, had seen the life lesson learnt. She had not forgiven herself. She smiled as she entered the guest room and placed the tray on the bed. He smiled his thanks and she left to see her mother.

She thought about Thomas, what a lovely man he was, he had also been kind as a teenager, at school, a good friend to Robert, even though she had been very mean to him, he too had forgiven her.

Her mother was awake and smiled. Cynthia said if she wanted something to eat and was happy to hear that she was very hungry. A good sign. She too was on the mend.

Going downstairs again she felt a tear roll down her cheek.

Why couldn't she forgive herself?

THE PAST; Period 5

The year 1867 Venice

The winter weather was harsh. The coldest temperatures for decades. The wind from the north was biting.

Eva and Isabella Umbrego sat side by side in the old library on St.Marks Square.

It was warm and it was quiet in the old building as they sat behind an oak table. Books and papers strewn around them.

A little over three years had passed since Eva had taken her twin sister to the old building that had once upon a time been the main house.

A lot had happened in those three years.

Their elder brother, Luigi, had married. He would be taking over the vineyard. When the girls turned eighteen and had already welcomed a nephew into the fold and another baby expecting, they decided to leave the homestead and travel to Venice. It was a decision they had arrived at after having discovered the painting and the scrolls., which they had told no-one about.

Eva, still in contact with young Carlos, the boy she had that day taken to the old house, asked him a favour, but it had to be a secret. Smitten and somewhat in awe of the stunning twin, Carlos complied with the request.

A month later they travelled to Venice to stay with their father's brother, Uncle Luigi, whom their brother was named after.

They settled down well and enjoyed their new life, both having already had quite some grasp of the Italian language, soon we able to converse easily.

It was Bella who had come up with the idea. To write a children's book.

And so it was that now, nearly another year later, they sat side by side in the old library, gathering their notes and compiling it all in preparation to have this little book published.

'The secret Princess' they had named it.

When they left their home, they took with them, the three scrolls they had found, using that information, with Eva reading it all once again, very carefully and with Bella retaining it all in her memory, they put together this story. Whilst it was all factual, drawing from the information on the scrolls, no-one knew, believing it to be wholly made up.

'Once upon a time, there was a princess, her name was Anna and she rode a white horse..' the story began.

A tale of three brothers who protected their sister, a tale of a crypt, a tale of secret levers, inner chambers, and hidden doors.

Apart from the arrival of a charming prince, and living in a castle happily ever after, most everything else was true.

Nobody would know.

Ninety years later, Alexa came across the little book and was elated when, reading through it she realised, that here were the clues, this was not just a children's story.

With her heart beating quite rapidly, she read through the whole story, then, carefully, concentrating fully, she copied every word that day.

THE PRESENT; Myrtle Creek

Saturday 2nd May

Twenty-five-year-old Claire Symonds punched in the numbered code and opened the door. Entering the room, she closed it behind her and headed for the desk upon which sat a large monitor. Placing her bottle of water down, she pulled the keyboard towards her as she sat down and typed in the password.

There was a wooden sign next to the monitor, which read, 'Search Engine'.

Claire smiled as the screen came to life. She was in what they now called the 'engine room'. Thomas had named it.

Thomas. She reflected that it had been almost a year ago now, that he had turned up. After Robert had died.

Tucking a few strands of blond hair behind her ear, Claire moved the mouse, clicked a few times, and began to check for any new e-mails.

Robert Pentegrass. He had been the one that had found her, he had been the one that, from this very room, had searched and searched. This had been his domain.

Suffering from a form of Asperger Syndrome, he came alive in this room and for nearly two decades, he worked on clues and police reports and newspaper clippings as he made it his project, to try and locate missing people, helping the Portland police department.

Over the years he had located thirty-five people and assisted in their rescue.

Claire had been taken. Had been drugged, a revenge action.

She had been taken from her apartment and transported to a large villa about twenty miles north of Sacramento, where she had been forced to work.

The arrival of Thomas was a big surprise, she was initially wary, as she was of men in general. He had been given the house, had been a friend of Roberts for many years, since high school. Though by that time she had lived as a housekeeper with Roberts for three years, he had never mentioned him. It didn't surprise her as he was a very private man. He would not allow her to come into this room, he alone would work from here and had outside helpers to assist. Claire thought the world of Robert, he saved her life.

Thomas was different. She soon warmed to him, and he involved her straight away when a call had come through, a request needing urgent attention, a request that Thomas, without hesitation, took on, which had impressed her.

He had arrived back at the house earlier and was asleep, having flown from Scotland to Nova Scotia and from there to Oregon.

Initially Claire had thought about locating her own case file, read through and discover how Robert had managed to find her, but thinking back to the situation that she had been, the circumstances, the hardship, upset her, so, she wisely, she thought to herself, decided to let sleeping dogs lie.

A ding sounded.

An incoming e-mail.

'Yes' Claire said to herself.

It was from DP, who she now knew to be retired detective, Desmond Peter Janssen, who lived in Bexleyheath, London.

Claire clicked on the message and began to read.

THE PAST; Period 6

The year 1879- Florence

Eva knocked on the tall wooden double door, Bella stood by her side. Moments later the right-hand door opened, and they were invited inside.

Ten days earlier, the now thirty-two-year-old Bella had suggested to her twin sister Eva, to go to Florence, to see the house for themselves, to follow the clues they had found all those years ago in that old trunk. The follow the clues they had themselves, so cleverly hidden withing the story book they had written between them.

She had picked up the news about the house, formerly the residence of Petrus Kastanje and his wife Odette. She had also learned that this was now a school for orphans and came up with the idea of going there, reading their book to the children and investigating the secrets of the crypt.

Eva marvelled at the idea, and so between them they made plans.

Both had, since writing their book twelve years ago, married. Both had also each given birth to a child. Eva married a painter, and they had a little boy, Bella married a sculptor, and she gave birth to a baby girl.

They gave birth within a week of each other, nearly eight years ago.

Four days ago, leaving their husbands to look after the children, they left Venice and set out for Florence.

The previous day Eva had visited the school, explained who they were and of their interest in the house, especially the crypt, which they knew about through communications they had discovered from Father Dominic.

The very mention of his name had been received with gladness and they would be most welcome to see the crypt and they would love for them to read to the children.

Beaming, the head teacher escorted Eva and Bella upstairs, Eva helping her blind sister up the staircase.

Nearly three hours later, having read to two classes of boys and girls who were totally absorbed in the story they told, with Eva holding the book they had brought along, and Bella, with her incredible memory, speaking in all sorts of voices much to the amusement of all, and after a meal, the twins were led to the foyer, giving each a lantern to hold and the door to the crypt was unlocked and opened.

Eva nodded her thanks, adjusted the bag that was across her shoulder, closed the door and made sure she was careful to watch over Bella as she could see by the light of her lantern, that the stone steps before them were worn and uneven.

'Okay, Bella, you give the instructions, I'll follow them, but don't move without me holding you, alright?'

'Yes' Bella replied, feeling the warmth of the lantern she was holding and smiling as she thought about the fact that she should be holding a lantern at all.

But the teacher had said that two lanterns would be safer in the dark crypt.

'The lever comes first, you should see a ledge, to the right a wooden pole, grab it tight, then pull it upwards'.

Eva, holding the lantern with her right hand, reached out with her left hand, grabbed the wooden pole, gripped it, and pulled.

'Yes Eva, I heard a mechanism click' Bella responded.

Manoeuvring around her sister, Eva took hold of Bella's right arm, just above the elbow and carefully escorted her a step at a time until they reached the bottom.

'Okay, this is the main crypt, I can see the coffins of Petrus and Odette, and that of a child, though we know of course, that it is not Anna'.

'I know' Bella answered, staying where she was at the for of the stone steps, ' I still think how much planning this Father Dominic has done, not just then, but for the future, just think, it was over three hundred years ago that he conceived this plan, and the house, now a school for orphans, dedicated to our Anna, all secured, all safe.'

Eva had moved to where the coffins were placed and thought about what her sister had just said. He sure had planned well. She wondered about the little girl in that coffin. Then, whispering a prayer, she walked back to her sister, 'Next stage Bella?'

Bella stood still, felt the first step with the back of her shoe, then holding the lantern higher for Eva to see, said,' From the first stone, counted seven, then from the bottom, count eight, then push'.

Eva counted, then with her left hand pushed the smooth stone.

'Yes, well done Eva..'

'Come quickly,' Eva interrupted and grabbing her sister, steered her thought the opening, knowing it would close behind them.

'The inner crypt' Eva whispered.

'Describe it to me please' Bella asked.

Holding her lantern high, Eva walked around the smaller inner crypt, noticed the big table, upon which she placed her bag, then saw the lower table and the wonderful chest that sat upon it. As she did all this, she spoke what she saw, giving as much detail as she could. The chest itself was beautifully crafted, and it was kin moments like these, she truly felt for her sister, not being able to see. She thought back to when she gave birth to her son, then a week later her sister gave birth to a girl, a girl she would never see. She remembered crying then and was almost in tears now, studying the chest.

'It's alright Eva' Bella said, speaking softly, 'You are, and have always been, my eyes'.

Eva, turned, looked at her sister, saw her smile, shook her head in wonder and realised how much she loved her.

'Well, we have the clues, we have the scrolls, we made our way here, we found the chest...' Eva began.

'But we don't have the keys' Bella concluded.

'No, I think we shall leave the scrolls here, I'll place them on that bigger table, who know, one day someone with the keys, might also find this place.'

'That's a good idea, now, we need to find our way back, and parts of that, could be a bit tricky' Bella said as Eva took the three scrolls from her bag and placed them on the table.

Following Bella's instruction, going through the low wooden door, then along a stone corridor, and again counting the stones in the wall, they activated another lever, slipped through the opening and after some scrambling they finally both stood in the narrow kitchen. Eva turned the gas lit lantern off. Then the twins hugged, pleased with their effort and glad they had come. The secrets which they had read about when finding the painting of the monk and those scrolls, the secrets which then later they had created a book about, were all true. It had all worked.

'I wonder if anyone will ever find that crypt, will ever get to enter that inner chamber, ever see that chest' Bella said, then, hearing footsteps, whispered 'Someone is coming'.

Eva smiled and leaned against the kitchen bench as the head teacher arrived.

'Thank you so much, for allowing us to be here today' she said, 'Bella and I must go now, we are missing our children'.

'And husbands' Bella added.

'Them too' Eva said, smiling.

Leaving their lantern on the kitchen bench, they left.

THE PRESENT; Chicago

Saturday 2nd May

Felicity Smith stood by the kitchen bench. Drink of juice in her hand, two pieces of toast on a plate. Her diary open.

Not her current diary, she had been reading through some pages she had written twenty-two years ago.

Taking a sip of juice, she sniffed and thought about that time.

She was working from home, the pandemic had dealt the company she worked for, a severe blow, five people had succumbed to the virus, a further four were in hospital and two at home.

She was feeling well, thankfully. The insurance company had supplied her with a laptop, and she would be able to work from home. Choose your hours, her boss had said, and after an hour training session, she had gone back home. That had been three weeks ago.

She had easily conquered her new role and was grateful that she had been given this opportunity, though at the same time sad as people she had known, had lost their lives.

Being at home, she had also taken the opportunity to rummage through all the stuff she had taken when she had left her family home. Apart from some clothes, some jewellery, and a few books, she had also taken all her old diaries.

Taking another sip, Felicity, though she preferred to be addressed as Fliss, sniffed again, took her glass of juice, and walked over to the window.

Chicago. As with many cities all around the world, restrictions in place, notices everywhere, keeping distance, wearing face masks, only go outside for exercise, work from home where possible.

Twenty-two years ago! Where had the years gone?

It was a special year, a memorable year. Good memories and bad.

It was the year when she had for the first time visited the site, where her older sister had died. It was the year when she had met

Simon. It was the year when she had a final argument with her parents. It was the year she left home.

She had not returned since.

Simon.

A relationship that she felt was about to happen, didn't happen. Not then.

Felicity sighed, finished her juice, then returned to the kitchen. With time on her hand and stuck indoors she had tidied and sorted out some of her stuff.

Placing the glass on the bench, she took a bite of toast and looked around. Her apartment, renting at first, she had purchased it over ten years ago now. Though she could perhaps afford a new place, she liked it here.

Simon.

He found her, had come to her, they had bonded, clicked, loved. A three-year relationship that was joyful. There had been a time then, that she felt she needed to be sensible, make contact with her parents.

But then, one day, Simon had returned after a brief visit to his hometown, with devastating news. She recalls having immediately sensed that something was terribly wrong.

Taking another bite of toast, she closed the diary.

She ended their relationship.

Chewing the toast, she sniffed again, having so hard been trying not to cry.

She couldn't go home, couldn't see her folks, because she would then not have any option, other than tell them what she knew.

Are they alright? She wondered, then unable to stop the tears anymore. She sobbed.

After several moments, she calmed down. Picked up a diary that had belonged to her sister, she recalls having taken it when the police had returned her belongings that day, after the tornado strike. She recalls having read through it after meeting Simon, to hopefully get a better insight into someone named Conrad Shilton.

Flicking through the pages, she remembers the time she had called on Simon at his work. Had then thought the possibility of a romance.

Felicity puffed out her cheeks, then using a forefinger she wiped the tears from her cheek and then froze. She spotted something she hadn't picked up before.

With what she knew now, with what Simon had revealed to her, that day, over four years ago already, she sniffed once more, then carefully read through a couple of pages.

This was interesting information, this, she knew in her heart, she needed to share.

She wondered if Simon still lived at the same address. Searching and scrolling through her phone, she found his number.

Her throat was dry, she felt her heart beating faster.

Pushing a button, she sat on the edge of her bed and heard it ringing on the other end. Would he be home?

THE PAST; Period 7 - Part 1

The year 1963   Eastbourne

Roger Sutherland stood by the window and looked out to sea. It was a clear day, the midday sun stood high, the sea looked very blue, and the scattered clouds were a fluffy white.

Why do things seemingly all happen at once. Three days ago, he had returned to the house to find it had been broken into, to find that someone had taken only that, which they obviously had come for. The keys, the painting, the information he had so painstakingly translated from Latin into English.

He had tried hard to think of how it was, that someone knew he had it, someone knew about the keys, the clues, the paintings, the story of hidden treasure.

He decided to check with the neighbours and discovered that a courier van had arrived, and a parcel had been collected.

A man had been seen coming from the house and getting into a black BMW,

Roger then made up his mind and decided to involve the police after all, then, as he re-entered his house and was about to make the call, he noticed something.

The telephone. As he went to pick up the receiver, he stopped his motion. The handset was the wrong way around. Someone had used the phone.

Someone who was very likely left-handed.

He left the house, walked back to the neighbour, used their telephone, then returned home to await the police.

After they had come and had dusted the handset and had a general look around, they left, and Roger made a couple of calls. The first was to the telephone company, requesting urgently details of calls made. He thought about Kim, briefly wondered if she might have anything to do with this, he had lost touch some time ago now, she had moved away, was now married, and already had a baby, this much he knew. No, he was sure she had no part in this.

The following day he received a call that totally shocked him.

The call was from America.

It was Mercedes, Oliver's wife. A tearful call. Her voice was soft, she spoke slowly, she told him what had happened.

He could hardly speak, his voice broke, he thanked her, told her how sorry he was, and after ringing off, he sat down and cried. His friend Oliver was dead.

Having regained some sort of composure, he paced through the house, downstairs, upstairs, downstairs again. Thinking through what Mercedes had told him, the details of the robbery, the bravery of Oliver.

Had this been a random robbery gone terribly wrong. Was it in any way connected to the theft?

Two hours later, he received another call.

It was from the leader of an upcoming exploration aiming to study wildlife and wetlands on and around Lake Ontario. They had approached him a few weeks earlier asking if he would be interested in coming as an artist, capturing the journey through sketches.

He had said he would love to go.

The call was to say that he had been accepted by the committee and a date was given as to when they would depart.

Roger studied the notes he had written about the object of this expedition, glad of the distraction.

This would do him good, focus on something else.

Standing still looking out to sea he then thought about the last phone call he had received. This had come late yesterday.

From the telephone company, the call had been made to a number in Monaco, to Vanetti Vineyards.

He contacted the detective dealing with this case and passed the information on.

Taking a deep breath in, Roger sighed.

Then turned and headed back upstairs to pack.

He would leave in two days' time. He would never return home.

A little over 17 miles away, in Hastings.

Natalie studied the notes she had written in her journalist pad, took a sip of her coffee and thought through all that Kim had told her.

Something just wasn't right. She had a nagging feeling, but why?

Reading through her shorthand notes, she took in all that the English woman had told her.

Blocking everything out, she was in full concentration, the notes written reminding her of the conversation spoken, the discovery, the plans made, the journeys taken.

It had all started, with Roger Sutherland.

Three quarters of an hour later, oblivious of many glances that were thrown in her direction, having added a few comments here and there on her notepad, Natalie sat back.

She looked around the pub, thought about getting another drink, noticed it was a lot busier now and putting her notes away, got ready to leave.

Once back outside she reflected on all that Kim had told her, telling her how marvellous she had been in retaining all the information from six years ago. Kim needed to collect her child from pre-school and had wished her well.

Natalie had not told her about the chase, had not told her about the accident, had not told her about the phone call she had received.

So, Roger Sutherland, what else did you find out, and was it you who called me, warned me of impending danger, was it you, who knew where the centre panel was.

Natalie reached the railway station. Not wanting to drive on the wrong side of the road, and having seen the traffic in London, was glad she hadn't even attempted this. The roads were much narrower, the traffic dense, the pace frantic.

But she was thinking, almost aloud as she headed for the correct platform. How had he found out, why hadn't he come to Monaco, and why had he lost contact with Kim. She knew that their other friend, Oliver, had decided to stay in the States. The voice that she recalls so very vividly, had spoken in English, had been short, to the point, informative, had also been with a touch of concern and urgency.

Had this voice belonged to this Roger?

Kim had revealed that she had met a guy, was expecting, and had moved to Hastings, revealed that the last time she had spoken to Roger, was when he had, with great enthusiasm, told of finding the third key.

She had not spoken to Oliver since the day they all departed on their various destinations.

With a shrug of her shoulders, she had said, life goes on, and felt that as this German, this Rudolph, had not been able to find a treasure after forty years, wondered if it even existed.

Life goes on, she was a mother, was expecting a second child, was very much in love and content with her life. To search for a treasure that might not even exist held no excitement for her. Her heart was just not in it.

Natalie noticed that her train was still some twenty minutes away.

She had an address, Roger's address, in Eastbourne. She would go back to her hotel near the airport, then would set out tomorrow to hopefully locate Roger Sutherland.

Victoria station, London. Natalie stood and watched the board. It was busy, people arriving, people going, the sound of the times and destinations and numbers a pleasing sound as they clicked clacked regularly.

Searching through the board she had found the track where the train to Eastbourne would depart from. Now just waiting for it to show as ready for boarding.

She had slept well, had gone over all her notes again and was thankful that Kim had such a good recollection.

The board changed again, and Natalie turned to head for the platform.

However, a large suitcase had been placed right by her side.

She stumbled as she bumped into it, lost her balance and was about to come crashing to the floor when a hand grabbed her upper arm and managed to steady her.

'I am so sorry' the man said, 'my fault, shouldn't have placed it there, are you okay?'

Natalie looked at him, then as he released her, she brushed her skirt down, then looked at him, again. 'Oui' it's okay'.

Then, looking at the bag he had slung over one shoulder, noticed a label. A travel label. It had a name clearly written and she was momentarily stunned. Then, as he spoke and asked her again if she was okay, she studied his face.

'You are Roger Sutherland?' she asked, feeling herself blush a little.

Taken aback, he answered' Do I know you?' then followed it up with, 'No, I would surely remember, you are French?' picking up on her accent.

'You are from Eastbourne?' Natalie asked, then looked down to see two suitcases standing on the ground, 'and you're going somewhere?'

Looking up at him again, into his eyes. Strange, she thought, it was as if there was a connection, but the voice was not that of the one she had heard.

Taken aback once again, Roger smiled, raising his eyebrows, asking' Yes, I am, but...'

'Mon Dieu, this is, what you say, quelle coincidence? 'Then, taking hold of the label on the bag across his shoulder, 'I read your label'.

Roger following her, looked and nodded, then, 'but..'

'Ah, oui, 'Natalie answered, 'how do I know you? I am Natalie, Natalie Umbrego, from Monaco, yesterday I speak with Kim, your friend'.

'Wow' Roger said, looking at the woman before him, feeling himself blush a little now as he studied her face, admired her long red hair and those lovely eyes that were studying him. Before he could think of anything to say, she spoke again.

'Did you call me? Tell me to take painting and run?'

Roger put the bag down, frowned, then said, 'No..but, somebody broke into my house, three days ago, I discovered a phone call was made, to Monaco, to Vanetti Vineyards, so...'

'You have painting of a monk?'

'Yes, well, no, not anymore, they stole the painting, and the keys.

'The keys, yes, your friend Kim, tell me, tell me story of monks and keys..but then, ...

'Somebody called you, from my house, and told you to run?' Roger asked, as the board kept ticking over the times and platforms, as the people kept walking past them.

'Can we talk, somewhere?' Natalie asked, then, 'where are you going?'

Roger looked at his watch, then at the board.

Less than twenty minutes later they entered a nearby pub and Roger, insisting he get the drinks walked over to a vacant table, placed his luggage down and asked what she would like.

Natalie sat down, gave him the order, and retrieved her pad and pen. She shook her head at the incredible coincidence of literally falling into the arms of the man she had set out to see this morning.

Flicking over to some blank pages, she wondered what she might learn from this Englishman, this rather charming man who had set her heart racing a little. She watched him as he stood by the bar and ordered their drinks. She was determined to find out all about this man, this Roger Sutherland.

Saturday 2nd May

Claire took a swig of her bottle of water, opened the e-mail from Desmond and began to read all about Roger Sutherland.

'Dear Claire, lovely to hear from you, hope to meet you one of these days, not likely at the moment, not with all these restrictions. Now, with regard to your request, most interesting,...'

The report was detailed and lengthy. Claire read it through twice, then made some notes.

Just as she was finishing, she heard the numbers being pressed on the keyboard door and Thomas entered.

'Hey, good morning, have you had enough sleep already?' Claire asked, swivelling around on the chair, then seeing him look at the screen, said, 'don't peek! sit down and I will tell you what our English detective friend, had found out.'

'Okay, you sound excited, I'm all ears' Thomas replied and sat himself down in one of the armchairs.

'Okay, so' Claire said, swivelling the chair again so as to face him, 'We had Roger's address, this from Detective Inspector Mantell, as it turns out, the house no longer belongs to the family. But, our good friend, DP, did some sleuthing.

Now, I've been re-looking at all the information that we all have, so, bear with me, let me run this by you, this Roger Sutherland picks up some stuff from a market, finds out about a treasure hunt that started way back, by a Rudolph Meyer, who spent some forty years on the trail. Now, Roger and his friends, Kim, the air hostess and Oliver, a school friend, divide up and each go a different direction, Kim goes to Monaco, but has little success, Oliver comes to the States, he did find the painting of the monk and takes pictures, but meets this girl and stays. Roger travels to Turkey, he is successful and finds the third key. All of that took place back in 1957.'

Pausing briefly, she then asked Thomas, 'With me so far?'

'Yes, absolutely, carry on'.

Claire closed her eyes for a moment, then, continued, 'Now, nothing much happens after that. It sort of seems that the whole excitement of it just evaporates, then, we come to the year 1963, we know all about the painting that was given to the forger, Roberto, who, after his death, bequeaths it to Sophie, which, is where all of this treasure hunt starts for us , where it all begins, and you know all of what happened since, but, what you don't know, what nobody knows, is what detective Desmond has found out, so' Claire swivelling her chair to look at the screen and refresh her mind as to what she had read through earlier, 'So,' swivelling back to face Thomas, ' Somebody broke into Roger Sutherland's house, back in 1963, stole all the things that he had discovered, the painting he had and, the three keys, all the documentation, now, the house he lived in, no longer belongs to the family, but Desmond, obviously doing some good sleuthing, discovered about the theft, which led him to a filed report, which led him to a discovery that Roger had made, the burglar or burglars, had made a telephone call, from his house, this call was traced, it was made to the Vanetti Vineyards in Monaco, moreover, they subsequently discovered that the call had been made by a man called Hugo Visser.'

Claire paused again, looked at the screen once more and then continued, ' One more bit of information that our English friend had found out, two days after the theft Roger left to go on an expedition, apparently he was an exceptional artist and was taken on to sketch the wildlife in and around Lake Ontario in Canada, the thing is this, he was not heard from again, the expedition set out from Toronto but went missing, lost, a total number of eight, five men and three women. No sign of the ship, no sign of any bodies, nothing was ever found. '

'Goodness' Thomas said, taking in all what Claire had told him, then after there a silence in the room for some time, he asked, 'So, who is this, Hugo Visser?'

'Ah' Claire said, focusing again on the lengthy report that Desmond had written, ' a few more things to tell you' turning to face Thomas, she spoke again, ' Firstly, this man, Hugo Visser, flew from London to Amsterdam the day after the theft, also, a courier van had been noticed and the police subsequently found out that a shipment, marked first class delivery, was sent to an address in Istanbul. It was, through this discovery that they got his name, then back tracked to trace that flight he took to Amsterdam.'

THE PAST; Period 7 - Part 2

the year 1963 - Istanbul

Youseff Stood by the bodies. He was in thought as to what to do next. He looked at the man, Hugo. Noticed the bullet mark, small calibre, straight into his heart. Saw the big gun in his limp hand. This was the shot he had heard, looking at his employer, Madam, the damage was severe.

He concluded the following, she must have shot him first, then he, collapsing, had somehow shot her.

He looked at the blood on the beautiful rug. That would take some cleaning.

He hadn't touched anything, turned and moved to the door at the far end, entered the office and, again making sure he didn't touch anything, at least not until he had thought things through, he took in the scene.

Three keys, neatly in a row, side by side, then a thick stack of papers, and behind the desk to the left, leaning against the wall, the painting, the monk. This had arrived by special courier only hours ago. The keys and the information Hugo must have delivered himself.

Youseff walked back into the large room, thinking as to what to do next.

He had arranged for Kazim body to be returned. Huzar was out of danger and would be able to travel back in about three days' time.

Youseff also thought about the two men that had been sent to America, to San Francisco. No news from them, they had not reported in, as per instruction. Should have done so two days ago. He was aware of some of the details of Madam's plan but was not given the full details.

She had shot and killed him. Why?

He had managed to shoot her, had he suspected something, had she?

He looked out the window. The very window where she had often stood. It was getting dark.

He checked the time on his watch, then, having made a decision, he went into Madam's office, looking around, he noticed a bag, a small duffel bag, figured Hugo must have brought this in, to carry the documents and the keys.

Setting to work, Youseff grabbed the bag, put the stack of documents inside, followed by the keys, zipped it up. Then, taking the painting and the bag, he left and crossed the large room heading for the double doors and to his office beyond.

There was a wardrobe there, placing the bag on his desk, he shifted the single door wardrobe slightly, placed the painting, face against the wall, behind it, then pushed the wooden wardrobe back. Next, he picked up the bag, placed it on top of the wardrobe.

Youseff then phoned the police.

THE PRESENT; Paris

Saturday 2nd May

It was early evening and the three of them were in the lounge in Sophie's apartment.

Sophie and Tammy were looking at Terri expectantly as she had been on the phone for several minutes.

Finishing the call, Terri held up her hand with her forefinger pointing to the ceiling in a motion to stop any questions being fired at her whilst she scrolled through her phone with her other hand.

Sophie threw a look at Tammy and smiled.

Terri opened up an e-mail, read it through quickly, then looked up and across at the two women sitting side by side on the two-seater.

'Right, that was Thomas, so, some news from England, from a detective Desmond?' Looking at Sophie, 'You know this man?'

'Oui, yes, he assisted in a case that Thomas was working on, what has he discovered?

'Well, we know, from all that detective Mantell told my mother and me, that this Roger Sutherland had found the third key, so, he had one of the paintings and three keys. Now, back in 1963, in the month of June he was burgled, all the information, the painting, the keys, all stolen, by a man named Hugo Visser, and we now also know, that in all likely-hood the stuff stolen, was sent, by courier, to an address in Istanbul. I have that address here.'

There were several moments of silence, the three of them each with their own thoughts. Terri sat on a single chair, phone in hand. Sophie and Tammy side by side on the two-seater.

Then Sophie stood up, 'Bon' she said, speaking quite loud, ' right, this is what I feel we should do, she turned to look at Tammy, then turned to look at Terri, ' Sophie knew she had their full attention, then, sort of pacing in the small space between the chair and the sofa, she began to speak, now and then throwing a glance at either Terri or Tammy, but mostly just looking into space.

'We have to divide the assignments, with this pandemic, we are restricted to movements, so, my thoughts are these, first, this man, this Hugo Visser, he breaks into the house of Roger Sutherland, he obviously knows about the paintings and the keys and the story surrounding it, he flies out of London to Amsterdam, so, I'll get Martijn on to that, check out what happened to him, in that June of 1963. We now have an address in Istanbul, it's where the courier shipped the stolen goods, so, Tammy, you and me, we will look into that and see what we can find out, then' Sophie turning to look at Terri, ' we have two paintings here, and, we do know the secret of the third painting, we have the Roman numerals IV, on the right hand panel, we have the city crest of Florence on the central one and we have that symbol, of a three pronged crown set inside a triangle on the left hand panel, so, Terri, will you look at everything you can find about the city of Florence, and how theses clues might be connected?'

Sophie, having acknowledged the affirming nod from the young Terri, then continued,' that leaves Roger Sutherland himself, going on this expedition, also in June 1963, so, I'll get Sam onto that, see what he can find out, and finally, there is Natalie Umbrego, the woman who gave the painting to Roberto, she was running, she was being chased, we know the Turkish connection there, but, why did this Hugo guy, ring the Vanetti Vineyard from England, from the Roger's house, and who did he speak to? I will talk with Thomas, he and Claire can investigate that, what happened to her, why did she never return to pick up the painting?'

Sophie stopped speaking, looked at the other two in turn and smiled.

'Excellent' Tammy said, standing up and giving Sophie a hug, 'it all began with you receiving that painting from Roberto, you taking the lead is the right thing to do, so, let's do it.'

'Yes' Terri said, also standing up and coming in for a group hug.' it's like we are the three musketeers' she said, laughing.

THE PAST; Period 7 - Part3

June 1963   Lake Ontario

The wind was from the north, and it was sharp. She could feel her face stinging from the cold. The water was calm, almost like a mirror. Natalie shivered, but it was not from the cold, it was as if something wasn't quite right, it was as if something was about to happen.

Puffing out her cheeks she stood by the railing near the bow of the ship. It was late afternoon, and the sky was a strange blue and orange colour.

All the others were inside. Taking in a deep breath she shook away the strange feeling she had and thought back. Back to the moment she had tripped over his suitcase, the moment he had caught her, stopped her from falling. The moment she had, seeing so very clearly the label on the bag that was slung across his shoulder, that he was Roger Sutherland..

He had agreed to speak with her, and they had found a coffee shop not far away and having ordered their drinks, he sat and had looked at her expectantly.

'Why did you stop?' she asked, looking into his eyes.

She sensed he was not comfortable with her presence and wondered why.

'According to your friend Kim, you were so excited, explaining all your finding, showing those keys, the painting. Then, finding that third key, surely, you must have been so happy'.

Roger carefully sipped his drink, thinking about why it had been he had stopped'.

Natalie waited patiently for him to speak.

'I came back, 'he began, briefly looking into her eyes, then looking away, before continuing, 'yes, I was very happy, to have found that third key, after all the research the translating of the findings of

Rudolph Meyer, having now all three keys and one of the paintings, yes, I was excited., happy...'

Natalie said nothing, sipped her drink and waited.

..' It was my , quest, really, sure I had perhaps drawn Kim and Oliver into it, but, Kim had not been successful in finding out much, did tell me about you, and though she was happy about the key I found, she was also, which I didn't know before, in a relationship.. anyway, and then with Oliver having decided to stay in the states, having met, the love of his life, he said, well, to be honest, I was rather down, Oliver was my best friend, he was now gone, and Kim, well, I sort of fancied her, but, never said so, she was now gone...'

Feeling she ought to say something, Natalie spoke, her voice soft, 'I'm sorry, I think I can understand, but there is something else, I think, you are, well, sad?'

Roger took another sip, felt tears welling up behind his eyes, blinked a few times, then, clearing his throat, he said, 'I found out yesterday, that Oliver, ... he was shot, an armed robbery gone wrong, grocery store, shot dead, protecting his wife and son..'

Natalie reached across and took hold of his hand, 'Oh Roger, I am so sorry'..

With a gloved finger she wiped a tear away, sniffed and watched the calm waters of the Lake Ontario for a while.

It would soon be dinner time. She was glad she had come, had been able to come.

She smiled at the thought of how bold she had been, though at first, she had been confused as to what was happening, with regard to the mystery of the three monks, she again thought back to that moment in the railway station...

'It wasn't you who called me in Monaco' Natalie said, after some time of silence.

Roger looked up from his drink, again looked into her lovely eyes, briefly, before taking a sip and answered, 'No, I discovered someone had used my telephone, so, the police came, took prints, it seems that whoever it was that stole all the stuff, called you, but why?

'Yes, he asked for me by name, then spoke to me in an urgent voice, a voice I know now, wasn't yours, he told me to get the painting, told me exactly where I would find it, then to take it and get away, there were two men, bad men, who were after it, who would, according to him, do anything to get it, I was in danger, my family was in danger, get the painting and get away..'

But, if he was helping you.. then why..'

'Why steal what you had?' Natalie finished, 'this, is a mystery, maybe the two men from Istanbul, were rivals in the hunt for the treasure, I don't know, perhaps he was going to, at some point contact me, but, such was the urgency in his voice, I just went to the room, an upstairs bedroom, opened the wardrobe door, a panelled door, ripped the panel off and sure enough, the painting was there, I managed to take it out, but damaged it in doing so, it was then when I thought of this Roberto guy, he is a forger and he not only would be able to mend the painting, but leaving it with him seemed like a good option.'

'So, this, Roberto chap, he's got it?'

'Yes'

'And these two men, did you ever see them?'

'Oh yes, they got to me as I was getting in my car, I took off, they followed, thank goodness, I lost them as I drove to Cannes, then, had time to hand to painting to Roberto, all good timing really, the fact that I knew where he would be, it all fell together nicely, I then drove out of town, they followed, and, well, they ended up having a bad accident.'

'Goodness' Roger managed to say, looking across at the woman across from him, such beautiful long red hair, those lovely green eyes.

'You are going somewhere?' she asked, finished her drink.

Roger, looking at his watch, answered, 'yes, I am off of an expedition'..

Natalie was about to turn and head inside for warmth and for dinner, when she sensed someone behind her.

'Hey, 'Roger said, 'wondered where you got to'.

'Look at that sky Roger, it's so different, and rather strange, don't you think?'

'Oh, my goodness' Roger exclaimed, 'what's even more strange, is that!' pointing

Natalie looked.

Ahead was a white cloud, a low cloud, like a mist, settled upon the water, it was bright white and as they approached it, or as it approached them, it began to blot out everything around it.

'Get inside 'Roger said, grabbing Natalie and taking her with him to the door, 'that looks like some sort of ice storm'.

'But there is no wind' Natalie managed to say as he opened the door for her.

Roger took a last look before entered the interior of the ship. The whiteness was rapidly nearing.

He shut the door and headed for the wheelhouse.

THE PRESENT; Parma, Italy

Saturday 2nd May

Whilst in Paris, Sophie, Tammy, and Terri were ready to follow up with their research and investigations, each with their own assignments, Terri's former teacher, Millie Parker had completed hers.

As she stood by the river that flowed through city, she was reminded of the movie she watched as a teenager, starring Elvis Presley, the film 'Blue Hawaii' and almost audibly she started to sing, 'As the river flows, surely to the sea, ..some things are meant to be..'

Millie sighed. The evening was a little chilly. She stood looking at the water a while longer, designated a stream, it flowed through the city, then would flow into the river Po. 'Some things are meant to be' she whispered to herself, then turned and headed for her apartment.

A month ago, to the date, a month ago she had left her home in San Francisco, only a few days after her friend Alison had visited and had updated her in detail, all that had occurred, on the day the tornado struck, all that had since, particularly in recent day, been discovered and had come to light. The complete story. A lot to take in.

Then the following day she had a message, from friend she had made when she was studying and living in Milan in the late eighties. Not a close friend, but one whom she was in regular contact with.

She was very ill.

Millie made up her mind instantly, she needed to just get away, felt she needed to go and see her and despite there already were beginning to being travel and flight restrictions put into place. She was determined.

She flew to Miami, from there to Curacao, then onto to Amsterdam and from there to Milan. Her friend was very ill, she was determined to see her.

The last leg was a train journey to Parma where her friend now lived.

Unfortunately, due to hospital restrictions, she was unable to visit her, but did manage to speak to her on the telephone, briefly, all too briefly.

'Stay at my place' she had said and managed to organise a key.

Walking along the riverbank for a bit, she then turned towards the apartment.

'Some things are meant to be' she again whispered to herself.

Her friend never came home.

The apartment was cleared by her family and Millie took on the rent, it was a lovely place, it would do for a while.

She had set herself an assignment, to make public, all that she knew, though being careful not to make any accusations where she had no solid proof, but the story needed to be told, in its fullness.

Not long after her mother had died, she had come to Milan, to study fashion, had lived there for two years, of the several people she had met during that time, only one remained quite close. Nina.

Reaching her new place, she got the keys ready and smiled as she thought about the reaction her article would receive.

Still mulling through all that Alison had told her, still feeling a loss over her friend, she had made up her mind.

The story now needed to be told, all of it, the tornado, the gold, the deaths, all of it.

Getting all her files together, she began to write an article. Going over all the notes she had made, she made sure that she had covered everything.

Earlier today, she had completed it, then posted it online, also sending it to several newspapers across the States.

Millie was pleased. 'For you mum,' she said aloud as she entered her apartment.

A little later, glass of wine in her hand, she stood on her balcony, looking out onto the garden below.

Meanwhile in Bilbao , northern Spain;

Malcolm Lynch stood on the balcony of his apartment that overlooked the sea. There was a gentle breeze in the air, but it was still warm despite it being the early evening and the light was fading.

He was worried, there was a strange feeling in his stomach. His throat felt dry, and he had been coughing intermittently for the past couple of hours. He also felt that he must have a slight temperature.

Was he, or had he caught this dreaded virus. Or had this suddenly come about due to what he had read as he had been catching up with news items on his tablet.

Staring out to sea, his mind took him back. A long time back.

The night after the storm. The digging up of the gold coins.

So much had happened, The excitement of the nocturnal activities, the excitement of his affair with Constance.

But the killings had been a shock, when Constance had later given him the full version of what had occurred, what her son had done, the death of the professor, the death of two of the students. Realisation had struck and over the next days and weeks, he had become increasingly worried. They had split the coins, she had four hundred and he had taken three hundred and twenty.

Their affair was no longer exciting, coming to the university each day was no longer a joy. He feared that any moment the police would come for further questioning.

The original police enquiry had been short and there had been no suspicion cast anywhere, with the exception of a young lad who had gone missing , Eddie Philpot, what had happened to him, all he got from Constance was her advice to just lay low and act normally, if anything should come to light, that it would all fall on the head of the young lad who had disappeared.

But this had not alleviated his concerns.

Five months later, he chose to get away, to run.

Over thirty years ago!

The news he had picked up earlier in the day, news about the theft and return of a painting to the museum in San Francisco, had drawn his attention, for in a detailed report, about a possible international connection, he saw a name, Detective Inspector Roger Mantell.

On the balcony Malcolm shivered. The breeze was turning cooler, yet he felt sweat on his forehead.

He coughed again, for several moments, feeling a pain in his chest and struggling to breathe properly.

After a while, having almost doubled up from the coughing bout, he went back inside. Made his way to his bedroom and lay down.

He closed his eyes, he knew about Detective Inspector Mantell, for he had been the one who had arrested Constance.

Did she give him up, after she had escaped and been re-arrested some months ago now?

But nobody knew where he had gone. He had been careful.

What he would never see, was an article that would appear the following day, hitting many Sunday newspapers, one that would even make it to some television news casts.

And his name would be mentioned.

As his breathing became more and more shallow, the now sixty-five-year-old former Dean of the University in Albuquerque, decided he had better lie down. No sooner had he done so when he closed his eyes and slipped into a coma.

THE PAST; Period 8

The year 1989 – Bilbao- Spain

The train from Madrid rolled into the Bilbao-Abundo station and hissed to a stop just feet from the buffers.

After the floods of 1983 the station had been massively renovated, as Malcolm reached the upper level, he stopped to take in the massive stained-glass window, the late afternoon light creating a dazzling and most magical effect on the floor below.

The huge scene depicts the economic activities of the Basque region and was installed back in 1948.

Malcolm was about to move on when sirens stopped him. Then several policemen came rushing into the station.

He remained standing still, for a moment his heart felt as if it had stopped, then, it had begun thumping loudly in his chest. Had he been found out, had someone in the auction house been suspicious?

Malcolm tried ever so hard to relax, as the policemen, a group of three, headed towards him, he managed to set his feet into motion and started walking towards them.

The relief he felt all through his body as they swept past him was immense.

Walking on he tried to replenish his lungs and headed for the exit.

He had been to the country's capital, Madrid, for an auction. A week earlier he had made the decision to try and sell two of the gold coins he had. They had been eager to see them, but had asked many questions, as to how he had acquired them, how long ago and had he any idea of their value. They also needed to know his personal details, name and address. Though at one point, when travelling to the city that day, he had thought about providing a false address, in the end he felt the less he lied, the more confident he would be. So, his name and address were true. But the back story of how he came to have these old coins, was fabricated, but he had prepared the story well and it was, seemingly, accepted.

Now, as he had regained his composure, he felt relieved. The auction had gone well, the sum raised for just these two coins, was great. He was well pleased. He still had another 318 of them!

Deciding to take a taxi to his house, he learned of the reason for the sirens and the police presence.

There had been a theft. A painting had been stolen from the museum. A valuable painting, a Titian.

THE PRESENT; Chicago

Sunday 3rd of May

Felicity Smith also picked up the story of the theft from the museum in San Francisco, also picked up the name of the detective from Albuquerque.

She had been in the process of trying to reach Simon, had let the phone ring only a couple of times before ending the call. She would try again tomorrow, she thought, and left it at that.

Then, this morning, she was drawn to another story, the headline caught her attention as she was scrolling through her tablet whilst having some breakfast.

'Tornado with a twist'

She started reading as her mouth opened slightly, her heart raced a little faster, for as she read on, she realised, this was a story of the storm in 1988, the tornado that had struck the archaeological encampment near silver city.

'When I was told my mother had died because of a tornado storm that had practically destroyed an archaeological dig she was working on, I was devastated, however, when I was told over thirty years later that she had in fact been murdered, I was totally shocked..'

So began the article and Felicity was immediately hooked.

In Yonkers, New York, Raphael Morton also saw the headline featured in one of the Sunday papers. He too was drawn into the story written by Millie Parker.

Carefully reading it through he then knew what had to be done.

His name was mentioned, his findings were explained, his parents needed to know, but he couldn't travel, didn't want to speak to them on the phone, so, called a friend.

'Hello?'

'Hi Simon, it's Raphael, do you get the Sunday paper?'

'Hi, you sound concerned, did you try and ring me yesterday?

Simon, in the front room of his house by the river in Albuquerque asked.

'No, not me' Raphael answered, then' yes, little concerned, ringing to ask a favour'.

'Absolutely, how can I help, there's something in the paper?'

'Yes, the whole story, the tornado, the gold coins, everything, written by a Millie Parker?'

'Millie? Yes, I know that name, friend of Alison's, hang on, picked up a paper earlier this morning, haven't opened it yet, bear with me, what paper are you referring to?'

'It's in a local New York paper, it must be all over the country I reckon'.

'Got it!' Simon exclaimed, 'hang on Raphael, let me read this ...'

After some moments, Raphael patiently waiting, Simon spoke' Wow, it's all there alright, your findings, my involvement, Alison's as well, goodness, wonder what detective inspector Roger Mantell will make of it...so, what is it you want me to do?'

'Could you please go and see my folks? Talk to them in person?'

'Of course, yes, I'll go and see them straight away, then get them to ring you, is that okay?'

'Thank you so much' Raphael answered, relief in his voice, 'I appreciate this'.

'Take care, I'll go now' Simon answered and taking the paper with him, got ready to leave.

In Chicago, having read through the article twice, Felicity picked up her phone and dialled a number.

'Hello?' a voice said. A voice she knew, a voice she missed.

'Simon, it's me Fliss..'

There was a brief silence on the other end of the line, then Simon found his voice and said, 'Hi Fliss, listen, I'm just going out the door, Raphael rang just now, wants me to visit his folks, tell them in person, I guess that's why you're calling? The article?'

'Yes, though there was something else as well,' and her voice a little shaky, she rambled on for a few moments, then realised what Simon had said,

'I..I guess I should ring mum and dad?'

'Yes, definitely, sorry Fliss, they will have to know now, better you ring them, call them now, then call me later?'

In Chicago she felt tears welling up, her stomach was churning and she realised that she had made a mistake in letting Simon go..'Yes, yes, you're right, okay, I, ..I'll call you later'

Felicity broke the connection.

In the kitchen at his home in Albuquerque detective inspector Roger Mantell was reading the same article. He shook his head but had to admit that perhaps it was time for the whole story to come out, he knew full well that the initial investigation was poor at best. There would be questions, he drank his coffee and knew that his Sunday would not be spent with his family today.

In Myrtle Creek the Sunday paper was delivered. The newspaper every day was a standing order that Robert had put into place many years ago, so as to keep up to date on local news. Often it had been through this media that he had found directions and clues to help in his quest to find missing persons.

Claire fetched it inside, headed to the kitchen where she began to prepare omelettes, something Thomas enjoyed having. Flicking a few pages into the newspaper, she saw the headline.

Only just rescuing the omelettes as Thomas appeared, she said, 'You have to see this!' pointing to the paper as she continued to prepare the breakfast.

'Had a message from Sophie' Thomas said, walking up to the counter where he looked at the article that Claire had pointed to.

'How is she, what's the latest?' Claire asked.

But Thomas didn't reply, he was totally engrossed in the article.

Claire dished out the breakfast, poured Thomas a coffee and waited.

When he finally looked up, she asked him, 'I just spotted the headline when you came in, what does it say?'

'Everything' Thomas answered, 'everything, the whole story, Robert is mentioned, quite a detailed account'.

Thomas smiled his thanks to Claire and sat on the stool by the counter and tucked into the omelette.

Claire read the article for herself, and all was quiet for some time.

'So, what did Sophie have to say?' She asked, having finished reading.

'Ah, yes, well, we have an assignment, she wants us to find out everything we can about a French woman, Natalie Umbrego, she is the one who gave that forger that painting, the one Sophie now has, she disappeared, never returned to collect the painting, so, a missing person really, right up our street, don't you think?'

'Absolutely' Claire answered, then, 'Will anything come with regard to this article?

'Maybe, questions will be asked, I'm sure of that, but let us concentrate of what Sophie had asked us to do, so, what do you think, how shall we proceed?'

Claire took a bite of her omelette, gave the question some thought and was appreciative of him asking her for her view.

'I'll fire up Robert's search engine, he has a programme on there that will search through various newspapers for a particular name that I can input, if I go for French and English papers to start with, see what pops up, then if you can search further back, perhaps find out more of her ancestry, often clues can be found in the past?'

'Sounds like a plan there Claire, first though, I'll give Cynthia a call, see how she is and her folks, also give her an update'.

'Give her my love' Claire said, getting up and taking the dishes away.

Thomas nodded, then briefly looked at the article in the newspaper again before heading for the lounge, he would set up in there as Claire would be using Roberts upstairs, what he had named, engine room.

THE PAST; Period 9

The year 1999   - New years eve- Portland

The last day of the last month of the year. The last day of the twentieth century. The last hour of the last day.

The streets were glistening under the streetlamps. It was raining, it was cold.

Hands in pockets, the heavy rain jacket firmly zipped up, the hood in place, Robert Pentregrass stood quietly on the front porch. Inside his ailing mother was already in bed, asleep. His father was sat in the lounge watching the television.

Robert stood still, watching the house that was diagonally across the road from him. A large house, in large grounds. Many cars were parked in the driveway and along the street. The sound of music easily reached his ears, there were lights shining through every window that he could see.

The Rozzini house.

He had been invited. She had asked him to come. He had declined.

The rain became a little heavier, but it didn't drown the sound of the music from across the road.

He watched her go, he noticed the many others who had arrived and had gone inside.

She had nodded, had kissed him on the cheek and said she understood.

He knew she did. Not many understood his condition, not many took the time to know him. Robert had only few friends, only one that he had bonded with over the years. Thomas.

From the very moment he had led him away from an uncomfortable situation he was confronted with in the school cafeteria, Thomas had become a friend.

Standing on the porch, he reflected that had been nearly ten years ago.

Taking in a deep breath, Robert turned and walked to the other side of the porch, before turning and walking back to the spot where he had stood since she had kissed him and crossed the street.

Holly.

Breaking into a broad smile he thought back to when he had first seen her, only eight months ago. He was walking from the centre of the city, back to his house, taking a route he hadn't taken before, just going for a stroll and trying to think about what to do next. His mother was ill, his father wasn't coping well, his younger sister seemed not to care at all and had moved in with some friends.

Noise reached his ears, shouting and cheering, the sound of clashing. There was a sports field ahead and upon reaching it he noticed the field hockey game in progress.

Young ladies. Running, short skirts and long socks, wielding the sticks with amazing dexterity.

Mesmerized, Robert stopped and watched.

Then, by the very place where he had found a spot to stand and watch, the action came towards him. Two of them, racing to reach the ball.

Slithering, sliding, side by side they came, sticks reaching out in front of them, both eager to reach the ball, both eager to slice it back into to play.

One of them made contact, shouldered her opponent slightly to one side and whacked the ball across the field.

He caught her eye as she looked up, she caught his, smiled and was back into the thick of play.

She wasn't very tall, around five foot three he guessed, but she was quite sturdy, and he was impressed with her strength and turn of speed.

With the play now further along on the field, he realised his heart was beating faster.

He stayed and watched the game. Found himself almost solely focusing on her. When the game was over and her team had been victorious, he had walked along the side-line towards the sport pavilion and had then stopped and waited.

When the players came out, she had seen him, had come over and stopping in front of him, said, 'Hi, I'm Holly, come and watch me play next week'.

Unable to speak, Robert merely nodded, realising that he must have gone beetroot red. She had smiled and left.

Smiling at the memory, he noticed that the had rain eased a little, the minutes ticked over towards midnight.

Robert again took in a deep breath, began to realise that he was getting a little cold and again walked to the other side of the porch and back again.

A friendship had developed. Slowly. He had explained to her, his condition, that he had Asperger Syndrome, she had accepted him for who he was. All five foot eight of him, with curly brown hair, a fair complexion and dark blue eyes. She understood the reason he didn't want to go to the New Year's Eve party, but she wanted to be there with some other friends.

He understood and insisted she must go.

Robert checked his watch, three minutes to go.

He thought about his friend Thomas, who, ten days ago, had said goodbye as he had been offered a job with a Spanish airline. It would already be the new year for him, Robert calculated.

The sound of church bells and fireworks brought him out of his reverie, and he decided to go inside and wish his father a happy new year.

Then once more returning to the porch, seeing that the rain had completely stopped now, he waited. But as the clock ticked on, as people began leaving the house across the street in dribs and drabs, there was no sign of her.

His heart was heavy. But eventually he shrugged, figured she must have met up with some friends and left with them. He had merely missed seeing her leave.

He didn't remotely think that he would never see her again.

Two days into the new year his mother passed away. His father, already having struggled to cope with the situation, suffered a stroke and died three days later.

THE PRESENT; Myrtle Creek

Sunday 3rd May- 3pm

Thomas sat in the comfy armchair in the lounge. He had, not long after lunch, decided to ring Cynthia. Her parents were both on the mend and in a few days' time, she would see if she could travel back and see him. She had insisted however, that he talked with her and updated her on everything that he was now involved in regarding to all this monk business. And when Cynthia said everything, she meant everything, and so he was on the phone with her for quite some time.

It was as he was quietly sitting and reflecting that he sensed someone there. Thomas turned around.

Claire stood in the doorway. Arms folded.

He got up, could see that she had been crying.

'Whatever has happened?' he enquired walking up to her.

When Thomas stood before her, she moved forward, hugged him for a moment and felt comforted by his arms around her. She then pulled back and looked up at him, 'I know why Robert began searching for missing people' she said, then moving around him she sat herself down on the couch. Thomas turned and sat in the chair opposite, 'Go on' he said.

'Do you know a girl called Holly?' she asked.

Thomas thought for a moment, then answered, 'Yes, yes I do, gosh, a long time ago, Robert's, well, girlfriend I suppose, I met her once, maybe twice, why?'

'I was drawn to a story, felt there was information there that might be useful, so, I then delved into that, read more and more, got sidetracked really, but, well, Robert's mum had died, then his dad died too..'

'Yes, yes I remember now, it was early in the year, I had recently flown over to Spain to start a new job there, his mum had been ill for some time, she died, then his father suffered a heart attack due to stress, he died too, I flew back and was at the funeral, but, how does that connect to Holly, I don't remember much about her, I think she played hockey, field hockey, that's how they met, I was away quite a bit around that time, learning my piloting skills in Seattle...'

'Well, Holly went to a new year's party, across the road form where Robert lived, an Italian family, Rozzini?'

'Yes, the name rings a bell.'

'Well, anyway, she went, Robert didn't, well, it wasn't his thing, we know that, so, he thought she must have hooked up with someone that night, then his mum and dad passed away, he was in the thick of things, sorting all that out, then it was sometime later that he discovered, she had gone missing, never came back to her apartment that she shared with a couple of girls. It was one of those girls who one day called on Robert, thought she might be with him, well.. anyway, that's how it all began, that's how Robert started to find missing people, his girlfriend had disappeared...'

'Wow, I never knew, never knew he searched for missing people at all... I was well into my life in Spain, I wrote occasionally, so did he, but ...well , so? Did he ever find her?'

'No'

Both were quiet for a while, it was then Thomas who spoke, 'So, how did your search get to the point of finding all this out?'

'Ah, well, I hadn't been very successful in finding out much about Natalie, other than the connection to the Vanetti Vineyards in Monaco, anyway, you know how sometimes you look for something that you've mislaid, can't find it anywhere, then later, when you're not looking, you find it?'

'I know what you mean, so..?' Thomas replied, seeing a grin appear on Claire's face., 'you're smile is giving you away..'

'Guess I should never play poker! yes, well, as I was totally engrossed in reading that part of Roberts life, getting quite emotional as you saw, learning of his parent's deaths, I thought about that fact, finding something when you're not really looking.

I thought about this girl, Holly, thought it might be something to one day look into, I found out her full name, Holly Koppel, so, just to see where it might lead me, punched that name into Roberts search engine..'

Thomas gave Claire a friendly stare, who then smiled and said, 'A headline jumped out, a Wayne Koppel was the master and captain of an exploration vessel called 'The Taciturn' who went missing in Lake Ontario back in 1963!'

Across the other side of the country, in Boston.

'Found something!' Sam said, sitting behind his study desk in the fourth bedroom.

Chrissie looked up from her tablet and watched as he studied the screen for a moment or two, before swivelling the chair around to face her, then smiling, said, ' There was a vessel, an exploration vessel, called 'The Taciturn', it went missing on Lake Ontario, June 1963, it was a combined Canadian and British venture, the captain was, ' Thomas turned around to check the names, then turned, ' Wayne Koppel, and the team , well, come and see the list of names..'

Chrissie placed her tablet on a small table by her chair, got up and looked over Sam's shoulder at the screen.

'You need to ring Sophie' she said.

Whilst in Chicago,

Felicity lay on the bed on her stomach. Her ankles were crossed, and her head nestled in the crook of her right arm.

Her eyes were open, and she stared at the framed photograph that stood on her bedside table.

A family photo, taken at the picnic area of a forest park. With her sister and mum and dad.

Felicity had been crying.

She sniffed and closed her eyes.

The telephone conversation with Simon had been difficult. He had been somewhat hesitant. She had told him what she had come across in her sister's diary, she had tried to sound confident and upbeat, told him it was lovely to hear his voice. He told her of the conversation he had just had with Raphael, Josie's brother, and the task he was asked to do. She wanted to say how sorry she was, she wanted to say how wrong she had been, she wanted to ask him if they could get together. But, before she even had the courage to say all those things, he said it was now so very important for her to ring her folks.

He was not wrong, she had to do that, she knew, she also knew that she had lost him, sensed the uncertainty in his voice, she said she would ring her folks straight away and hung up. She knew that someone else had captured his heart.

Before even further considering that, she rang home.

'Hi mum' when the connection was made.

'Oh Fliss, how are you? Where are you? Oh Fliss, I am so sorry, we are so sorry, are you alright? We miss you so much...'

'Mum, yes, I'm fine, you need to get a local paper, you need to get one now, or have you had one today?'

'Eh, no, we haven't, what's up love, what's happened?'

'Get on your computer then mum, check local news, I'm staying on the phone, where's dad?

'He's out, taking the dog for a walk..'

'You have a dog?' Felicity asked, then, 'well, get on your computer mum, please'.

A little over ten minutes later, she had ended the call, promising to come and see them when travel was allowed.

It was then when she had broken down and cried.

Cried over the news that she and her mother shared when the article was read.

Cried over the fact that she knew she had lost Simon.

Felicity sniffed again, then rolled over onto her back and told herself to get it together, she needed to make another call.

She searched for the number of the police station in Albuquerque, rung it, then insisted she speak with detective inspector Mantell.

In Albuquerque.

Roger had just come home, practically a whole day without his family. His wife greeted him kissed him and then his cell phone rang.

Raising his eyes to the heaven he smiled and answered.

'Hello, who?' he asked, then,' Oh yes, put her through...

Miss Smith, yes, yes, I know who you are, I take it you've read the article too?'

'Yes, but it's not why I'm calling you' Felicity answered.

'Oh?'

'I know where Malcolm Lynch is likely to be'.

'The dean who vanished, possibly went to Spain? Do tell Miss Smith'.

It was approaching midnight in Paris.

When Sophie put her phone down and looked at the screen of her laptop.

Incredible, she was thinking, the phone call and the e-mail, both about the same thing.

The e-mail from Thomas was about how they found out about Natalie Umbrego, the phone call from Sam, about the report on Roger Sutherland.

They had been together, they had travelled to Canada, they had been part of the same exploration team that had sailed into Lake Ontario. They had vanished, the ship, the crew, vanished, without trace.

Back in Myrtle Creek;

'Thomas?' Claire said, poking her head around the door and looking into the lounge where he sat by the window.

'Yes?' he answered, looking up.

'You know this girl, that Robert knew, this Holly, well, I feel I ought to try and see if I can find her, for Robert, if you see what I mean, if that is okay with you of course.'

'That's a great idea Claire, we've discovered, well, you've discovered a lot today, I'll carry on with further research on this exploration vessel, but, yes, you go for it, it's a great idea.'

Claire thanked Thomas, then bounded up the stairs, saying softly to herself, so, what happened to you Holly, where did you disappear to?'

THE PAST; Period 10

1st January 2001- Rozzini house- Portland

Despite the rain, though fortunately it had eased a little, the firework display was going ahead, and the party had all come out to the back veranda of the large mansion house. The church bells had chimed, the hugs and kisses and well wishes had been done, drinks were still flowing, and the buffet table still had ample goodies to tuck into.

Holly moved with the others and waited. She decided she would watch the display, then cross the road to see and wish Robert a happy new year. She knew he would be waiting. She felt a little dizzy, realised she probably had a little too much to drink, despite telling herself to be careful.

The host, Nico Rozzini, had spoken in a loud voice and had called everyone out to the veranda.

The fireworks began.

Then there was a woman who was suddenly there beside her, her shoulder pressed against hers and she leaned closer and spoke in her ear, a loud whisper, so as to be heard above the noise of the sparklers and rockets that were fired into the night sky.

'I know what happened to your grandfather' the voice said.

Holly turned to look at the woman beside her, looked straight into her eyes, frowning and was about to say something, but the woman spoke, 'Very confidential, you need to come with me'.

Then Holly felt the gun pressing into her ribs.

As she registered this, she sensed someone else, another woman, on her other side.

'Don't try anything silly, just come with us, all will be explained' a voice whispered into her other ear.

THE PRESENT; Parma-Italy

Monday 4th of May

The sun rose in the east. Her balcony faced east, and Millie stood there, leaning on the wooden handrail that secured the sizeable balcony. There were several plants, originally having belonged to her friend who had sadly succumbed to the dreaded virus. Her family had asked if it was okay to leave them. She had tearfully nodded, sad not to have been able to see her friend at all, due to the restrictions.

There was also a sun-lounger and a small glass topped table.

The clouds in the sky were few and far between. It would be a warm day and already Millie could feel the strength of the rays.

She wondered how much she had shaken up the world she had left behind. Taking in a deep breath, she squinted as the sunlight hit her face, then turned and went inside.

She would have some breakfast, then check the world news. She felt good, she felt relieved, she had done the right thing. It had tired her out, she had gone to bed early, but had awoken fresh. She felt light, a burden had been lifted. She knew it would certainly have put the cat amongst the pigeons, but so be it. She smiled to herself as she prepared something to eat, wondering what kind of response there would be. She knew in her heart that what she did, had to be done.

In Paris.

Sophie was up and about early. She had showered and made herself breakfast before settling down in the dining room, placing her laptop there and opened it up, to her right were several sheets of paper and placing these in order, the punched in her password and sipped her orange juice.

It wasn't much later when Tammy entered the kitchen and dining area. She too had already showered and was ready for breakfast.

'Terri?' Sophie asked.

'Fast asleep' Tammy answered.

'Not an early riser then, did you sleep well?'

'Very well, lot's going through my brain of course, with all that is happening, but once I fell asleep, that was it. You?'

'Same, hope to hear..'Sophie began.

'Soph?' Tammy asked, bringing in her juice and some cereal.

'Just reading that e-mail again, from Thomas, and thinking about that call last night, incredible really, this Roger Sutherland and this French woman, Natalie, both ending up together, both then going on this expedition, then, vanishing.'

'Do you think it's all connected?' Tammy asked.

'I've been thinking about that' Sophie answered looking at her friend as she sat down on the opposite side of the table, 'if it is all connected, then it's worrying, that would take a lot of planning, not to mention involving some unscrupulous people.'

'Who's unscrupulous?' Terri asked, entering the kitchen wearing a pink towelling bathrobe.

'We were thinking about the mysterious disappearance of Roger and Natalie, on this expedition in Lake Ontario.' Tammy answered.

'Yes, do you think it is all connected with the monks?' Terri asked entering the dining area.

'We don't know, but it is suspicious' Tammy answered.

Just then Sophie phone rang.

'It's Martijn!'

Sophie answered and listened for quite some time.

In Amersfoort

Martijn relayed all that he had found out regarding Hugo Visser and what had occurred in 1963, then made a little small talk with Sophie, before hanging up.

The next call he was going to make was going to be to Sam's friend, the chief of police in Rotterdam.

Back in Paris

'Hugo Visser was shot and killed in Istanbul,' Sophie said, looking at Tammy and Terri in turn, 'Martijn is going to see if he can get permission to investigate'.

For several moments no one spoke. Then Terri, heading back into the kitchen area to prepare some breakfast, said, ' I had a thought, in the middle of the night' reaching for a cereal box, finding a bowl and pouring some of the contents into it, 'about the clues on the monks tunics', adding some milk to the cereal, she took the bowl and re-entered the dining area, noticing that Sophie and Tammy were looking at her expectantly.

Sitting down at the table, Sophie spoke, 'And?'

'We have the crest of the city of Florence, right?'

'Yes' Sophie answered.

'Then we have a number, the roman numerals for the number 4, right?'

'Yes' Tammy and Sophie replied in unison.

'Well, I think it has to be an address, the other clue, though we were thinking might be a crown, but, what if it is the rest of the address? We have the city, we have a number, so, I think it must refer to a street'.

Terri took a mouthful of her cereal and Sophie got up and headed for the lounge, saying, 'You are right Terri, it does make sense, but a crown inside a triangle, what could that mean?

Sophie picked up the large map of Florence that was spread out on the coffee table and noticed something. She looked at Terri who smiled broadly.

'I got up in the night, had this thought, took another look at the map, pretty sure I found it.'

Sophie smiled back, looked at Tammy who was looking at Terri and placed the map on the table.

Tammy looked to where Sophie was pointing, the circle that was penned on the map.

Both reading aloud what was written.

'Santa Trinita'

'I'm thinking that means something like triangle?' Terri asked.

Sophie and Tammy looked across the table at Terri, both grinning, 'Clever girl Terri, well done you.' Sophie said.

Tammy gave Terri and appreciative nod, then said to Sophie, we could perhaps see if we can locate this on one of those satellite mapping programmes?'

'Ooh, yes, yes, Terri said,' like google earth, great idea, may I try?'

Sophie looked at Tammy, then both looked at Terri, 'This is your find, you do it.' Sophie answered, 'I have such a programme on my laptop, I'll get it.'

Less than twenty minutes later, Terri exclaimed, 'Found it!'

Tammy and Sophie joined her and all three of them looked on the screen.

Then Tammy spoke, asking, 'Do we know anyone in Italy?'

The light of the new day slowly made its way across the Atlantic Ocean and would soon be touching the east coast of America.

THE PAST; Period 11

The year 2005 — Istanbul, Turkey

Thirty-five-year-old Danielle Vitali unlocked the roller door of the old garage and lifted it open. Nearby a train rumbled across an iron bridge. The noise momentarily distracted her. She then looked once more into the garage that seemed to be stacked with all sorts of things. Taking a step inside she found a light switch. Three tube lights flickered for a moment, made a buzzing sound, and then settled to bring plenty of light all around.

Where to start, she was wondering, taking in all that she could see.

Dressed in dark blue jeans, a red, long-sleeved sweatshirt over a white blouse. Her feet in leather dark brown short ankle boots with a small square heel and her long auburn hair tied into a ponytail, she had come prepared to get her hands dirty and sorting through what had been described to her, a garage full of junk.

Standing still for a moment, arms folded, she pondered her options. It was early morning and already quite hot outside. She heard another train rumble over the iron bridge adjacent to the garage.

Her mother had recently died after a long illness. She didn't know who her father was, and her own marriage had failed after less than five years. She had no children.

It was when sorting through her mother's belongings that she made several discoveries. Standing there, in this old garage miles and miles away from her home in Trieste, Italy, Danielle thought back....

..The first one was a revelation that left her stunned. Her mother had been adopted.

She had stood in the mother's bedroom, had stared at the paper in her hand for a long while, before sitting down on the edge of the bed and took in what she was reading. How had she not known that, how had her mother not told her. She had never been told who her father was, perhaps she could find out information that had been withheld for all her life. With her marriage having ended almost seven years ago, maybe it was time to re-invent herself, to find out about her ancestry, to search for information about her father, to look for documents about her mother's adoption. There and then, sitting on the edge of the bed that day, Danielle made a promise to herself, to dig, to discover, to unearth the truth..

Making her mind up, she decided to start on the left-hand side of the old garage, work her way from the front to the back and then across from the left to the right.

A little over two hours later, she rubbed her back, wiped the sweat from her brow and decided she needed a break and something to eat and drink.

Shutting the roller-door she walked up the narrow street that was situated in the south-west area of the city and thought about her next move.

Not far away was a café and speaking in English, Danielle ordered coffee and cake.

Full of junk, she was told, well, some of it, yes, it was of little value, but she had come across some heavy drapes which were of good quality, a small desk, and a leather chair which, though rather dirty and with signs of mould, could be restored, and also a lovely lamp.

Sipping her coffee she thought back to how she came to make her way to Istanbul..

After dealing with all the funeral arrangements, the cleaning of the house and the preparation to ready the house for sale, Danielle had put together all the papers and documents that her mother had secreted away, placed them all on the dining table in her apartment and spent many hours reading them and following this up with research on her computer. She had taken some time off from her work as a senior nurse at a private clinic and was totally gripped by all that she had found out, about her mother, the possible identity of her father, but most of all, about her mother's biological mother, her grandmother, a woman whose name was Alexa Grossman. Intrigued, Danielle delved deeper, and after some searching, she discovered that, in the year 1963, she had been shot and killed. In Istanbul..

Taking a bite of what appeared to be a type of fruit cake, she savoured the taste, drank some more coffee and again reflected on her current situation..

The story of her grandmother having been shot and killed drew her into the past and determined to find out why this had been, what had occurred. Over the next weeks, though she returned to work, in her spare time she would research, follow clues, trace clues, trace connections. Totally absorbed she was often surprised as to how many hours she had spent on this quest.

Then, one Saturday afternoon, she came across some names, and following these connections, this led to a man. ...

Arriving back at the garage, Danielle unlocked the door and again rolled the shutter door open. She realised she had left the light on and, as she entered, she noticed some shelving at the back, near the ceiling. Making her way there, she found an old table, manoeuvred this where she wanted it and stood upon it.

The long shelf, stretching all the way across the width of the garage, held several cardboard boxes, most of them less than a metre in width and only about eight centimetres in depth. Reaching up, she pulled one of them down, got off the table and opened it up. It contained a painting. She immediately could see that this was a valuable oil painting. Her heartbeat had increased, and she proceeded to take all the other boxes down.

Having created a clearing on the garage floor, she looked down at what she had found. The sun was high in the sky, the temperature had risen sharply, and Danielle was perspiring quite a bit inside the old garage.

It was a quiet street, occasionally a car would drive past, and the frequency of the trains had diminished as the morning peak time was now over.

Ten paintings lay before her. Each one of some value. Then there was an odd painting, a wooden panel, depicting a monk. Lastly of the things she had pulled down, was a brown leather satchel, having only briefly looked into this, it seemed to be full of papers and documents, though there was also a wrapped bundle of something as well, casting her eye over the paintings, she then again reached for the satchel and took out the bundle, wrapped in what appeared to be a couple of small handtowels.

Unrolling these she was amazed, for there, in her hand, shining under the tube lighting of the garage, lay three silver keys.

Furthermore, she suddenly realised, glancing at the panel with the monk painted on it, that around his neck, hung a key, just like the ones in her hand.

This was most intriguing, valuable paintings, silver keys, a monk. What could it all mean?

Time to sort things out, time to carefully wrap the painting up again, time to arrange transport.

Time to leave Istanbul.

Whilst in the late afternoon Martijn was with the chief of police in Rotterdam, preparing documentations and permits for him to travel to Istanbul the following day to liaise with the Turkish police, across the Atlantic in was early in the morning and the seminar room at the university of Albuquerque was beginning to fill with reporters, television crews, university staff and members of the public.

Several people were on stage preparing microphones and lighting.

Detective Inspector Roger Mantell waited calmly in the wings. The dean was in conversation with his assistant and the other guest was the curator of the city's museum of culture.

At the doors to the seminar room, two members of staff stood by a table that held several bottles of disinfectant for folks to wash their hands upon entering and a few boxes of masks as everyone was required to wear them.

Only those who were to speak would be exempt.

Simon Lightfoot had earlier in the day already spoken to the detective, wished him strength and asked if his former girlfriend, Felicity Smith, had spoken to him.

She had, he informed him, and had told him of a likely city in Spain where the previous dean might now be living, this according to some information she had found in her late sister's diary.

The detective said he would contact his counterpart in Bilbao after his televised meeting to arrange an investigation.

Simon again wished him well for the press conference and ended the call.

He thought about the brief chat he had with Felicity, Fliss, as she preferred to be called, late the previous evening. He himself had gone around to Josie's folks, at the request of Raphael. They had not been aware of the article written by Millie Parker. Simon had brought a copy and had sat down with them.

When Fliss called, he first asked her if she had spoken to her parents, and how did that go.

She was tearful in replying, telling him, in between sobs, how she had spoken with her mother who was reading the article from her computer.

She then also told him of what she had discovered in her sister's diary and how she felt that the dean who went missing, could well be in the city of Bilbao, in Spain.

He had suggested she contact detective Mantell with this information, and she had replied that she had already done so.

After that the conversation was somewhat stilted and it was Simon who ended the call, wishing her a goodnight and that she would be able to go and see her folks soon.

Simon stood by the window of his front room, looking at the river that flowed just across the street.

He was in love with Alison, this he knew, this he was sure of. Yet, the brief conversation with Fliss had brought back memories of their three-year relationship.

Was he over her?

At the university the press conference was in progress.

Statements were made, by the current dean. Statements were made by detective inspector Mantell. An announcement was made by the curator of the museum of culture. Questions were asked.

In the audience were several of those who had been students, who had been on the archaeological dig that fateful day, thirty-two years ago. There were tears when some, for the first time, grasped the fullness of what had occurred that day.

When it was all over, the dean, William Armstrong, and detective Roger Mantell walked of the stage after shaking hands and both relieved that it was over.

The truth was told.

A truth that Simon had been looking for. A truth that Robert Pentegrass had begun to search for. A truth that Alison, Millie, and

Raphael had played their part in finding. A truth that Eddie Philpott had contributed to.

Constance Shelton was in prison. Her son Conrad had been killed in Italy and Malcolm Lynch was thought to be in Spain.

Professor Emily Parker's discovery would find a prominent place in the museum.

In San Francisco Alison was reading the long e-mail that her daughter Terri had sent. She was pleased that she had bonded so well and quickly with both Tammy and Sophie and felt a little left out as she hadn't, as yet, met either of them.

Her phone buzzed and she saw it was Simon. Great timing, she thought as she answered.

In Boston, sat behind his desk and scrolling on his laptop, Sam was about to take a sip of recently brewed coffee, when his hand stopped the motion and putting the mug down, he looked at what he had come across. Reading it through twice, he made a decision, he saved the information and followed a new trail.

Twenty minutes later he picked up his phone, pressed some numbers and waited.

'Sam?' Sophie answered.

'Hi Sophie, sorry it's late, but I have come across some information, and, since then have also made another discovery, the wonderful world of the internet, so, to elaborate, still following and trying to establish more on this woman Natalie Umbrego, I found out about a children's book, it's titled 'La Principessa Segreta' written by, wait for it! Eva and Bella Umbrego. You had mentioned something about a princess, well, this little book, was published in Italy, in Venice, back in 1867! My Spanish is good, not too different from Italian, it means the secret princess, this could well hold some clues, maybe, I don't know, what I do know, what I have since found out, that there is a copy of this very old little book, in a small library, specialising in ancient manuscript and books, not too far away from where you live, I'll e-mail you the

details of the book and this library, perhaps, with your connection
with the Interpol guy, you might be able to gain entry, as it is closed,
of course, at present.'

'Goodness, wow, that sounds an interesting trail, clever you, I'll
get on it, hopefully sort something out for tomorrow.'

'Excellent, how are Tammy and Alison's daughter?'

'They are fine, looking at me expectantly, so I'd better go and
tell them, you know what Tammy is like! 'Sophie said, laughing and
breaking the connection.

Sam smiled, turned around in his swivel chair and got up to tell
Chrissie the latest.

THE PAST; Period 12

19th January 2015- Paris

Only a few streets away from both the Gare Du Nord and Gare de L'est railway stations was the Paris Fine Arts Auction House. A set of three wide marble steps led to the entrance. The foyer was warmly decorated with various paintings and accommodations hung on the wall. Through a door to the left was a gallery where one could view the various items that would be auctioned later in the day. This had now been cleared. Through another door leading from the foyer, one could enter the auction room. It was spacious, well-lit and could comfortably seat around a hundred and twenty people and there was standing room at the back as well.

The podium was around ten metres wide and close to four metres in depth. A large monitor was hung high above the right-hand side. The rostrum was in the centre and to the left two women sat behind a desk keeping an eye on their laptops for the on-line buyers. On the other side of the rostrum a smaller table was placed. Sophie Pontiac, the manager, sat there, several sheets and books before her, as well as her own laptop, to keep a record of the proceedings.

She looked up at the people gathered, not a full house, around eighty or so, she estimated. She spotted him. Sitting near the back on the right. The Dutchman. The man who, earlier in the day, as he was viewing the items for sale, had questioned the Gauguin. Her boss, the director, Emmanuel Sauvonne, had taken him to his office and had summoned her. She had been short with him, questioned his expertise, told her of her own experience and had, at the time, felt that he had left with his tail between his legs. Watching him for a moment as a few more people entered, she was thinking that she may have been a little too harsh. He was sat quietly, and she knew, having been informed of his registration, that his name was Sam Price, from Rotterdam.

The auctioneer came on stage, stood behind the rostrum, sorted out his array of papers, checked to see that the monitor, which would clearly display the items, was working, checked the microphone for sound with a tap of his finger, looked up at the big clock on the wall and turned to look at Miss Sophie.

She nodded.

He was no longer a young man, well into his seventies, was of very slight build, had greying hair, wore glasses that were perched almost on the end of his nose and began to speak. His voice did not at all match his appearance. It was clear, it was deep in timbre and rather voluminous.

Sam Price glanced at the programme, the catalogue, then up at the auctioneer. He spoke first in French, then immediately in English. He was clear and fluid in both, even though he was originally from Prague, Sam had read in the brochure. The crowd settled and the first item was brought out.

Sam had also spotted the woman, the manager, Sophie, sitting behind her desk on the podium. He smiled as he recalled her face, quite red, and her eyes, big and piercing, as she practically berated him.

What a day this was. What a mix of emotions. His mind was in turmoil, jumping from one thought to another, he had found it hard to hang on to any of these thoughts that rambled through his mind, for any length of time. But as the day had gone on, he was beginning to feel more relaxed. The episode earlier, when he had asked the director, about the Gauguin painting of the woman on the shore, asked whether it had a good provenance as the was just something that nagged at him about it. He hadn't expected to be marched off to the director's office, hadn't expected to be questioned and challenged by the manager, by Miss Sophie Pontiac, but it had been a distraction, a welcome distraction.

When he had left the hospital in Rotterdam that early morning. He had been in a daze. Found himself entering the main railway station, then having look at the departure and arrivals board, had purchased a return ticket to Paris. He needed to just get away, away from the city, away from the hospital. He needed to find a place to breathe, a place to sort out the jumbled mess in his mind. His throat was dry, he could feel his heart beating and as he sat in the train a little later, he half smiled and wondered how it was still beating at all.

The smooth ride across the rails on the high-speed train was calming. Looking out the window as the landscape rushed by, he kept trying to get his thoughts in some sort of order, trying to focus, trying to establish some sort of timetable, some sort of organisation. Though his heartbeat had settled down and his throat was relieved of its dryness by a coffee, he still felt it difficult to concentrate.

It was sometime later, as he had existed the station in Paris and had aimlessly walked about for a bit, that he came across the auction house. Noticed that there was a sale on today and entered.

It was then that he had stopped by the Gauguin, it was then that something in the painting had stopped him, had nagged at him.

Before he could even begin to think what that might have been, he had been asked to come along with the director, with monsieur Sauvonne.

Sam sat and listened to the auctioneer for a while and looked at the screen as to the item that was auctioned. It was a painting, an oil, a landscape featuring an old wooden bridge. Glancing down at his catalogue, Sam noticed it was by a well know Turkish artist, Hikmet Onat.

Seated five places along from where Sam sat, was a woman. Her brunette hair was cut short, exposing a slim neck. She wore glasses and her brown eyes were focused on the auctioneer. Danielle Vitali wore a white blouse under a soft pink cashmere pullover and the beige trench coat she had worn upon arrival, now lay folded on the seat next to her. She wore a long skirt, a patterned material with predominantly burgundy tones. Her feet were into calf high leather boots.

She was pleased she had come. The price of her painting was going up and up. It was the first of two that she had offered to be auctioned today.

Danielle thought back, shaking her head a little, realising how the years had passed, it had been nearly ten years ago.

Ten years, since she had travelled from Trieste to Istanbul. Ten years since she opened that old garage door.

As the auctioneer banged his gavel down Danielle smiled, was well pleased with the sale of her first painting and her mind drifted back, to that day, in that street, with the trains rumbling across the iron bridge..

.... knowing she had a garage with stuff to sort through, Danielle had hired a transit van. She closed the roller door, walked up the street and to where she had parked the vehicle. Minutes later she pulled up, drove partway up on the footpath and got out.

It was still very warm, having already perspired in the old building as she was rummaging through all that it contained, she was now perspiring a lot more as she worked hard to load much into the van.

The ten paintings, the panel portrait of the monk and the leather satchel, had been the first to be loaded. Forty minutes after that she had taken everything that she deemed had value, turned off the light, closed the roller door, closed the side door to the van and got behind the wheel. Having been informed that there were several bulky items in the garage, Danielle had sourced a shipping company, but felt she needed to check out the contents first. Stopping briefly, she checked her bearings, then drove on. The shipping company was near the airport, and it wasn't long before she arrived. Danielle insisted she was present as they unloaded the van to note and describe every item as it was being packed..

Her next item would not be for a while she noted and sat back to enjoy the proceedings, though she had registered in case she wanted to purchase something, there really wasn't anything she particularly took a fancy too.

Five seats along Sam watched as the Gauguin was brought to the podium.

There was some bidding, but it never made reserve and was cleared for the next item.

Sam got up and left. It was time to go back, time to catch the train, time to head back to Rotterdam, time to go home.

It would only be then, once inside the apartment, that the realisation struck home. In the early morning his wife, after an illness, had quietly slipped away. She would not come home again. It was only then, closing the apartment door behind him that he broke down and cried.

THE PRESENT; Paris

Tuesday 5th May

Tammy and Terri sat in the back of the dark green Mercedes and Sophie sat in the front. Walther was driving.

He had smiled at them all upon arrival, through the mask he was wearing and was pleased that all the women were wearing their mask also.

Getting into the back Terri smiled, said good-morning Walther, and received a teasing nudge in her ribs from Tammy.

They were heading towards the Rue des Ecoles, near the university, where this small library was situated, specialising in old books, manuscripts, and maps, from a variety of European countries, Greece, Italy, Spain, and Germany in particular, along of course with French and Flemish literature.

The streets were a lot quieter these days. Many people, where possible, working from home. Every day more people were admitted into hospitals. Special barrack, not used since the second world war, were being cleaned and prepared. Equipment transported in. Beds made ready. The army was involved in additional transport.

The virus was not, certainly for the moment, showing any signs of subsiding.

Walther drove in almost silence. This assignment still had all to do with the world of art and he had been instructed to be of help in any way he could. Knowing the manager of the auction house and her predicament from a previous case, he was more than happy to be of assistance. To have an extra two beauties along was a bonus and he threw a look now and then in his rear-view mirror at the blonde woman from New York, wondering what her story was.

An elderly man, whose width seemed to match his height, was waiting by the front door as Walther pulled up. He too was wearing a mask.

The man from Interpol showed his credentials, introduced the three women and the man invited them inside.

Sophie spoke to him, explained about the Italian children book from the mid fifteen hundreds, titled 'La Principessa segreta' and told him of research that led them to believe it was here.

He bowed his head, thought for some time, then looked up and answered that he recognised the title, it would probably be on the second floor, there they would find a whole section in Italian, it was there somewhere, he was sure.

Sophie thanked him and whilst Walther stayed with the man, the three women climbed up an old steel circular staircase.

Less than ten minutes later Tammy called out, 'Got it!'

Meanwhile, detective Martijn Vogel landed at the airport to the south-west of the city of Istanbul and was soon after, transported by an un-marked police vehicle to the centre of the city.

Taking his mask off, speaking in English he explained his findings about Hugo Visser, the connection with art theft and the address where the man had been shot and killed. His counterpart, not wearing a mask at all, having been made aware of the incident that had occurred way back in 1963, had located the relevant files and explained that they would be going to the very building, and the very room, where not only this Hugo Visser was shot, but also a woman, named Alexa Grossman.

Events in Bilbao also unfolded. A concerned neighbour had contacted the apartment block management, who in turn got hold of the maintenance company who then showed up and gained entry, into the flat belonging to Mr. Malcolm Lynch. An unpleasant aroma hit the nostrils of the maintenance caretaker as he opened the door and it only took a few steps to see that the occupant, lying on the three-seater couch, was dead.

An ambulance was called.

A detective arrived as the body was taken out, he showed his credentials, asked a few questions, then entered the apartment. A telephone call, the previous evening, from a counterpart in

Albuquerque in New Mexico, to his chief, informing him of the circumstances, had brought him here.

He searched for some time, though first opening a few windows to clear the smell away. He found some interesting documents, found information about an auction in Madrid where Mister Lunch had gone to, over thirty years ago, confirming that he had placed two gold coins to be sold. This added to the information received from America that the man had stolen over three hundred old Spanish gold coins. But he was flummoxed and quite sure that wherever they were, it was not in this apartment. It was when he was about to leave, that a thought occurred to him.

The bicycle.

He had seen it earlier, had wondered why it had been placed in the second bedroom, leaning up against the wall. There was something about it and he decided to take a second look. It was very clean. The tyres were new and not worn anywhere. It was as if it had never been used. He took hold of the rubber grip of the handle, pulled it towards him and was taken aback by its weight as he pulled it towards him.

Smiling now, he put his other hand just below the saddle and lifted the bike. Putting it down he was smiling even more now, and nodding his head. It should not be anywhere near this weight. Studying more closely he figured that it had been rebuilt. All the metal bars of the frame were larger in circumference than standard. Checking it all out in his mind, he figured that there was no doubt. The gold coins must be inside these bars.

Standing back, he took pictures, then, made a call.

'Do you have a photocopier?' Terri asked, leaning forward to speak to Sophie in the passenger seat. Walther was driving the elated trio back to Sophie's apartment. In the back seat Tammy was looking at the small book and thinking about the fact that it had been written and printed all those years ago. The cover was a little worn, the pages were beginning to yellow, and though the binding was loose, it was not falling apart. Sophie was chatting in French to Walther as he drove through the much quiet Parisian streets and Terri had been quiet for a while, in thought.

Sophie turned, 'Oui, I have one, but, not at home, in my office'.

'Can we go there? I know someone who speaks Italian, she lived in Milan for some years if I remember right, she's nice, mother knows her, she was my teacher at school'.

Without hesitation Sophie gave Walther new instructions, then turned back to talk to Terri. 'You know how to reach her?'

'Mother will,' Terri answered, and not thinking about the time difference, she took out her phone and pressed some numbers.

'Terri?' a sleepy voice answered, 'Are you okay? What's wrong?'

'Oh, no, I'm fine, sorry mother, forgot about the time difference, so sorry, but, well, do you have a contact number for Miss Parker?'

Noticing that it was just after three o'clock in the morning, Alison shook the cobwebs from her eyes, scrolled on her phone, found the right place, and spoke, 'Got it here, sounds important, it's not to do with that article, is it?'

'What, no, what article?' Terri asked.

'Never mind, here is the number..'

'Thank you, mother, sorry I woke you. It is all very exciting, I will tell you all about it later, love you' Terri said, then hearing here mother say 'Love you too' broke the connection.

In the back seat Tammy looked across to Terri who was now dialling another number.

Sophie sat turned around also watching the youngster.

'Hello?'

'Hello, Miss Parker, hi, its Terri'

'Terri, goodness, how are you? I read about the break in at the museum, were you involved in that?'

'Ah, yes, but I am fine, thank you, so sorry to call you at this hour, but I would like your help, you lived in Milan for some years I remember you telling the class once, do you still speak, or more importantly, read Italian?

'Why yes, and by the way, did you think I was in the states? I am actually in Italy at present, and yes, I speak it reasonably well and, yes, I can read it too, what is this all about? I can hear excitement in your voice, and there must be some urgency? by the way, how is your mother?'

'She's fine, just spoke with her, she gave me your number, didn't say you were in Italy, asked about some article you wrote?'

'Yes, long story, it's not about that is it?'

'No' Terri replied as Walther brought the car to a stop outside the auction house.

'We have a book, a children's book, written, goodness, like hundreds of years ago, but we need to know the exact translation of the story, sorry, can't say more at the moment as to why, but it is very important'.

'Goodness, sounds intriguing, of course I will help, your mother helped me greatly not long ago, and I will do my best, how will you get it to me?'

'We are going to photocopy the book, there are not a lot of pages. so, can you give me your e-mail address?'

In Parma Millie pondered over the conversation, was curious, wondered what kind of children's book would be so important and thought about Terri's mother Alison. She felt a little guilty that she hadn't spoken to her since the time she had come to her house to give her the whole account of what had occurred that fateful day all those years ago. She needed to talk with her, explain the situation, explain the reason for the article, and certainly to thank her for all her help.

Fixing herself a drink of tea, she opened her laptop and awaited the forthcoming e-mail from Terri.

Sipping her tea, she thought about the amazing technology of the day as she began to read the attachment on the e-mail sent, registering also, that it had come from the Paris Fine Arts Auction House. Terri was in Paris?

It was indeed not a long story and after having read it once, Millie split her screen and began to translate.

A fairy-tale love story. A princess and a prince. The white horse, the castle. As she read the story on the left-hand side of her screen and as she carefully wrote the translation on the right-hand side. She paused after some time, thought about her own love story. Though about a young man she once knew. Would she ever fall in love again, she wondered, as she continued her translating.

As the dawn broke and early flights from O'Hare airport in Chicago were already soaring into the sky and flying over her apartment, Felicity woke, flew the covers aside and headed for the shower.

Would she ever fall in love again? She inwardly asked herself as the turned the taps.

Afterwards, towelling herself dry, she wiped the steamed-up mirror and looked at the reflection. Should she give up on Simon? Should she try and re-connect? There was someone else in his life, she could sense it, was it serious?

As she dressed, she wondered who this, rival, might be.

Preparing breakfast, she decided to try and get Simon back into her life. They had been so good together, hadn't they?

In San Francisco Alison heard her phone ring. Picking it up, hoping it would be Simon, she saw it was a different number.

'Millie?'

'Hello Alison, before anything else, I must apologise to you, you have been so very helpful to me, I have treated you badly, doing this article without telling you, I am so sorry... '

'Oh No Millie, there's no need, reading the article did come as a surprise, but, hey, it did need to be told, good for you, and your mother, bless her, needed to be recognised for what she had achieved... did, did Terri call you?'

'Yes, she did, she, like you, didn't know this, but I moved to Italy, I will stay here a while, yes, she wanted me to translate something, it all sounded very mysterious, she will no doubt tell you all about it, I asked her if she had been involved in that break in at the museum, she said she was, is she alright Ally, did she get hurt?'

'No, yes, she was there, but she was fine, very tough is my Terri, she called me in the early hours, to get your number, very intriguing, I'm waiting to hear from her.'

'She is in Paris I gather?'

'Yes, it is all to do with the break in, but I can't say any more...'

'Terri said she would tell me later...' Millie said, 'Sorry again, I really should have told you about the article, have you any response about it? '

'Detective Roger Mantell gave a press conference yesterday. Your story made it into several papers and on television, they will be creating a special section of dedication to your mother in the museum in Albuquerque, you will come to the opening of that?'

'Very likely, maybe, I don't know, I have to go...thank you again.'

The connection was broken.

Alison sighed. Then thought about what her daughter had asked Millie to do, a translation? Of what? Come on Terri, call me!

Two days later   *Thursday 7th May*

Letitia Teremos checked the instrument panel. She smiled as she thought back to the telephone conversation she had with Thomas.

Thomas, the handsome pilot. As she tapped a few instruments, she then set about to start the port engine, she sighed as she remembered how she had been quite taken by him. It had been a strange set of circumstances, but the end had turned out alright. She had seen how taken he was with the woman he was with, Cynthia, who, she had not failed to notice, was making sure that he was her man.

The port engine was up to speed, Letitia started the starboard propellor.

She looked at the house, the hacienda style residence, and saw her manservant standing in the doorway.

Her orchard plantation was not far from a town called Ampuero, in Northern Spain. Engines up and running. She made a call on her radio.

Thomas had rung to ask if she would be able to help out. She had, without hesitation, said of course.

He explained the situation, explained what, if she was willing, she had to do and told her that all the flight plans and permits would be granted and that all her fuel would be paid for.

Letitia, her almost black hair tied in a ponytail, began to roll the plane forwards.

Something quite different for her birthday, she thought, celebrating her forty second this very day.

She raised her hand to farewell Augustus, her driver and manservant who was a long serving and loyal friend, threw the engines into full throttle, released the brakes and the plane shot along the runway.

Augustus waved in acknowledgment and went back inside.

The front door closed. They were there, Sophie, Tammy, and Terri. Standing in the foyer and taking it all in. They had found the address, Terri had worked it out, they had seen an aerial photograph, Santa Trinita, the clear view of the house number, in Roman numerals to the left side of the tall double doors. Then a further sign, that of a three- pronged crown, in the stonework above the door. The address was right, the clues led them there. Tammy, with her resources and wealth, had again provided the costs of transport, Sophie with the help of her friend Walther from Interpol had secured the required permits and when Millie had sent the translated script, they felt they had all that they needed to find the treasure.

What they didn't have, were the keys. The silver keys that the three monks had taken away from the very place they were now in, some four hundred and forty plus years ago.

Sophie had sent a huge thank you to Millie and then had printed the translation of 'La principessa segreta and made a copy so that the three of them would be able to read it though individually and make notes.

That had been late morning the previous day.

Before even beginning to try and figure how this children's story would provide the clues they needed, Sophie called Martijn. He had spoken with her the night before, explaining his findings, relating the story of Hugo Visser and a woman called Alexa and that he was reading through a substantial account of the shootings and other activities this woman was involved with.

Sophie told him all about the book written by twins who were related to Natalie Umbrego and that there were clues to be found to help find the treasure.

Martijn said since they last spoke, he had discovered a lead, he would follow this up, a lead that would take him to Trieste.

Sophie told him she loved him and missed him and to be careful.

He responded by saying he loved her and that she too, should be careful.

By early evening they had grouped together and shared their thoughts.

Together, they had, they were sure, worked out the various clues.

A decision was made, they would go to Florence, they would go to the house, they would follow the clues, they would find the chest of which they had learned about.

A chest with three locks.

Sophie had contacted Walther. Tammy had contacted Thomas in the hope he would have contacts that would secure them a flight.

Terri, in the meantime, made a detailed sketch of the keys that hung around the necks of the two monks of which they had the painting.

Thomas did indeed have a contact, a contact with a plane. A Spanish woman, Letitia Teremos.

She landed the twin propped plane smoothly and followed the instruction of a young man who was giving her signals with his hands.

A week ago, at the same airfield, Thomas had landed, bringing the three ladies to Paris. She would be flying these three women to Florence.

As the prop engines were winding down, she saw a man appear. He was sturdy in build, had dark hair, a tanned skin and most handsome, she thought. He wore a mask which reminded her to don her own as she prepared to open the door and swing the steps down.

Standing now at the top of the steps, Walther noticed and admired her. She was slim, about five foot four and rather attractive, he thought, wary of the propellors as they were slowly coming to a stop.

Clipboard in hand, he climbed the steps. Letitia drew back inside and watched him enter. He stopped, lowered his mask, then, speaking English, 'Miss Teremos, thank you for your assistance, my name is Walther, I am an Interpol agent, I have your flight plans and permits for Florence, also we have fuel here, if you will allow that young man out there to see to that?'

'Ah, hello, Si, of course, and please, my name is Letitia, I have three passengers to take I believe?'

'Yes, but please, come with me inside the building, some refreshment before you continue your journey?

Fifty minutes later Letitia once again went through the starting procedure. She was introduced to the three women and led them to her plane.

'One of you can sit with me, I have two seats in the cargo area' she said, climbing the steps and taking off her mask. Sophie insisted that Tammy would sit in the cockpit and she and Terri settled themselves in the port and starboard side fold-down seats in the empty cargo space.

Tammy threw a sideways glance at the Spanish woman, she had noticed how she had interacted with Walther, and he with her. Smiling she wondered if she wasn't just a little bit jealous.

Letitia, sensing perhaps that she was being observed, turned, threw a quick smile at the blonde woman from New York and, as she fired up the starboard engine, asked, 'Do you know Thomas?'

'Yes, but only from last week when he flew us, that is Terri and myself, over here, Sophie knows Thomas better, she is the one that contacted him, and he, contacted you, thank you very much for this' Tammy answered.

Letitia spoke on the radio, received the go ahead and turned the plane towards the runway.

Moments later, the small plane left the tarmac and flew into the blue skies, heading east towards Florence.

Upon arrival there and having showed their permits and travel documents, they were driven to the centre of the city and deposited only a stones' throw from the address.

A man, wiry in built, with greying hair nodded a greeting to them as he was awaiting them in the doorway. Spoke to them briefly in broken English and invited them in. He then closed the door and left them.

The three of them looked at each other for a moment, then took their masks off.

'Okay, well, according to what we have learned from the book written by the twins, we need to go through this door' Sophie said, walking towards the door on the far right of the foyer, passing two doors on the left and two doors on the right.

Tammy and Terri right behind, Sophie opened the door.

According to the man who let us in, there is no electricity down there, no lights, but there should be...ahh, yes, here we are, on the shelf, three torches'

'It's like they were expecting us, I mean, you only rang this morning Soph' Tammy said, taking a torch from Sophie who then grabbed another to hand to Terri.

'It's all coming together' Sophie answered, switching on her torch, 'the person I called is from a well- known auction house, here in Florence, we have had dealings with them over many years. When I told him of this address and mentioning Walther, from Interpol, he was most accommodating. When I asked how we could gain entry, particularly to the crypt, to view the coffins of Petrus and Odette, he said he would arrange someone to let us in.'

'Indeed, and, although he only spoke Italian, I picked up on the fact that there was no electricity in the crypt, but still, three torches, I can't remember you mentioning that there were three of us.' Tammy said, a slight concern on her face.

'True' Sophie replied, 'I hadn't'.

'There!' Terri said, pointing the light of her torch to what looked to be a wooden pole.

Both Sophie and Tammy shone their torches at the same place.

'Yes! do the honours Terri' Sophie said, excitement in her voice.

Young Terri stepped forward, grabbed the pole with her left hand, then pulled it upwards.

There was the sound of a faint click.

Making sure they walked carefully on the stone steps going down, they reached the crypt.

'Next part' Tammy said, shining her torchlight on the wall, silently counting a number of stones. Then, her light stopping, 'This one!'

Tammy pushed and the wall moved. With a slight scraping noise, it opened up.

She quickly slipped through, followed by Terri and then Sophie.

They were in another crypt, an inner chamber and all three were startled when behind them the wall had closed.

'Oh, my goodness' Terri whispered, her torchlight shining onto the object.

Sophie shone her torch in the same place, and Tammy did as well. In the brilliant light of their three torches, stood a beautifully crafted chest sat upon a low wooden table.

Three copper bands were across the curved lid and down the sides. Three steel locks showed prominently just below where the led closed. Built into the chest itself.

All three women were silent for some moments.

Terri was the first to move closer, bending down to look at the locks.

'These are strong,' she said, studying the ornate lock that was crafted into the chest.

'Yes,' Sophie agreed, also bending down and looking at the lock on the right- hand side. We do really need the keys!'

Tammy in the meantime, had decided to look around the inner

chamber, shining her light into the various areas, then stopped, for behind where they stood, was a table, an old wooden table, but what had caught her eye, there placed neatly in a row, were three silver keys, and beside them, also neatly in a row, were three scrolls, tied with ribbon.

'Guys' Tammy said, her voice only barely above a whisper.

Sophie stood upright, then shone her torch where Tammy was pointing hers and gasped.

Terri, hearing the gasp, also stood up, turned, and saw.

Again, there was silence in the room.

Three torchlights playing their beams on the table.

'But' Terri began..

'I know,' Tammy said, throwing a look at Terri beside her, 'How..'

'Did they get here?' Sophie completed.

'They have to be used in a certain order' Terri said, 'from what we learned from that book, three keys to choose...'

'Indeed' Tammy said, moving towards the table, 'there is a sequence, but which key is which, are they placed here in order?'

'I have the sketches!' Terri said, fumbling in the bag that was slung across her shoulder, 'we can figure it out,' pulling out the sheet of paper.

'Okay,' Terri began, looking from the table to the drawing she had made, 'yes, they are in the right sequence, the one on the left is that of Bonifatius, the monk who went to Santiago de Compostela and whose painting ended up in San Francisco, the one I brought to Paris...'

Sophie looking at the drawing Terri had made, said, 'yes, and the one in the middle, is the one Flavius had, his painting is the one that was sent to me by Roberto.'

'Where it all began,' Tammy said, 'well, for us anyway, which leaves that the last key must be that which Ignatius wore to Izmir'

'Okay, 'Terri said, picking up the right-hand key, 'we agreed that the sequence must be the address that were the clues on the paintings, and in order that an address would be written'.

'Yes, so,' Tammy said, reaching for the key on the left, 'the number first, the number 4, so, ...'

Sophie took the last key from the table and the three of them turned around to face the chest. 'So, the right-hand key, should be for the left-side lock, go for it Terri'.

Terri moved forwards, placing her drawing back into her satchel, bent down and holding the torch steady, she pushed the key into the lock with her right hand, then, taking a deep breath, she turned it.

In the silence of the musty inner chamber, the noise was audible and echoed around. A distinct click. The lock was open.

Terri stood up and Tammy moved into place, the number of an address, was followed by a street, in this case, Santa Trinita, the key that Bonifatius travelled with. Tammy bent down, inserted the key, and as did Terri, she took a deep breath and turned the silver key.

Again, much to the relief of all three of them, an audible click as the lock opened.

'Well,' Sophie said, now bending down to the third lock, 'this has to be right, the key Flavius carried, the centre piece, the clue of the city. The last part of the address.

She inserted the key and turned. Click.

The three of them stood in front of the chest.

'What are we waiting for?' Terri wanted to know.

Sophie smiled, 'I don't know Terri.

Tammy said, 'Go, Soph, you open it'.

'You take the right-hand side, I'll take the left, ready?'

Without a squeak, the lid opened and stayed upright.

THE PAST; Period 13

the year 2017- Florence, Italy

November, and a cold wind was blowing through the piazza as the woman, carrying a parcel and a small leather bag slung across one shoulder, knocked on the right-hand wooden door.

Number 4 carved into a stone to the left of the double doored entrance, in Roman numerals.

Danielle Vitali heard the door being opened.

A smile and a brief conversation and she was invited to enter.

The door closed.

She was asked, with sign language, to remain in the foyer and the elderly lady disappeared through one of the five doors that led from the spacious and marble tiled foyer.

She was about to place the parcel that she carried under her arm, on the floor, when the same door opened and another woman, smiling, came out.

'Miss Vitali, welcome to St. Anna school for orphans, I am Catherine.'

'Thank you, 'Danielle answered, then, presenting the parcel, 'this, is for you, it's the painting I mentioned.'

'Thank you, yes, please' the woman, somewhere in her thirties, Danielle guessed and the person she had spoken to on the phone two days ago, took the parcel and turned, 'please, come with me'.

'Would you like some coffee, or tea? Something to eat? Did you travel from Trieste today?' the woman asked as she walked into a large rectangular room.

Danielle took in the furniture, the walls, the paintings, the lighting.

'Oh, yes, please, some coffee would be great, and yes, I travelled here today, thank you for seeing me, somehow, when we spoke on the phone, I felt that you knew about this painting, about its story..'

There were three desks in this room, various cabinets, a couple of bookcases, two chandeliers suspended from the ceiling and to one side of the large room, two armchairs and two three-seater couches surrounded a glass topped low table.

The woman, Catherine, placed the parcel on the table, gestured for Danielle to be seated, then took a phone from her pocket and made a call.

'Well, well let's have a look, shall we?' she then said and proceeded to unwrap the parcel.

Danielle took the leather bag from her shoulder and chose one of the comfortable looking armchairs to sit in, watching as the parcel was unwrapped.

'You know the story of this painting?' the woman asked, turning to look at Danielle, 'I mean, all of it?'

The door through which they had entered opened, and a young man came in, carrying a tray with cups, plates, some cake, milk, sugar, and a coffeepot, which he set down upon the other end of the glass topped table.

He nodded a greeting to Danielle, received a thank you from Catherine and left the room.

The wrapping was discarded, and Catherine took hold of the wooden panel, studying it for some time.

'That's Ignatius' Danielle said, the aroma from the coffee reaching her nostrils, 'and yes, I believe I know the whole story, well, perhaps not quite the whole story, I know it all began with Father Dominic?'

Catherine laid the painting down, then proceeded to get the drinks ready.

'Would you like milk, sugar?' she asked pouring out the strong looking black liquid.

'Just some sugar please, and, that cake does look tempting' Danielle answered.

'So, this is Ignatius' Catherine said, having distributed drinks and cake and sitting down in one of the three-seater couches, 'you don't know here the other two are?

Danielle shook her whilst taking a bit of the fruit cake.

'So, yes, Father Dominic, he sure was quite the planner, this school for orphans is entirely thanks to him you know..'

'Of course! St. Anna, after..'

'Yes, named in honour of Anna Kastanje..' Catherine filled in.

'We are grateful to you also Miss Vitali, and I'm sure you would like to complete your search?'

'Please, call me Danielle, and if you mean would I like to go down to the crypt, with all its secret doors..then yes, absolutely!'

After the coffee and cake and some general chit-chat, Catherine took Danielle on a tour of the house. Now having been renovated and modernised with several classrooms and a new kitchen, Danielle thought about the young Anna, who at the age of three had become an orphan. This was a wonderful legacy.

Arriving back in the large marble tiled foyer, Catherine opened the door on the far side, reached inside and handed Danielle a torch. 'You'll need this'.

'Thank you, I will need by bag first' she answered and headed for the room where earlier she had enjoyed her coffee and cake.

When she returned to the door, Catherine had disappeared.

Switching on the torch, the bag across her shoulder, Danielle stepped through the door. Closing the door behind her Danielle studied the ledge in front of her and spotted the wooden lever.

Taking a deep breath, she reached out with her left hand, grabbed the pole and just as Eva Umbrega had done a hundred and thirty-eight years ago, Danielle pulled it upwards.

She heard a faint click.

Being careful to go down the stone steps, she reached the bottom, slightly adjusted the bag over her shoulder and took time to look around, standing for a while by the three coffins.

Bowing her head, she thought about what she knew about Petrus and Odette, their kindness, their influence, their impact upon this city.

Daniuelle then walked back to the bottom step of the stone

staircase, shone the torch on the wall and counted the stones, from right to left and from bottom to top.

She placed her left hand on a stone, pressed hard.

The wall moved, the opening appeared, and she slipped through into the next chamber.

Shining the light from her torch around, she stopped it when she spotted the chest. It was beautifully made, and the brass bands were gleaming in the light, and she saw the locks. Three of them, built into the woodwork of the chest.

Turning, she then noticed the other table, saw the three scrolls placed there.

She frowned. What were these scrolls, had they been placed there by Father Dominic? Had they appeared at some later time? Had someone been there before her?

Shaking her head, she turned again to face the chest.

Then reaching into her bag, she took out the three keys.

No, she thought, she was sure, that without these keys, no one had unlocked the chest. She too would not be able to open it, for although she did have the keys, she knew they had to be inserted in a certain order, and having had only one of the three paintings, therefore just one of the clues, she knew that she would not be successful. But she didn't mind that.

She had returned the painting that she had found in that old garage. She would leave the three keys here, on the table, in the inner chamber.

Maybe one day, someone else might make it to this point.

Danielle took another look at the chest, placed the three silver keys on the table then headed for the small wooden door through which Father Dominic had left, nearly four-hundred-and-forty years ago.

Again, focusing on the number of stones she needed to count, she pressed the right connections, and it wasn't too much later, that she found herself in the narrow kitchen. Though no longer used as a kitchen as a new and much larger kitchen had been built to provide the meals for the school's orphans and staff.

Pleased with herself, she sought out the headmistress and having declined to stay for lunch, she left and was back in the street, with the cold November wind still blowing. Time to go home, back to Trieste.

∿

THE PRESENT; Thursday 7th May

In Trieste, Danielle opened the door.

'Hello, Miss Vitali? I am Martijn Vogel, from the Dutch police, looking into the death of a Miss Alexa Grossman, this was in Istanbul, in 1963, your name came up in an enquiry...' Speaking slowly in English and showing her his credentials.

Danielle looked at his identity card, then into his face. Smiling, she asked, 'Dutch police?'

'Long story' Martijn answered, observing the woman before him.

'Well, in that case, please come in and tell me this story' she said, stepping back to let him in.

In Florence, at the airport, sitting in a private lounge area close to the airport apron, from where she could see her plane, Letitia was enjoying something to eat and had already noticed the attention that was given her by several men as they passed through.

Smiling she thought back to not that long ago, when Thomas and Cynthia had come into her life. What a turn of events. To hear his voice again yesterday was a pleasant surprise. Yes, she thought, he was involved with Cynthia, but a girl can dream, can't she? She thought to herself, smiling, and drinking some juice.

To yet again be involved, though be it in a small way, to another adventure, was exciting.

She wondered how they were getting on. They had been away for some time now already and the day was drawing to a close. Though she hadn't been told of all the details, Letitia knew that it was all to do with a treasure hunt that was set in motion centuries ago. Her curiosity, she was told, would have to wait to be fed, but they would tell her everything upon their return.

Drinking some more juice, she pondered as to what this treasure might be.

In the inner chamber, Sophie and Tammy had opened the lid of the chest. It had opened smoothly, without a sound. It was suddenly incredibly quiet in the semi darkness. Terri, along with the other two, shone their torches into the chest.

It was the young Terri who moved first, she handed her torch over to Tammy, then leaned into the chest to retrieve what was there. A small scroll, tied with a ribbon, lay on top of a large book. Not a word was spoken as Terri lifted the book, with the scroll on top, out of the chest.

'I guess it's not what you expected' a voice said, in English and speaking softly.

It startled the three of them, Terri turned, book and scroll in hand, Tammy and Sophie reacting by swinging their torches into the direction of the voice.

Standing there, having very quietly entered through a small door, stood a woman, holding a lantern.

Whilst in Chicago, Felicity had made up her mind. She was packing a suitcase. Sure, she thought to herself, it had been her fault. She had broken it off with him. Sure, she thought, it had all been for the right reasons, or so she felt, at the time.

Since her, very brief, conversation, she knew, she was not over him, she had feelings for him and getting cross with herself for how she had reacted then, wasn't helping. She had to try, she had to go to him, she had to fight for him. Moreover, she reasoned, it was time to see her parents.

Despite the travel restrictions, despite the warnings of staying indoors, when possible, she knew also, that some people were still travelling, some people were still heading into work, or seeing family. She would do the same.

She had booked herself a ticket on the train. Flights were almost impossible to get, but the train, it was still running.

She booked a ticket on the Southwest Chief, a train that ran from Chicago to Los Angeles. It would be leaving later today, at two-forty-five, and reach Albuquerque the following day at around three-thirty.

And in San Francisco, Alison too had made up her mind. The last conversation she had with Simon, had been, different. She sensed a change in him, in his voice. It made her tummy feel tight and she put it down to women's intuition, something was definitely not right. Searching for a way to get to see him, she had decided also, to go by train. She would travel first down to Los Angeles, then, board the Southwest Chief Amtrak service, heading east. Leaving at around six pm, she would arrive in Albuquerque just before lunch the following day. She just needed to see him, to be with him, to hold him.

The following day, Friday 8th of May

Stepping from the train, she had only just taken the small suitcase that was handed to her by the porter, when she turned, and there he was.

Alison practically dropped the case and flung herself into his arms.

Initially she had wanted to surprise him, but as the journey went on and as she got nearer her destination, she became more and more uncertain.

Had she picked up a wrong sensation, was her intuition playing with her mind, what if he was with someone!

An hour before her estimated arrival, she dialled his number.

Afterwards she took some moments to get her heart back into a regular rhythm. All was well, he was surprised to hear she was on her way, but she could tell the joy in his voice. Her fears had been unfounded.

She pulled back from him, stared into his eyes, could feel tears welling up behind her own.

He pulled down his mask, then slipped her mask down and kissed her gently, before saying, 'Are you okay?'

'I am now' she managed to say. They both put their masks back on and Simon steered her towards the exit.

Her arm firmly around his waist as he wheeled her suitcase with one hand and his other hand around her waist, Alison felt like she was practically floating. She knew with certainty, that her heart, which she could feel beating in her chest, belonged to him.

Still over four hours away, on the Amtrak Southwest Chief, heading for Albuquerque, Felicity was restless. She knew in her heart, that he was involved with someone else. Was it serious? Should she just come knocking at his door?

Looking at her watch she calculated the time that was left for her to decide.

Watching the landscape go by and listening to the sound of the wheels on the track, she felt herself fall doze off.

When she finally arrived, a little before four in the afternoon, she hailed a taxi and gave the address. Time to see her parents, time to mend bridges, time for hearts to heal. Simon was in the past.

As she got out of the taxi, her mother came running from the house. Her father was not far behind.

The taxi driver placed her case on the pavement and got back into his cab.

Felicity hugged her mother, and both were crying.

She tearfully smiled at her father.

She was home.

Epilogue; Myrtle Creek

Monday 11th May

As the sun occasionally peered through the scattered white clouds, Clair stood still and reflected. She had gone for an early morning walk. Thomas was due to arrive shortly, having once again flown the private jet across the Atlantic. He had collected Tammy and Terri, had dropped them both of in Yonkers as Terri would spend a few days with Tammy at her New York apartment. Had then flown the jet back to Portland and was on his way home.

Cynthia was already there, eagerly awaiting the return of her boyfriend.

Claire found herself passing by the war memorial monument. An eight feet tall obelisk with names carved into it. A fortnight later it would be Memorial Day and there would be a service held there.

She stopped, looked at some of the names, falling soldiers from the small town of Myrtle Creek. Casualties from the second world war, a couple from the Korean war and a few from the war in Vietnam. There were two names from the conflict in Afghanistan, both women, the only women carved into the obelisk.

A light early morning breeze played with her hair as she stood there for a moment.

Claire thought about her grandfather who had been killed in action when deployed to France in the second world war. She thought about her uncle, her father's older brother, who had fought in Vietnam. But her main thoughts went to a young man she knew.

Luke.

A memory she had consciously pushed away for many years. She had only briefly mentioned him to Thomas one evening, recently, when they were just chatting.

It was time, time to recall the event.

Luke.

Five years ago already. When she was living in Sacramento. She had moved there for work, had, through a Christmas party, met Luke. He was in the military and due to be deployed. That night, as they were walking back to her apartment, a group of thugs, two of which knew Luke, made fun of him being in the military. They were well intoxicated. They wanted to fight. Of the four, two of them came forward, Luke placed himself between them and her.

He was well-versed in un-armed combat.

Seconds later he escorted her away. The two who had attacked him were moaning on the ground, the other two decided it best to leave.

Claire took a deep breath.

She began to walk back home. It hadn't been that memory that she had been pushing away. Three days later he had departed to Afghanistan and that same evening, three of those four thugs, had taken her, overpowered her, forced her into a van...

It would be nearly a year later, that she was rescued. When she met Cynthia, when she heard about a man named Robert Pentegrass, known as 'The Searcher' who had been the one that had located her and arranged the rescue.

Claire headed back, pleased that she had been able to properly think back on those events, thankful, of course, to Robert who, sadly, had now passed away. Thankful to Cynthia and thankful to Thomas, who had so quickly taken her into his trust and to be part of all that Robert had so many years ago started.

Walking up the steps onto the veranda, she smiled and thought back to that day when Thomas had arrived, when she had challenged him.

Still smiling she entered and joined Cynthia and Thomas, who had arrived back, in the lounge.

'Claire' Cynthia said, 'come on, make Thomas tell the whole story, I still only know bits here and there, I'm sure he hasn't told it all, make him Claire'.

Claire smiled, looked at Thomas who smiled back and said, 'Better tell her everything Thomas, or else I might tell the story, and maybe get a few things mixed up, like the fact that you were flying a plane with three women in it, all that way....'

'Okay, okay, Thomas said, throwing a friendly scowl at Claire, then turning to Cynthia, 'right, well, here goes, a recap then, of the mystery surrounding the three monks from Florence.'

It was late evening in Paris and Sophie had just completed writing everything down. Sitting back, she looked at the last words written that showed on her laptop screen.

Shaking her head, she thought she would have liked Father Dominic. He sure had carefully planned and plotted it all in incredible detail, and furthermore, had made preparations for the future, the far away future, for this had all taken place, over four hundred and forty years ago.

Sipping a little of her red wine, Sophie reflected, so much to think back on, her romance with Martijn, her good friend Tammy, her new friend in the young Terri, both of them safely back in the States by now.

Sophie pressed the print button and stood up, she would file this adventure, she would add some photos and it would surely be talked about for some time to come.

Heading for the kitchen, she poured some more wine into her glass, looked at the clock which showed it to be just after eleven in the evening, sat herself on the comfy two-seater and taking a sip of wine, she closed her eyes and thought back to the moment a voice startled the three of them, there in that inner chamber, just as Terri was lifting the book and scroll from the chest....

.. 'I guess it's not what you expected' the voice had softly spoken in English.

Terri turned around, book and scroll in hand, Tammy and Sophie pointed their torches in the direction of the woman.

She squinted in the light, but was calm and stood still, holding the lantern.

'My name is Catherine, 'she said, her voice still soft, but clear, 'I am the head mistress here, of the school for orphans, named after a girl who was orphaned, at the age of three, whose name was..'

'Anna' Sophie interjected, pointing her torch downward, as did Tammy, also still holding Terri's torch.

'Yes, Anna' the woman said, then, 'please, follow me, though the secret doors still work in the way they were designed to enter this space, the exit is no longer working, renovations and a fire that occurred some time ago, led to the discovery, please, follow me and I will explain it all, and, congratulations for being able to open the chest, well done, you are the first to do so, since Father Dominic locked it, also, please bring what you have discovered..'

With that the newcomer, Catherine, turned and the three of them followed, Sophie closing the lid of the chest before joining Terri and Tammy.

They entered a narrow corridor, then turned right into another corridor that sloped upwards, then in and through a door, which, by the light of the lantern and torches, they could see was new.

They were now in the kitchen.

The cable operating waiter system, through which Father Dominic had crawled, was no longer there.

Catherine placed her lantern on one of the kitchen benches, turned the light off, looked at the three women behind her and said, 'This way'.

Terri, still holding the book and scroll, followed, Tammy and Sophie turned their torches off and placed them beside the lantern.

Leaving the narrow kitchen, which was obviously not in use now, Sophie looked around and tried to figure out where, according to the children's book, written by the twins, the original wooden dumb waiter system would have been.

Through another new door, they went into the room where three years earlier Catherine had invited Danielle Vitali into.

Sophie, Tammy, and Terri took in the vast room.

Then it was both Tammy and Sophie who gasped at the same time.

For on a wall, opposite the three windows that looked out over the piazza, hung a painting.

Painted on a wooden panel.

'Oh, my goodness!' Tammy exclaimed.

Then Sophie said,' It's, Ignatius!'

'Indeed, do you perhaps know where the other two are?'

Sophie turned to the woman, approached her, extending her hand, 'I am Sophie Pontiac, these are my friends, Tammy Wilson and Terri Hudson, and yes, I have the other two, Bonifatius and Flavius..' then looking at the wall, went on to say, ' I can see that you have placed this painting so as to accommodate the other two, it is right that they should come here, be put together..'

'Thank you' Catherine answered, shaking Sophie's hand, and turning to shake the hands of Tammy and then said to Terri, 'please, young lady, put that book and the scroll on the coffee table, after which she also shook her hand, turning again to Sophie 'that would be much appreciated. I take it then, you have them?'

'Yes, we have them, you were expecting us?' Sophie answered, walking over to where a glass topped display case stood, below the painting of Ignatius, and smiled. There were three scrolls on display inside...

Sophie turned and gave Catherine a quizzical look.

'The three keys normally are on display in there as well, I heard of your coming yesterday, who you were, your reason for coming, so I placed them in the inner chamber, wondering if you would have the information to successfully unlock the chest' Catherine said, as Tammy and Terri Joined Sophie by the cabinet. These scrolls were given, some years ago, they were found in a library in Venice, and someone connected them to belong here. They are duplicates that Father Dominic wrote, these ones originally were given to Anna, the ones you saw in the chamber were left there by Father Dominic.'

He sure was very detailed in his planning' Sophie remarked.

Catherine smiled, then indicated to them, 'Please, come and sit,

I long to hear your story, the quest that has brought you here, I have arranged drinks to be brought...'

And at that moment the door opened, and a young man entered carrying a large tray....

...Taking another sip of wine, Sophie shook her head as she remembered. It sure wasn't at all as any of them suspected..

....' I see that the book, that was in the chest, is a bible.' Sophie said, noticing the cover for the first time. It was worn, it was old, the brown cover had faded, and the lettering was only just visible.

'It's an old Vulgate Bible,' Catherine answered, ' I recognised it, it most likely belonged to Father Dominic.

'So, he placed it in the chest?' Sophie asked.

Catherine smiled again, then said, 'open up that scroll'.

Tammy had decided to be mother and poured the drinks. Dark coloured and strong-smelling coffee.

Sophie nodded to Terri, who sat nearest, to open the scroll.

Terri, who had shaken her head at the coffee, which, she could smell, far too strong for her liking, chose a glass of juice and took as sip, then picked up the small scroll, put her glass down then untied the ribbon and opened it.

'I can't read it, it's short, in Latin I suppose, but I can see a reference at the bottom, a bible reference, I think, if I am translating right, it says Matthew six and verse, XX1, so that's 21.'

'Very good young lady' Catherine said, 'In English, the verse says this, 'For where your treasure is, there your heart will be also'.

Contemplating in her apartment in Paris, Sophie recalled the moment, all of them thinking about that verse, all of them trying to understand what exactly the meaning was..

... Terri leant forward to hand the scroll over for Sophie to read. It was beautifully written.

'Father Dominic himself, wrote it' Catherine said, 'I recognise his writing, we have no duplicate of that one, it shall go in the cabinet, with the others'..

'So, 'Sophie began, thinking it all through, 'So, Father Dominic, placed the bible in the chest? And the scroll with that verse?' she asked.

'Yes, indeed,' Catherine answered, ' quite some time ago, I did some research too, and, finding out about Father Dominic, also finding out about how he had secured the riches of Petrus and Odette and ensured the safety of Anna, I was quite sure that the chest would not contain a treasure of jewels and gold. The wealth of the possessions held by Petrus and Odette was placed, and put to use, so that now, today, it still funds the running of this school for orphans.'

Catherine looked at them each in turn and continued,' When I made my way to the chamber, hearing that you had arrived there, I watched as you opened the chest, and when I saw what you lifted out, young lady, I knew what it was. This was the treasure, 'Catherine explained, patting the bible that lay on the table, pausing briefly, she continued, 'He first had to make sure the baby, Anna, was safe, he then set out this plan, quite an intricate plan, this was all to be revealed to Anna, when she became of age, when she turned eighteen.' Taking a sip of coffee, she again looked at the three women in turn, then continued, ' you see, the plan, the clues , the keys, the chest, he designed it all for her to follow, for her to go into this quest, to journey, to use her initiative, to then, eventually, come back here, follow the clues that Father Dominic had left with her, and reach the chest. Three keys, three clues, then, upon reaching the chest, three locks to choose.'

'That is quite.., 'Tammy began, looking for the right words, 'quite an undertaking, particularly for a young woman, especially in those days, I mean, like four hundred or so years ago!'

'Rather dangerous, I agree' Terri added.

'True' Catherine answered, ' But she would have had finances available, people around her that she could rely on, however, although Father Dominic had to also make sure that the house, this house, must not fall into the hands of those who were desperate in obtaining it, along with other riches that were held by Anna's father and mother, he didn't quite count on one thing. Yes, he was clever in making sure, that the wealth that they had, would be put to use , for the good of the town, for the good of the people, and mostly, for the good of the orphans, but, Anna never took up the challenge, she made her way to Monaco, to the Vanetti Vineyards, to see Viana, a woman that was mentioned by Father Dominic in the instruction he left her. Here she left the scrolls that are now in the cabinet, here she ended the quest that she never wanted to start. She wanted to see the portraits, the panels of the three monks, wanted to see what they looked like. She then came back home, to look after the woman who had raised her, the woman who had brought her up, not her birth mother, but her mother none the less, it was where her heart led her.'

After some moments of silence, Tammy and Sophie drinking their strong coffee and, Terri sipping her juice, it was Sophie who spoke.

'So, how do you know all this? How did the scrolls end up here, and the keys? I mean, I, we, know of some of the story, we know of a German man, Rudolph, who found a letter, mentioned a treasure, we know he found two of the keys and secured one of the portraits..'

'And then there was an Englishman,' Tammy said, continuing the story,' we know that he found the third key, he also had the two that Rudolph had discovered along with that single portrait..'

'But,' Terri spoke, also wanting part of this conversation, 'His house was broken into, and all those things were stolen, taken to Istanbul.'

'Goodness, yes,' Catherine said, smiling at each of them, 'Quite some sleuthing, and you obviously came across that book written by the twins, which led you here.'

Pausing briefly, she then went on to say, 'There is another person who has been involved, it was this person who discovered the scrolls in the library in Venice..'

.. Sophie finished her drink, stood up and headed for the kitchen. Recalling how Catherine then told them the story of a woman named Danielle Vitali, who had inherited some belongings from a long lost relative, discovered the painting of the monk and various documents, and too followed a trail, which led her to visit here about five years ago. She brought the keys, the portrait, and the scrolls.

All three mesmerised with the story, the trail, and the search that Father Dominic had set in motion. Rudolph Meyer had been the first to take up the treasure hunt, it was Roger Sutherland who took on the search a long time later and it was this Italian woman, Danielle Vitali, who it was, that actually completed the search.

Then, as they left the big house in Florence, as they once again donned their face masks, Sophie promising Catherine that the paintings would be couriered to her, they made their way back to the airport where Letitia was waiting to fly them back to Paris, Sophie had a call from Martijn.

He too told the story of Danielle, who he had been to see, in Trieste, and the rest of the tale fell into place as he explained the long conversation that he had with her. Which she would make him tell her, every word, when they got back home.

'It's all about the heart' she whispered, thinking of Martijn, who, true to his word, spoke with her over the phone, after she had said goodbye to Tammy and Terri at the airport, where Thomas was waiting to take them home.

She had then meticulously written everything down. From the very moment her door ball had rung, and she had received that parcel from Roberto.

Seven minutes later she snuggled herself into bed and fell asleep almost immediately.

In her lounge, on the coffee table, the laptop was still on, on the screen were the words that Father Dominic had so beautifully written, centuries ago.

'For where your treasure is, there your heart will be also'.

THE END

www.ingramcontent.com/pod-product-compliance
Lightning Source LLC
Chambersburg PA
CBHW071411300726
48976CB00006B/2066